A RACING MURDER

A HAM HILL MURDER MYSTERY

FRANCES EVESHAM

D1492979

B

Boldwood

First published in Great Britain in 2021 by Boldwood Books Ltd.

This paperback edition first published in 2022.

1

A CIP catalogue record for this book is available from the British Library.

Paperback ISBN: 978-1-80415-277-5

Ebook ISBN: 978-1-80048-075-9

Kindle ISBN: 978-1-80048-074-2

Audio CD ISBN: 978-1-80048-067-4

Digital audio download ISBN: 978-1-80048-069-8

Large Print ISBN: 978-1-80048-073-5

Boldwood Books Ltd.

23 Bowerdean Street, London, SW6 3TN

www.boldwoodbooks.com

For Ed and Marina, Pete and Wendy, Ron and Sheila, our racing buddies.

MAP OF LOWER HEMBROW

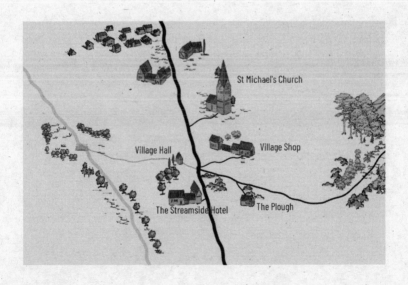

1

COUCH TO FIVE

Imogen Bishop squinted at the sky. Those black clouds looked about ready to burst, but if Harley, her faithful canine companion for the past year, didn't get his walk right now, he was going to complain all day.

One pleading look from the friendly brown mutt's enormous eyes could persuade the most hard-hearted of Imogen's guests to scratch behind his ears, rub his stomach or even – although The Streamside Hotel's rules forbade the practice – sneak him a mouthful of bacon from breakfast. As a result, he was developing quite a tummy. Imogen fought the tendency with more and longer walks, pleading notices in the hotel foyer, and instructions to her hotel staff to police Harley's diet.

This morning, she'd been tempted to let him exercise within the hotel grounds. It was a race day at nearby Wincanton Race-course and the hotel was full to bursting with racegoers in khaki tweeds, poring over the *Racing Post*, arguing over promising newcomers and planning bets, so she had plenty to do.

But Harley needed his walk around the village at least twice a day, so Imogen gave in. The early-morning February wind had, in a spirit of adventure, morphed from the mild south-westerly of the past few days to a chilly north-easterly, so she marched more briskly than usual down the lane that ran at right angles from Lower Hembrow's single paved road, Harley by her side.

She longed for better weather, so she could walk Harley up Ham Hill. It rose, temptingly, above the village, only a ten-minute walk away, but the slope from the village was steep and she'd no intention of climbing up to the country park in this wind.

Harley trotted quietly, close to Imogen. After several months of hard work, she'd finally trained him not to pull on the lead, so his sudden bound forward took her by surprise. 'Hey, slow down, Harley. Heel.' She took a tighter grip on the lead, turned a sharp corner in the lane, and stopped dead. She was just in time to avoid cannoning into a short, bald man in horn-rimmed spectacles. Dressed in brand-new running gear that strained over a sizable paunch, he swerved to avoid her, skidded to a halt and doubled over, wheezing, his round face damp and bright red.

Tail wagging furiously, Harley pounced.

'Get down, you daft ha'porth,' the man gasped.

Harley dropped back onto all fours, leaving two muddy pawprints on the man's sweatshirt. Imogen's lips twitched.

'When I've got my breath back,' panted Adam Hennessy, Imogen's friend and the owner of The Plough Inn, Lower Hembrow's public house, 'I'll have something to say about Harley's manners.'

'You're the only one he ever jumps on. You know he adores you –he chose you when he was a stray and wandered into Lower Hembrow. He's happy at the hotel, but he misses you and gets over-excited when you appear. He's perfectly behaved the rest of the time. Well, almost...' Imogen's voice tailed away. There'd been an unfortunate cushion-chewing incident last week.

Adam's breathing now back to normal, he pulled off his

glasses and polished them on his top. 'I'll forgive him for trying to bowl me over if you promise not to tell anyone you saw me running. As a pub landlord, I have a reputation to uphold.'

Imogen considered this. 'I didn't exactly see you running,' she pointed out. 'You appeared round the corner, skidded a bit and stopped, but I'll take your word for it. Are you sure you're not overdoing it? You look shattered.'

'Nonsense. I'm fitter than you think.' Adam squared his shoulders. 'Don't forget I used to be a police officer. I'll have you know I've passed a few fitness tests in my time.'

She contemplated his stomach. 'Recently?'

He chuckled. 'Not for years.'

'Well, don't kill yourself.' Imogen looked him up and down. 'Why the sudden rush to get fit? Oh—' A sudden light flashed on in her brain and she fell silent. They were good friends, she and Adam, but there were some boundaries they hadn't yet crossed.

She eyed the new kit. Was this sudden desire to get trim anything to do with Adam's interest in Imogen's friend, Steph Aldred?

'Take it easy, won't you? We'd all rather have you in one piece than on a slab at the mortuary after a heart attack.'

He opened his mouth but before he could speak she grasped the nettle and said, 'By "we", I mean everyone who cares about you, including Steph.'

Adam looked away, narrowed his eyes and tapped his Smartwatch briskly 'Actually, I've been running for a while now. I'm doing Couch to 5K. It's a nine-week programme.'

So, he wasn't yet ready to talk about Steph. She'd let it go for now. 'I've heard of the programme, but I haven't seen you running before.'

'I try to avoid sightings. Hence the early hour and the back lane.'

'How many more weeks do you have to go?'

'Eight and a bit.'

'Out of nine? Nearly there, then,' she spluttered.

Harley, eager for exercise, pulled on the lead and they all walked on together.

'We're on our way to the shop,' Imogen said. 'It'll be open now and I want a loaf of bread before it all goes.'

'Don't you have bread at the hotel?' Adam raised his eyebrows in mock surprise. 'Wyatt's already baked ours for lunch.'

Imogen grinned. 'Nice one-upmanship. Gerald, our snooty chef, bakes every morning. He prides himself on his rolls and the guests love them but I want a loaf of lovely, unhealthy, sliced white bread for my toast – just for a change.'

'Wyatt would agree. He complains he can't get Texas Toast here. Apparently it comes in a special packet and it's extra thick.'

Imogen groaned and kissed her fingers. 'That would be perfect. Unfortunately, I don't think Mrs Topsham sells anything so exotic in the village shop. Warburtons Toastie would be the nearest thing.'

Adam turned back. 'I'll give the shop a miss today. I'm improperly dressed for shopping and just a bit sweaty. Also, it's starting to rain.' He raised his hand. 'See you later.'

* * *

As Imogen pushed the shop door, its bell rang cheerfully. She stepped inside. Jenny Trevillian from the nearby farm turned, nodded and went back to her shopping list. Edwina Topsham, perched on a stool behind the counter, leaned on one elbow, her ample chest engulfing half the worktop where her 'Present from Llandudno' mug of strong brown tea balanced precariously on a roll of toilet paper. She beamed at Imogen over cans of beans, packets of rice and bottles of sunflower oil.

Alfie, the Saturday boy, stopped stacking boxes of apples and grinned. 'Where's Harley?

'I tied him up outside. There's not much room in here...'

Edwina eased herself around the counter. 'Nonsense,' she cried. 'Bring him in, m'dear. We can't leave the poor chap outside, can we? Not in the rain.' She bustled across to fling open the door, unhook Harley's lead and usher him inside. 'And you, Alfie Croft, can stop gawping and start fronting up those cans if you've finished with the fruit.'

Harley accepted Edwina's enthusiastic hug with no more than a resigned glance at Imogen. At last, Edwina struggled to her feet. 'Now, what can we do for you, Mrs Bishop? Running out of supplies, are you, what with all these foreigners up at your place?'

To Edwina, all visitors from outside South Somerset were 'foreigners.' In fact, the description covered anyone who'd been resident in Lower Hembrow for fewer than twenty years.

Imogen had inherited her late father's hotel a little over twelve months ago but she wasn't a total incomer. She'd lived at The Streamside Hotel as a teenager when her father first bought it.

Alfie's eyes slid to Harley then back to Edwina. Imogen took pity on him. 'Harley needs dog biscuits.' She reached for a box from the nearest shelf and shook it. Harley's ears pricked.

She handed the box to Alfie. 'Will you give him a couple? Not too many, mind.' She brushed raindrops from her coat and shivered. 'You're right, Mrs Topsham. The hotel's full this weekend. It's not the best weather for racing, though.'

'Don't you believe it,' Edwina returned to the counter. 'Soft going, they call it. It suits some of the horses better than others. Take Butterfly Charm, from Leo Murphy's yard up the road near

Misterton. She's running today and she likes a bit of give in the ground. Leo's offered young Belinda Sandford her first professional ride on the mare.'

Alfie piped up, 'My dad says she don't stand a chance. No stamina in that 'oss, he says. Can't stay the pace. Needs a jockey with the guts to use the whip on the final straight, not some girl.'

'Nonsense.' Jenny Trevillian thrust her shopping list in her pocket, juggled a variety of cereal boxes and frowned at Alfie. 'Young Belinda knows what she's doing. Butterfly's only a four-year-old and she needs encouragement, not punishment. You bring a young animal on with kindness. That's my opinion.' She dumped the boxes on the counter with her other purchases.

Alfie grunted. Jenny Trevillian's word on upbringing was pretty much law in the village. With her husband, Joe, she ran the nearby mixed farm, rearing cattle, sheep, pigs and six noisy children with equal fearsome efficiency.

'In any case,' Edwina agreed, 'the final furlong at Wincanton slopes downwards and the drainage is good. It's a perfect ride for Belinda. She's the most promising apprentice in Leo Murphy's yard, you know, and a local girl, at that. Lower Hembrow, born and bred.' She glowed with pride. 'All her mother's family lived here.'

Imogen was nursing a precious piece of gossip. Now, she savoured her moment of triumph. 'Belinda and her mother are staying at the hotel this weekend.'

Three sets of eyes turned her way. 'In fact,' she continued, 'we have several members of Butterfly Charm's syndicate dining with us. They're very excited, especially Belinda's mother, Diane, of course.'

Jenny Trevillian beamed, smugly. 'I was at school with Diane Webber. Of course, she's a Sandford, now. Maybe I can catch up with her while she's here.'

'Maybe.' Secretly, Imogen wondered if that would be wise. Reunions could be horrendous, rekindling all sorts of ancient jealousies and grievances. When Imogen's husband and father had died within weeks of each other, turning her world upside down, she'd met many old school friends for the first time in years. Those encounters had thrown her life into turmoil for months.

Still, at least she'd met Steph and Dan again. Her heart flipped over at the thought of Daniel Freeman. It was ridiculous at her age, turning fifty, just as she'd decided romance was over, to be as excited as an eighteen-year-old. She felt a hot blush creeping across her cheeks and quickly bent over, fiddling with Harley's collar to hide her face. No need to give the village grapevine more fertiliser.

2

RACECOURSE

That afternoon, the rain stopped and a watery sun shone over the gathered crowds at Wincanton Racecourse.

Diane Sandford's stomach clenched with nerves. Her maternal fears never left her. They'd first appeared when she watched Belinda, as a toddler, struggle up a rope ladder on the climbing frame in the park. The terrors flourished when Belinda moved on to her first bike, and almost overwhelmed Diane as her daughter played rugby, swung a hockey stick and rode her first Shetland pony.

But no fear could scramble Diane's stomach more than the thought of Belinda riding the sleek, excitable, head-tossing racehorse, Butterfly Charm, in today's steeplechase.

Her smile stitched firmly in place, Diane wished Rupert, her late husband, were here to experience the agony and pride of watching their daughter in her first professional race. Rupert had encouraged Belinda's love of racing. Diane had never liked horses – they were far too big and strong, with potentially deadly hooves – but nevertheless she'd kept her share in the horse's ownership syndicate even after her husband died.

She watched, outwardly calm, as Butterfly Charm sashayed round the parade ring for the last time, watching the spectators from the corner of one eye. The beautiful grey lapped up the admiration; as big a diva as an opera singer, she knew all eyes were drawn to her sleek coat and immaculate oiled hooves.

Diane would never admit her fear of horses to her horse-mad daughter. She was shielded from the animals today by Belinda and the other owners and trainers in the parade ring, but she still wished she could watch from a safer distance.

The bell rang and the trainers approached for final checks, and to give the jockeys a leg up into the saddle.

'Quite a girl, your daughter.' Diane started as Henry Oxon's voice boomed in her ear. He slipped an arm round her shoulders. 'Rupert would be proud.'

One of Rupert's oldest friends and colleagues, Henry, along with his wife, had been a tower of strength during the depressing months of Rupert's illness and eventual, inevitable, death. 'Time to get to the rails and watch young Belinda see off the competition.' All Henry's statements sounded like commands.

Diane accompanied Henry and the other three members of the Butterfly Charm owner's syndicate to the rails at the edge of the racetrack, close to the finishing post.

Henry's wife, Ling, smiled at Diane. 'Look at the odds.' She pointed to the line of bookies, whose boards proclaimed which horses were most – and least – fancied to win. Butterfly Charm merited only a humble 25-1.

'Belinda's going to surprise everyone.' Ling squeezed Diane's arm. 'She's an outsider so no one's expecting her to win, but that's because they don't know her. Their eyes are all on Season's Greetings, the favourite, but I think Belinda's in with a great chance.'

'I can hardly bear to watch,' Diane confessed.

'She'll be fine,' Henry insisted. His voice grated on Diane's already stretched nerves. All the words used to describe successful barristers applied to Henry. He was confident, gregarious and clever with a wide streak of ambition – a very different man from Rupert, who'd spent much of his working life on legal aid cases.

Somehow, Diane was never quite sure how, Henry had persuaded Butterfly Charm's trainer, Leo Murphy, to take Belinda on as a stable hand. It was due to merit alone, though, that he'd sponsored her through jockey training and offered her this, her first professional race as a conditional jockey.

Belinda was fond of Ling. Sometimes, Diane thought with a spark of envy, she seemed closer to Ling than to her own mother.

Nevertheless, Diane would be eternally grateful to Henry and Ling for their friendship; grateful enough to forgive Henry's habits of loudly discussing money, sneering at anyone who hadn't attended public school, and standing, always, just a little too close for comfort.

She stepped sideways, closer to Magnus and Laura Wilson, the other couple with shares in Butterfly Charm. Magnus murmured, 'Nervous?'

She nodded.

'Don't be. Just enjoy yourself. Belinda has nothing to prove. No one expects her to win.'

Diane managed a smile. 'I don't care whether she wins. I just want her to get round safely.'

Magnus squeezed her arm. 'She'll be loving every moment.' He turned away, holding a pair of binoculars to his eyes. 'Here they come. What a sight.'

* * *

Just then, as the rain returned, the first horses thundered past on their way to the start. The ground trembled beneath pounding hooves. There was Belinda, crouched forward, eyes straight ahead, focused. Butterfly Charm stretched her legs, glad to be active at last. The Ham Hill Handicap Chase was a two mile race with six huge jumps, taken twice, and including a dicey-looking water jump. Diane squeezed her eyes shut, terrified at the mere thought of it.

Now the horses and riders were at the starting tape, under starter's orders. Diane squinted at the big screen as the flag dropped and the runners headed for the first jump, their jockeys' silks a riot of colour.

Hedge trimmings flew as the horses lifted over the fence. Diane let out her breath. They were all over. Belinda was safe – for now.

But there was a long way to go.

The crowd gasped. A horse had fallen at the fourth. The jockey, an old pro, curled into a ball for safety and let the rest of the field swerve past.

'Not Belinda,' Diane muttered under her breath. 'Not Belinda.'

Butterfly Charm galloped smoothly, keeping in touch with the front runners, gliding over each obstacle with graceful ease. Diane forced herself to breathe evenly. It was going to be all right. Belinda was round safely and on the second circuit.

Another horse fell, unloading his rider, and the field was down to six with Butterfly Charm in fourth place.

The horses thundered down the track towards the rails, two riderless runners by their side. Diane's friends cheered, hoarse with excitement, almost drowning out the commentary. Ling bounced up and down on her toes, shrieking encouragement.

Butterfly Charm moved up to third place. There was just one

more fence to go. Belinda's purple cap bobbed in the air as the elegant grey lengthened her stride and, slowly, inch by inch, overtook the dark bay in front of her.

Diane clenched her hands at her chest, the knuckles white. 'Go on,' she whispered. 'Go on, Belinda.'

Butterfly Charm was at Season's Greetings' shoulder, still fighting, as the two horses took off and landed together over the final fence, galloping neck and neck, stride for stride, every sinew straining.

Diane gasped. Season's Greetings was tiring. Slowly, Butterfly Charm was moving ahead.

Then, unbelievably, she was in the lead, a short head in front of Season's Greetings.

Was it all over?

No, not yet. The other horse was fighting back. There was a long, downhill run to the finishing post, and Diane knew Butterfly Charm's chief flaw was a lack of speed in the final stretch.

Surely, Butterfly Charm couldn't possibly win? Diane's heart thudded as Butterfly Charm put on a burst of speed, gaining ground until she was ahead. Astonishingly, against the odds, she was going to win.

But then, she lurched. She jinked, swerved to the right. Quick as a flash, Belinda switched her whip to her right hand. She touched Butterfly's shoulder and the horse straightened and speeded up, leaving Season's Greetings in her wake as she thundered pass the post in first place.

Tears of joy sprang to Diane's eyes. Belinda had won. Her first proper race, and she'd won, against all the odds.

But something was wrong.

The cheering died away.

The crowd was murmuring.

Diane turned, confused. All around, people frowned, shaking their heads.

What could be wrong?

The loudspeaker blared and Diane's heart plummeted.

There was to be a Stewards' Enquiry.

Ling squeezed Diane's arm. 'What a shame.' The queue of punters in front of the bookies broke up into chattering groups.

Diane forced herself to breathe. She felt sick. Belinda's first race. Had she won, or lost? Diane couldn't tell. It was all in the hands of the stewards.

* * *

Belinda arrived at the Stewards' Room, her stomach churning. Alex Deacon, the jockey who'd ridden Season's Greetings into second place, was already inside.

The stewards sat behind a long polished table. Belinda was ushered to a plain wooden chair, a few metres from Alex.

Alex, several years older than Belinda and riding in her fourth professional race, held her racing helmet cradled on her lap. Golden blonde waves flowed over her shoulders. Belinda's own hair had partly escaped from an elastic band on top of her head and stray wisps, damp with sweat, stuck to her forehead. She wished she'd taken a moment to wash her face and brush her hair.

Alex oozed with confidence as they watched a video of the race. She couldn't wait to put her side of the story.

'Butterfly Charm came up on Season's Greetings' shoulder and began to pull ahead. I knew my horse would make a great finish and I waited to time it right. But just as I was about to whip him on, Butterfly Charm moved to the right, crossing my path, so I had to pull him up.'

She glanced at Belinda, flicking her hair back over one shoulder.

Belinda kept her eyes on the Chief Steward, but she could see Alex's smirk. She'd seen her smile like that on the dance floor at Young Farmers' events. The boys fell for it every time.

The Chief Steward was in his late fifties, a well-built farmer with a reputation for being firm but fair. Even so, Belinda could have sworn his cheeks flushed a little.

It was her turn to speak. Leo had trained her for this but she was still terrified.

She thought about Leo's instructions. 'Keep it simple,' he'd said. 'Don't try to be clever.'

'We came down the straight,' she said.

'Sorry,' said the steward. 'Can you speak a little louder?'

She swallowed and tried again. 'After the last jump, we were neck and neck and then Butterfly Charm drew ahead.'

'Yes.' The steward tapped his pen on the table. 'And what did you do next?'

Do? What had she done? It was all a blur. 'I tapped Butterfly with my whip. Just once, to encourage her.'

'Which hand?' asked the Chair.

Belinda thought back. Horses raced clockwise at Wincanton. 'We were on the outside, with Season's Greetings inside, next to the rails, and my whip was in my left hand.'

She closed her eyes, reliving the heady excitement of the moment. 'I tapped Butterfly Charm's flank, to keep her going, but she moved in a little to the right. I couldn't see Season's Greetings, for we were well ahead by then.' It didn't hurt, did it, to point that out?

'As soon as I realised my horse had moved to the right, I corrected her.' Her voice faded away. She admitted the truth to herself. In a rush of adrenalin, with the finishing post so close, she'd lost control of the horse. Just for a split second. And, in that instant, Butterfly had drifted.

Belinda licked dry lips. The Chief Steward nodded. 'Thank you. I'll ask you both to leave the room and we'll deliberate. We'll make our decision known as soon as possible.'

Fighting to keep any sign of emotion from her face, Belinda left the room behind her rival. Alex turned and raised an eyebrow. 'Not the greatest debut,' she said, and her eyes glittered.

Belinda bit back a retort. She was sure Alex had deliberately pulled up. 'Let's wait for the result,' she said.

'Oh yes. My uncle, the racing journalist, is here. The news will be in the evening editions.'

'You're assuming you'll get the decision?'

'Of course.' Alex smirked. 'You'll learn. Just a rookie error.'

Belinda looked Alex in the eye. 'Did you pull him up deliberately?'

Alex leaned in and smiled. 'What do you think?' she murmured.

She'd known it. Belinda clenched a fist in fury. She longed to slap Alex's smug face.

At that moment, a camera whirred.

Alex smiled and turned away. 'Uncle John. Nice to see you.'

Smirking, she took her uncle's arm and walked away. After two steps, she glanced back over her shoulder. 'Can't wait to see that photo in the *Post*.'

3

DINNER

The dining room at The Streamside Hotel buzzed.

Diane had booked a table at seven thirty for the Butterfly Charm syndicate. Belinda had wanted to stay away, but Ling had persuaded her to come. 'Win or lose,' she'd said, 'we always celebrate.'

Belinda had groaned. 'They'll all be so disappointed. I won fairly. I really did.' She shook her head. The enquiry had been a nightmare.

'Cheer up,' Ling said. 'That was the most exciting race we've seen all season. Of course, we wanted you to win and we all had a little flutter, but we joined the syndicate for fun, not profit. You did a terrific job to come second.'

Belinda chewed her lip. She hoped her mother hadn't put money on the race. She could barely afford the annual fees for the syndicate, but insisted on staying in it all the same. Perhaps it was because Dad had been such an enthusiast. Belinda knew Mum was scared of horses, no matter how much she pretended otherwise.

Belinda's eyes filled with tears.

She wished Dad were here to laugh and wink at her. 'It's sport, Belinda, not real life,' he'd say, with a hug to show he understood his daughter's disappointment. He'd never shared her competitive instincts. As a criminal lawyer, he'd fought hard for truth and justice and had lost, when necessary, with grace. He'd also had very sharp eyes. Belinda was sure Alex had deliberately held back her horse, making it seem as though Butterfly Charm's small swerve had seriously impeded her progress. Dad would have seen it.

Belinda blinked hard and took a breath. Dad would tell her to accept the verdict. It didn't matter that Alex had been sneaky. That was all part of the game, like a clever defence in court. There was no point in sulking.

Instead, she made herself sit straight at the elegant table, where every place was set with spotless cutlery and sparkling glass. The champagne was ready, the first bottle already open and nestled enticingly in an ice bucket. Belinda must put on a good face. She stitched on a smile.

Henry Oxon raised his glass in her direction. 'Remember, you passed the post first. Nobody can take that away from you. A jolly good show for your first professional race and the stewards recognised that. You haven't been fined, or penalised.'

'Not by the Jockey Club,' Belinda admitted, 'but I'm sure Leo will have something to say in the yard, although he was kind today.'

'Stop worrying,' Ling said. 'It happens to everyone. You told me that yourself.'

'Not in their first race,' Belinda sighed. 'With their mother watching – and the syndicate – and Alex laughing at me.' She groaned. 'I'm sure she held Season's Greetings back deliberately, to make me look even worse.' Then she bit her lip. She was whining and Dad wouldn't have liked that.

Henry was on her side. 'Probably. Racing's a battle, Belinda, just like the law. I show my clients in a good light, so I win the case even when I know they're over-egging their side of the argument and maybe even stretching the truth. It's all a game.'

Ling said, 'Belinda's Dad didn't see it that way. He wanted to punish the ones who deserved it, not play games just to win.'

Henry gave a bark of laughter. 'Poor old Rupert. A great guy, honest as the day is long, but not really cut out for the real world.'

Magnus Wilson, an anaesthetist at the local hospital, leaned closer to Belinda. He was a handsome man, about the same age as her father and Henry, and a long-time friend of both. He had the brightest blue eyes Belinda had ever seen, although he hid them behind a pair of silver-rimmed spectacles. He removed the glasses and smiled at her. 'Take no notice of Henry. He has no morals. Your Dad was a good man who wanted to make the world a better place.'

Laura, Magnus's wife, said. 'We could use a few more men like that around here.' She glared at Henry.

There was a short silence. Henry took a breath, as though about to speak, but Ling rested a restraining hand on his arm.

* * *

Just inside the dining room, Imogen was chatting to Emily, her hotel manager. She heard raised voices and glanced across the room, listening, ready to deal with any trouble.

The big, red-faced man at Belinda Sandford's table emptied his glass of wine in one long draught. It probably wasn't his first. His tiny wife wore an embroidered silk dress, her hair in an elegant chignon, immaculately neat, complete with a white flower. She smiled at the young girl on the other side of the table. 'Don't take any notice of Henry,' she advised. 'Lawyers love to argue and even more, they love to win. Henry forgets he's not in court and that he might hurt people's feelings.'

The big man refilled his glass, laughing loudly. 'Quite right, Ling. Take no notice of me, Belinda. Get back on the horse tomorrow. Onwards and upwards, that's the spirit.'

Imogen raised her eyebrows at Emily. The awkward moment had passed. The staff wouldn't need to break the tension by making enquiries about the food, or topping up water glasses.

Emily grinned at her boss. 'Race days can be tricky,' she said. 'Owners are either celebrating or commiserating, and whatever's happened they all drink too much.'

Although Emily was still in her twenties, she'd run The Streamside Hotel efficiently for several years, first for Councillor Jones, Imogen's father, and now for Imogen. Imogen had soon found she could rely on the younger woman's common sense and experience.

Imogen's own area of expertise was the garden. Her gaze slid through the window, enjoying the new floodlighting that lit up the snowdrops, so they mirrored the myriad stars in the night sky. Imogen had brought all her landscaping expertise to bear on the hotel's grounds during the past six months, and this year, the garden would look wonderful. The earliest of the daffodils were already in bloom under the hawthorn trees by the stream.

She breathed a sigh of pure happiness. The bluebells and crocuses would flower soon and the hectic spring work begin. She'd barely be indoors for the next few months and there was nowhere she would rather be than outside in the fresh air.

She heard a noise in the reception area and turned. Adam Hennessy was hurrying through the lobby, waving, his face serious.

Imogen's throat tightened. 'Something's wrong,' she muttered to Emily, and crossed the foyer. 'What is it?'

Adam stopped in his tracks. 'Came to warn you. The police are on their way. They want to speak to some of your guests. I thought you'd want to head them off, keep things calm.'

'Too right. The last thing we need is a visit from the police. I suppose it's not just parking offences?'

'No such luck,' he said. 'Trouble at the racecourse, apparently.' He dropped his voice. 'There's a body.'

'A what?' Imogen stiffened. A surge of adrenaline tied a knot in her stomach. Not again. Not another death. It was less than a year since her own husband had been murdered.

In a sudden rush of feeling, the rawness and pain of that time returned. Her legs trembled.

Adam took her arm and led her to a chair in a quiet corner, almost hidden behind a huge pair of potted ferns. 'Sorry, that was thoughtless. It's no one you know. At least, I don't think so. One of the jockeys.'

'An accident in a race?' The knot in Imogen's stomach began to untie itself. This time, the bad news was not for her. 'Who do they want to speak to?'

'According to my old mate, James Barton, who rang to let me know—'

'The forensic pathologist?'

He nodded. 'The police want to talk to Butterfly Charm's jockey.'

Imogen jerked her head towards the dining room. 'She's having dinner with friends. And they're not too happy. There was an incident during the race, I heard. I'll bring her out of the dining room if I can, without causing a fuss. Belinda, that's her name.'

He nodded. 'Are you up to it?'

'Of course. It was just the shock. It brought it all back – you know, Greg's death and everything.' Shakily, Imogen stood up, squaring her shoulders. 'I'm fine, now. I'll get Emily to head off the police and take them somewhere quiet.'

She slipped back into the dining room and murmured in Emily's ear. As ever, the manager caught on fast. She gave a short start and a long stare. 'They can use one of the conference rooms.' She was already on her way to organise things.

Imogen swallowed hard, took a breath, let it out slowly and approached the guests at the syndicate table.

She leaned close to Belinda. 'I'm so sorry to disturb you. We need to talk. Would you mind just popping out for a moment?'

Belinda turned, frowning. 'I'm sorry? What's the matter? Is it the Stewards' Enquiry?'

She looked terrified. Imogen said, 'Please don't be alarmed. Come with me and I'll tell you in private. It's too public here.' Belinda's eyes slid past her. Already, one or two diners at other tables had stopped eating and turned towards the syndicate table.

Belinda scrambled up, dropping her napkin on the floor.

The big man at her table rose to his feet. 'Is there something wrong?' he boomed.

His wife touched his hand. 'Be quiet, Henry,' she murmured. 'No scenes in the hotel, please.'

He grunted, hesitated, and subsided. 'Can't we have a little peace and quiet while we're eating?' he growled.

Belinda followed Imogen from the room and another woman – Belinda's mother, Diane Sandford, Imogen realised – tagged along with her daughter.

The rest of the syndicate exchanged glances, shrugged, and refilled their glasses. The other diners in the room, losing interest, went back to their meals.

4

THE PLOUGH

Adam was waiting in the entrance foyer. He said, 'Emily's taken the police officers to the Hazel Conference Room. We thought your guests would rather not be escorted by the police.'

Belinda's eyes were like saucers. 'I haven't done anything. Why do the police want me?'

'Don't worry, dear.' Diane Sandford's hand was at her throat. She seemed almost as anxious as her daughter.

Imogen showed them to the conference room and returned to reception. She grabbed Adam's arm. 'You'd better tell me everything you know. Come into the office.'

He sank into an office chair, eyes gleaming. Imogen had seen that look on his face before. A retired policeman, Adam was never going to lose his fascination with crime.

Imogen said, 'Thanks for diverting the police. Hardly anyone's noticed they're here.'

'I thought you'd rather not have a fuss. The body's at the race-course and they'll just be asking for a preliminary account from your guest.'

'Belinda Sandford's her name. She grew up around here – her mother's a local girl.'

Adam blinked. 'How do you know all that?'

She grinned. 'You should have come into the shop with me this morning, and then you'd have heard the gossip. Anyway, as the police are here, I assume this unfortunate jockey's death wasn't caused by an accidental fall from a horse?'

'Nothing so simple. James says the winner of the 3.15 was found with her head stuck in a trough of water in one of the stables. The jockey was a woman – well, a girl, really. Someone called Alexandra – or Alex – Deacon. Apparently, there was a Stewards' Enquiry into the race and your Belinda Sandford was found guilty of tactical obstruction of Alex's horse. That must be why the police want to see her.'

'And that accounts for the air of gloom at her table this evening,' Imogen said. 'They glugged down champagne as though there was no tomorrow, but none of them looked as though they were enjoying it. Emily and I thought we'd need to fend off a shouting match. The other people at the table are members of the horse's syndicate. They each own a leg, or something.'

'Ah. Interesting.' Adam nodded, frowning.

'Why especially? Stop teasing.'

He laughed. 'Sorry. Trying to maintain my aura of mystery.' Imogen smiled. Adam's moon face and twinkling eyes really weren't designed to look mysterious.

He said, 'I know very little about horse racing, but I've heard that the members of a syndicate share any prize money. They'll be out of pocket over the race.'

'Aha. I see what you're thinking. A motive?'

He held up a finger in warning. 'We're getting way ahead of ourselves. I imagine this poor woman, Alex Deacon, might have had a heart condition or bumped her head or something. There could be any number of reasons she died.'

'There's going to be plenty of gossip when the news gets out. If I know Lower Hembrow, the place will be buzzing with speculation by tomorrow.'

Adam laughed at that. 'Tomorrow? I bet it's already a hot topic across the road in The Plough. Which reminds me, it's busy over there this evening. I need to get back, reluctant though I am to drag myself away from the action over here. I'll see what the locals have to say, but I'm not getting involved.' He folded his arms. 'And, what does that snort mean?'

'You know you can't wait to start piecing together the evidence.'

'Not much evidence available at the moment. I'm keeping a beautifully open mind and I refuse to see murder around every corner. Most unexpected deaths are perfectly innocent. But I need to get back to the pub. It's Saturday night, so it'll be heaving by now. Can you deal with the police?'

'We can cope,' Imogen smiled. 'Emily will keep an eye on the syndicate, make sure there's no trouble. As soon as they finish eating, she'll spirit them away to take coffee somewhere private. The hotel's bursting at the seams but I think we have one suite spare, a rather gloomy one that needs redecorating at the back of the hotel. If I know Emily, she'll keep the police well away from the rest of the guests.'

'Worth her weight in gold, your Emily.'

'Meanwhile,' Imogen said, 'I'll go back up and wait to catch Belinda and her mother when the police have finished. I think they'll need strong coffee.'

* * *

Adam crossed the road, enjoying the velvety darkness despite the cold. He loved Lower Hembrow village when it was like this – quiet, peaceful and a million miles away from his former life with the West Midlands police in Birmingham. The sky had cleared at the end of the day and the brightest of late February moons glinted, surrounded by the sparkle of millions of stars.

He'd made a good decision, moving here. Who wouldn't want to live in Somerset?

Adam felt he could almost reach up and touch Venus, as it dipped below the horizon.

He pushed open the door to The Plough. Light and noise flooded out, with all the force of a breaking wave.

'Here he is.' The voice of the new barman, Rex Croft, soared above the racket. Adam had a soft spot for the Croft family. Rex's younger brother, Alfie, had named Harley, when the stray animal had arrived and adopted him.

Harley now lived across the road at The Streamside Hotel. Adam, having never before owned a dog, had discovered the role was trickier than expected; Harley had all but wrecked his bachelor quarters at The Plough.

Searching for a solution, reasoning that Imogen was fragile after her husband's death and a dog might help her adjust, Adam had suggested Harley should live permanently at the hotel.

Imogen and Harley had soon bonded, spending hours together in the hotel gardens, but sometimes, Adam discovered with surprise, he missed the dog's friendly presence.

Not tonight, though. The Plough was packed with locals and a dozen heads in the bar turned to watch Adam's progress between the polished tables. He nodded cheerfully at them all, let himself through the folding countertop and stepped behind the bar.

One of the young farmers shouted, 'Come on then, Adam. Tell us all about it. What's going on over there? Who died?'

Adam had been right. The news had already hit Lower Hembrow.

Oswald, the ageing gardener from The Streamside Hotel, raised his glass of cloudy local cider. His weathered cheeks glowed from the drink. They were almost as red as his nose which, large and leathery, was permanently flushed, a victim of his all-weather outdoor life. A few strands of grey hair wavered on top of Oswald's skull.

'There's been a spot of excitement over at the racecourse,' he said. 'Some poor girl's dead, I hear.' He shook his head. 'Drowned, that's what I heard. Drowned in a water trough.'

An aggressive voice interrupted. 'I'll bet that was murder, then. You don't drown yourself, do you? Stands to reason.' That was Joe Trevillian, escaped from his farm and family, and making the most of an hour or so of freedom.

'Where did you hear that?' Adam asked.

Joe grunted. 'It's all over the county. Ann Clarkson's not too pleased. The dead girl worked at her racing yard, over Ditcheat way. An up-and-coming young jockey, she was, so I hear.'

He scratched his head. 'Ann will be upset. She and Leo Murphy have been rivals for years. She's hoping to steal his place as the top trainer in the county any way she can, and she had her eye on young Alex to help.'

He took a gulp of cider and wiped his mouth on his sleeve. 'Two up-and-coming female jockeys, from rival yards, in the same race? You mark my words, two women in competition will lead to nothing but trouble. Jealousy, that'll be behind it.'

Adam was about to suggest that maybe the dead girl's family deserved more sympathy than her employer, when the sudden crack of glass on wood shocked the drinkers into silence.

Rex Croft had slammed a pint glass on the bar, sending a wave of beer across the surface. 'What do you mean by that? You accusing Belinda or something?' Adam had never before heard the normally gentle Rex raise his voice.

Joe held up his hands in mock surrender. 'Not accusing anyone of anything, young fellow. Just a passing comment. Keep your hair on.'

Rex's eyes flashed. 'You'd better watch your tongue, Joe Trevillian. If you were twenty years younger I'd take you outside...'

'You and whose army?' sneered Joe.

Time to step in. 'Let's calm down,' Adam said. 'This is just speculation. All we know is that this young jockey died at the racecourse. It was probably an accident – and it's a tragedy for her family. So, let's show some respect, shall we?'

Why was Rex so indignant on Belinda's behalf? Adam had only a vague recollection of seeing her once or twice, when she'd dropped into The Plough with friends.

Maybe Rex had more than a passing interest in her.

The drinkers in The Plough, disappointed to find that no one was about to throw a punch, turned back to their own debates. Joe Trevillian waved his glass. 'Same again.'

Adam shot a warning glance at Rex and moved to serve the farmer. 'Sheppy's?'

Joe nodded, rested his elbows on the bar and asked, 'Are the police calling you in on this one, Hennessy?'

Adam passed over a glass of cider and eyed the farmer. For some reason he'd never understood, Joe Trevillian had taken a dislike to him. He never missed an opportunity to sneer at Adam's policing background.

Adam's last case had ended in disaster when someone leaked details of a police raid, and a colleague had died. Adam had lost his taste for policing, ended his career early, taken his Detective Chief Inspector's pension and his pot of savings – one of the benefits of never having married – and bought The Plough.

He sometimes thought he learned more from the gossip of locals like Joe Trevillian, Rex Croft and the evergreen gardener, Oswald, than he had from any of his officers' laboriously typed reports.

Why did Trevillian feel such antipathy towards him? Was it just a cantankerous nature? The man had no links, so far as Adam could tell, with anything that had happened in Birmingham.

Maybe the man just objected to overweight, undersized, unathletic ex-policemen moving into his village. 'Give it another thirty years,' Adam had told Imogen, 'and maybe Joe and I will be best buddies.'

But, he rather doubted it.

He smiled at Trevillian and blinked, mildly, through his thick spectacles. He liked the way they disguised the workings of his active mind. 'I'm a private citizen, these days,' he said. 'I don't know any more than you about this poor woman.'

Trevillian snorted. 'Bet you could find out, though, if you wanted to.'

A young farmer buying a round for himself and six mates saved Adam from the need to reply. By the time he'd filled their glasses, Joe had lost interest and turned away.

5

GARDEN

On Sunday morning, The Plough's chef, Wyatt Logan, arrived early. 'We've got a bit of a crisis around here, Boss,' he drawled. 'Extra lunch orders and we're plumb out of beef.'

Adam sighed. Wyatt was a great cook, introducing jerk rubs and cornbread to The Plough, and recalibrating local residents' understanding of 'gravy.' To Adam's surprise, The Plough's locals, those most rural of English folk, lapped it up. But Wyatt's forward planning was disastrous. If his food hadn't been so good, he'd be long gone.

At least, today, he had the grace to blush. 'I guess we might be able to borrow from The Streamside.'

'That's the second time this month,' Adam pointed out. 'We ran out of lamb chops a couple of weeks ago. It's getting embarrassing. Maybe we should just offer vegetarian food. Or vegan, so you don't have to order meat?'

Wyatt's eyes were brown puddles of horror. 'No way, Boss. Sure, some of the locals love their greens, but those farmers out in all weathers? They'll just fade away without their steak. Why don't I hop across to The Streamside and beg from Emily?'

Adam paused. Maybe he should go himself. His policeman's antennae were twitching. Imogen might know more about Saturday's death at the races by now.

'Don't bother,' he said. 'I'll go this time. Just make sure it doesn't happen again.'

Wyatt's face fell. He seemed to like visiting the hotel. Adam wondered why. Maybe he hoped for a job there. Adam imagined Gerald, The Streamside's chef, who longed for a coveted third AA Rosette, shuddering at the thought. No. The man would starve rather than serve Wyatt's signature cheese dip and fries.

Adam arrived at the hotel and waved at Emily through the office window. She pointed towards the garden. 'She's on her way out,' she mouthed.

Adam found Imogen wearing her favourite brown gardening cords, flannel shirt, sweater and gilet. 'Gardening today? A bit chilly, isn't it?'

'Layers,' she told him. 'They're the answer when it's cold. You start off wearing as many clothes as you can find. Then you warm up a bit and shed one item at a time until you're down to a T-shirt.'

Adam shivered. 'You look determined.'

'Harley and I are pruning,' she said. 'Have you come to give us a hand?'

Harley was already at her side, alert, his tongue hanging out in anticipation.

'I've never pruned, but give me the secateurs, tell me what to do, and I'm your man,' Adam said. 'But first, I need a favour. Can you loan us a few pounds of beef from your kitchens? Wyatt's underordered again. Do you have any spare?'

She chortled. 'With Emily in charge? Of course we have. You could have rung her directly. I think,' she nodded, solemnly, 'in fact, I'm absolutely certain that you came here this morning because you wanted an excuse to pick my brains and find out more about this racecourse affair.'

Adam grinned. 'I can't deny it, but I really do need beef, so...'

Imogen sighed, rolled her eyes, and led him back to the office. Emily was hard at work, her computer keyboard clattering like gun shot as she typed.

Imogen explained The Plough's problem. 'Can you organise someone to take any beef we can spare across to Wyatt?'

'I'll sort it out,' Emily promised, clicking 'save' and logging off the computer. 'I'll take it over myself.'

Imogen opened her mouth to object. Surely someone from the kitchen could go? But Emily was already on her way.

Harley, tail wagging, led the way through the garden to the potting shed, where a huge variety of forks, spades, shears, loppers and secateurs hung neatly along the walls. Adam touched a finger on the sharp edges of one of the hoes and whistled.

'I'm sorry to say all I have for my pathetic little garden is a spade, a fork and one of those wooden dibber things I've never actually used. But this year I'm going to get it all in shape. The paddock's too big for a beer garden so I plan to steal a little corner for myself for my own garden. Though how I'll find the time, I have no idea. My retirement's proving anything but restful at the moment. I meant to spend every day painting, but I've hardly touched my brushes this year.'

Imogen stroked the shining surfaces of a range of different sizes and shapes of spade. 'That painting of the village you gave me at Christmas is lovely. The guests adore it. One wanted to buy it, remember?'

'It was New Year's Eve and he was drunk.'

'True, but it's something.'

Adam grunted. The truth was, since meeting Imogen's old

school friend, Daniel Freeman, he found his own amateur efforts embarrassing.

Daniel was a well-established artist, working from a proper studio, with an exhibition in Yeovil in a few months' time. He was also far too handsome for a man of fifty, with a full head of hair showing only an elegant streak or two of grey.

Imogen liked him, a lot. Was it just a crush from their school-days, or something more serious? And, if it was serious, could Dan – Adam noticed Imogen called him Dan, these days– be trusted not to hurt her? After all, he had an ex-wife and a son living in the South of France. Not exactly a good omen.

Still, Imogen was an adult. It was none of Adam's business.

She pushed open the potting shed door.

'It's beautifully warm in here,' Adam said.

'It's Oswald's favourite place. He hides in here and drinks tea. It wasn't always a potting shed – it's brick-built and very sturdy. I think it was a barn or a stable, once. One of the family who owned the estate before my father bought it, used it as a study. They put in these windows – one on either side. This one,' she pointed, 'looks out over the stream, and you can see the main building from the other.'

'I like the smell in here. Earthy,' Adam inhaled. 'I could enjoy painting this place. A still life, you know, with all these shiny tools hanging on the walls – so beautiful, yet menacing.'

She grinned. 'Menacing? That's the policeman talking. These tools are Oswald's pride and joy. When it's pouring with rain, or freezing cold, there's nothing he likes better than cleaning and sharpening all the blades.'

She took down a pair of secateurs and handed them over. 'Talking of freezing weather, I need to start work. I've heard there are winter storms on the way, and I won't get anything done if the garden's covered with a foot of snow for a week.'

She gripped the handles of a hefty wheelbarrow and steered it, refusing Adam's offer to help, out of the shed and towards a tall row of fiery stems. 'Dogwood.' She gathered half a dozen bright red shoots in one hand. 'I grow them for the colour. They've been beautiful this winter, but it's time to cut them right down so they'll grow again next year. I'll collect the best stems and put them in water in the hotel. They'll soon grow new leaves and bring spring into the place.' She cut down the branches and waved them in the air. 'Lovely, aren't they?'

'Meanwhile,' Adam said, unable to raise much enthusiasm for pruning, 'what happened last night? Did DCI Andrews march your guest away in handcuffs?'

She piled the stems in her wheelbarrow. 'The police were only here for a few minutes. I gather they were just getting a handle on events at the racecourse.'

'The whole affair was the talk of the pub,' Adam said. 'Tempers were running high. Rex seems to have an interest in this Belinda Sandford, and I thought he was going to land a punch on Joe Trevillian's nose. Not that I would have minded. The man's a grumpy old so and so. I don't know how I've offended him.'

Imogen stopped work and stood a moment, hands on hips. 'He's like that with everyone. Some kind of chip on his shoulder, I suppose. He thinks the world's against him.'

She pointed to another clump of bright stems. 'You can chop those down, if you like.' Adam grinned, took the hint and bent to the task.

'Young Belinda was in quite a state last night,' Imogen confided. 'Luckily her mother was here to look after her, although she seemed as upset as her daughter. Belinda left for work first thing this morning – you know how it is with racing yards – they start work at the crack of dawn, but Diane's staying for another night.'

'I hoped Belinda would still be here.'

Imogen raised an eyebrow. 'Why? Did you want to cross-examine her?' Her lips curved in a knowing smile. 'Are you going to get involved?'

'Not likely. I'm retired, and I want to stay that way. But I'm just as nosy as the next man.'

Imogen gave him a look that his friend, James, would describe as 'old-fashioned.' It involved raised eyebrows, pursed lips and a brief shake of the head.

Adam ignored her and attacked a tall branch of dogwood, his secateurs slicing neatly through the stems.

She said, 'To be honest, I don't know any more details. Just that this other jockey, Alex Deacon, was found dead in the stables at the racecourse. I tried very hard – well, moderately hard – not to eavesdrop when the police were talking, but I did hear something about her body in a trough of water.

'She'd just won a race, rather acrimoniously, I believe. It depended on a Stewards' Enquiry and Belinda was deemed to have obstructed Alex's horse. There's no love lost between the girls, I hear.'

'Who told you that?'

Imogen had the grace to blush. 'One of the guests at Belinda's table. There were two couples, plus Belinda and her mother. They all have shares in the horse, Butterfly Charm.'

'Quite a set of potential suspects by the sound of it. Did you hear anything about them?'

Imogen wrinkled her nose. 'Belinda told me their names. She'd thought the police were about to arrest her, and she was so relieved after they left that she couldn't stop talking. Let me think, now.'

She closed her eyes for a moment, then opened them. 'They sat at the big round table by the window. Belinda's mother,

Diane, sat with Laura Wilson, a glamorous blonde, on one side and Laura's husband, Magnus, on the other.' She broke off to think. 'Yes, that's right. Then, a noisy, opinionated barrister, Henry Oxon, sat on the other side of Laura with his Thai wife, Ling.'

She grinned. 'There, are you impressed with my memory?'

'Brilliant. Anything else strike you about the syndicate?'

'Well, the champagne flowed rather freely and things became a bit rowdy. I thought the barrister was going to start a fight but his wife headed it off. Belinda's mother was necking the wine like water. She was a touch wobbly on her pins when we went up in the lift, and a bit hysterical about her daughter.'

'Anything about the other couple?'

She nodded. 'The man, Magnus, works at the hospital. He sees himself as something of a ladies' man, I think. After the meal, he tried to persuade Emily to join him in a glass of whisky.'

'And did she?' Adam was curious.

'Not Emily. She's far too sensible to drink on duty. In any case, he was with his wife, so it was all perfectly innocent.'

Adam, with a grunt of satisfaction, removed a long, bright red stem of dogwood, and laid it on the pile. Harley sniffed at the branch, sighed, and lay down.

'Exhausted, are you?' Adam asked. It was good to see Harley contented. There was plenty of space to run here. Not that Harley showed any inclination to move at the moment.

Imogen looked at her watch and straightened up, one hand on her back. 'Ouch. Getting old.' She shot Adam a glance, smiling mischievously. 'By the way, Steph's coming tomorrow for the Spring Fair committee meeting. They call it the Spring Fair, although it doesn't happen until early May, so shouldn't it be called the Summer Fair? Anyway, we're holding it outside in the hotel garden. Optimists, all of us.'

Adam laughed. 'With alternative arrangements in case of rain?'

'Of course. Marquees. Big ones. You're coming to the meeting, aren't you?'

Adam made a face. He'd forgotten all about it. In a weak moment, he'd agreed to join the committee, his arm twisted by both the energetic vicar, Helen Pickles, and Imogen. Finally, Maria Rostropova, known in The Plough as the Most Glamorous Woman in the Village, had battered down the rest of his defences.

He hadn't known Steph would be there.

He turned away to keep his face hidden. He thought about Steph, one of Imogen's old school friends, far more than he'd admit to anyone, even Imogen.

Steph was bright and lively, a journalist who'd made her living delivering witty columns for magazines but planned to write a book. 'All I need,' she often said, 'is a decent subject.' Her face, with its upturned nose, large brown eyes and wide mouth always on the verge of laughter, surfaced much too often in Adam's daydreams. He grew tongue-tied in her presence, like a schoolboy. It was all quite ridiculous for a man of his age.

He glanced at Imogen, wondering what she thought, about to confide in her, but lost his nerve at the last moment and drew back.

It's blindingly obvious, he told himself, that Steph, the successful journalist, is not going to be interested in a middle-aged ex-copper who's spent his entire adult life proving himself unsuccessful with women.

He snapped the secateurs shut and stuffed them in a pocket.

6

COFFEE

On Monday morning, Harley greeted Imogen by dropping his disgusting toy rabbit, covered in dribble, at her feet. Michael, Emily's deputy, had given the thing to him and he was meant to keep it in his basket. Imogen often had to steal it when he wasn't looking, leaving him bereft and puzzled while she threw it in the washing machine.

One of the disadvantages of 'living over the shop,' as she called residence at the hotel, was that Imogen felt on almost permanent show.

Harley, on the other hand, loved the guests. On Saturday, Imogen had only just prevented him dropping his rabbit on Laura Wilson's ivory silk skirt.

Laura had roared with laughter in an earthy, deep voice, startlingly at odds with her elegant appearance. 'Gorgeous dog,' she'd enthused. 'We had two or three mutts like him on the farm while I was growing up. Mum and Dad still keep a couple of sheepdogs.'

Imogen wiped Harley's drool from her shoes just as Steph arrived for the Spring Fair committee meeting.

Small, dark-haired, and dressed in cheerful blue and yellow, Steph waved the morning paper in Imogen's face, bubbling with excitement. 'What do you know about Wincanton? It's all over the papers – one of the jockeys died in suspicious circumstances on Saturday. Have you heard anything? And have you seen Adam? I'm eaten up with curiosity and he gets inside information from his friendly pathologist, doesn't he?'

Nothing excited Steph more than hot news.

'You can ask him yourself,' Imogen grinned as Adam arrived, spruced up with neatly combed hair and, Imogen could swear, a new pair of horn-rimmed glasses. 'Let's go up to the Hawthorn conference room. I booked it for this morning's meeting. Emily will show the others up when they arrive.'

The Hawthorn Room was one of Imogen's favourites, for the window looked out over her beloved gardens and the sun peeked cheerfully through the window. When the room was unoccupied, Imogen often sat there alone, drinking coffee and planning.

As she led the way to the lift, past the dining room where Emily was overseeing preparations for lunch, a commotion in the foyer stopped her in her tracks. A high-pitched voice was shouting, 'I don't care, I'm going to ask him.'

Diane Sandford, face distorted, hair unkempt, ran to Adam and clutched at his sleeve. 'Please help us,' she sobbed. 'Everyone thinks my daughter killed that jockey, but Belinda wouldn't hurt a fly. They told me you're a policeman...' The rest of her sentence disappeared in a flood of tears.

* * *

Adam glanced at Imogen. 'Can we use the office?' he asked.

She nodded and he ushered Diane Sandford away from the fascinated gaze of the guests in the foyer, mentally rehearsing his response to her plea. Despite years of dealing with anxious, distraught members of the public, his heart still went out to parents whose child was under threat – no matter how old the child.

He motioned for Diane to sit down, but she stayed on her feet, pacing restlessly backwards and forwards across the room, hands clasped. Her face was white and Adam could see that tears threatened. 'You have to help us,' she begged.

'I'm no longer a police officer,' Adam pointed out. 'I know this is hard for you and your daughter—'

She faced him, 'That's just it,' she said. 'Belinda isn't taking it seriously. She says she has nothing to worry about – but if that's so, why did the police come?' Her voice tailed off.

'Please sit down,' Adam said, firmly.

Emily's face appeared at the window. 'Coffee?' She mouthed. Adam nodded his thanks and gestured at the chair. 'Take your time and tell me what happened.'

At last, Diane sat, hovering on the edge of the chair as if ready to run away at any moment. 'Belinda's a jockey at Leo Murphy's stables,' she said. 'She loves the work – every moment of it. She was born to ride. My husband encouraged her.'

They paused as coffee arrived. Diane heaped sugar into her cup.

'Your husband?' Adam queried.

'Rupert died,' Diane said. 'Eighteen months ago. It was cancer, of course. It all happened so quickly. Luckily, Belinda kept busy at the stables.' She tugged at a gold chain around her neck. 'That sheltered her a little from – from most of it.'

She winced. 'I don't see much of Belinda these days, because she's doing so well. She's ridden for the yard once or twice as an apprentice, but Saturday's race was her first proper, professional ride.'

She leaned forward, keen to explain clearly. 'She wouldn't earn much money from it, but winning would take her higher up the ladder.'

Adam knew almost nothing about this arcane world of horse racing. How did you even become a jockey? He'd assumed only wealthy people rode, but Diane didn't look rich. Her husband had been a barrister, but Adam knew criminal lawyers outside big cities often earned far less than their clients imagined.

He sat quietly, letting Diane talk. She was getting into her stride. The tears had dried up and her hands lay still in her lap.

'Belinda was so excited. The race was her dream come true. I don't think anyone expected her to win. Not on her first ride. In any case, Butterfly Charm isn't the best horse in the yard. That's why I could afford to keep my shares after Rupert died.'

She blew her nose and sat up straighter. 'Henry and Ling have been very kind. I sometimes think they only hold on to their shares in Butterfly Charm to keep me company.'

'And Henry is?' Adam asked, gently. Diane's take on the other syndicate members would be useful.

'Oh dear, I'm not telling this very well, am I? Henry was the head of my husband's chambers. Rupert had known Henry for years and they're almost like family there. They look out for each other. Henry was always trying to persuade Rupert to drop the legal aid side of the work, but he wouldn't.'

She took a deep breath and leaned back in the chair. 'Sorry, I'm rambling, aren't I? You don't need to know all this.'

'Tell me about the race,' Adam suggested. 'I gather there was confusion over the outcome.'

Diane sniffed and blew her nose, tucking her handkerchief away in her pocket. 'That's one way of putting it.' She tried a watery smile. 'Belinda made a silly mistake at the end of the race. It was such a shame. She says she lost concentration for a split second, when she was in the lead. I suppose she got overexcited, and who can blame her? It was her first race, wasn't it? I mean, anyone can make a mistake...'

'Of course they can. It's all part of the learning process,' he soothed, wondering how serious a mistake Belinda had made.

Diane nodded, her hungry eyes fixed gratefully on his. 'I knew you'd understand. But the stewards said she'd impeded the other horse.'

She shook her head, angrily. 'Belinda came in first, but they gave the race to Alex Deacon.'

Her eyes blazed, suddenly. 'All the cheering stopped and there was this awful announcement, saying there was going to be a Stewards' Enquiry.'

She shuddered and her voice shot up the scale. 'I didn't know where to look. It was as though Belinda had committed a crime.'

She frowned, and her eyes flashed. 'Henry thought Alex Deacon – the girl who died – held her horse back deliberately, to make Belinda look bad. Cheating, I'd call it.'

She shrugged. 'Still, what's done is done. We decided we'd carry on with our dinner.' She gave an unconvincing attempt at a laugh. 'Henry had already ordered the champagne.'

Adam tried to keep her on track. 'What happened after the race?'

She paused a moment, as though trying to remember, and then the words flooded out, tumbling over one another. 'We all stayed at the racetrack while Belinda went back to check on the horse, before one of the stable lads drove it back to the yard. Then, we came back to Lower Hembrow for dinner together, all six of us – that's me, Belinda and the rest of the syndicate. We'd asked Leo, the trainer, but he couldn't make it. Just as well, I suppose. It would have been embarrassing, wouldn't it?'

With a sudden, jerky movement, she grabbed her cup to gulp

down the coffee, replacing it with such force that Adam feared for the hotel's elegant saucer. 'Belinda could only stop for one night, but I stayed for the rest of the weekend. I enjoyed my spot of luxury. Rupert and I often spent the weekend in a country hotel.'

She was on her feet again, moving restlessly from one foot to the other. 'We were eating dinner, trying to enjoy ourselves, although Henry was – well, Henry likes an argument when he's had a drink. Then, the next thing we knew,' she finished with a rush of words, 'two policemen arrived to talk to Belinda and it turned out the rider of the other horse, Alex Deacon, was dead.'

She swept the back of one hand across her eyes and Adam edged a box of tissues nearer to her. Her handkerchief must be soaking wet by now.

'Can you imagine? It was such a shock. At least the officers didn't stay very long. They just wanted a few facts from Belinda, because she knew Alex. After they left, Belinda said it was nothing to worry about. She did know Alex but they weren't really friends. They rode for rival yards, you see.'

She was talking earnestly, now, trying to explain, 'Belinda is with Leo Murphy, while Alex rode for Ann Clarkson. But then, then,' her breath shuddered, she sniffed and scrubbed at her eyes. 'This morning the police telephoned and asked Belinda to go into the station again. And I just know, after the way that race ended, that Belinda is going to be their main suspect.'

She looked directly at Adam, her eyes red from crying. 'Mr Hennessy, if there's anything you can do to help prove her innocence, please do it. Henry will do what he can, I know, but he has his position to think of.'

That sounded very much like a quote from the man himself. Diane seemed desperate, searching for someone – anyone – to lean on, in the absence of her husband.

Adam couldn't be that person, but he wasn't about to make her feel worse. 'As I said, Mrs Sandford—' he began gently.

'Please call me Diane. And I can pay, of course. I can't afford a lot, but...'

Adam held up his hand.

'There's no need for that, Diane. I'm not a policeman any more, I'm just the landlord of The Plough over the road, and I wouldn't dream of taking your money. You should stop worrying. The police are very thorough, very honest and always determined to find the truth.'

He resisted the temptation to cross his fingers behind his back. The police had been willing to jump to conclusions when Imogen's husband died, and he had a suspicion that if he had not intervened, Imogen might even now be in custody, accused or even convicted of her husband's murder.

'I'm not sure there's much I can do,' he said, as much to himself as to Diane. 'But I'm sure your daughter has nothing to worry about.'

As long, he thought silently, as she's telling the truth and didn't shove her rival into a trough of water in a fit of jealousy. He kept that thought to himself. If it were the truth, Diane Sandford would know it soon enough.

7

COMMITTEE

Next morning, Helen Pickles, the vicar, threw open the door of the Hawthorn Room. 'The perfect place for our committee meeting,' she hooted, arms aloft, as though offering a blessing.

Harley trotted past her, made a brief visit to Imogen and Steph, and then settled down close to the door as though on guard.

Helen processed across the room, stately as a Thirties cruise liner, while the assistant manager, Michael, breathless, staggered in her wake with his arms full of boxes.

'Wonderful, Michael. You are a true star, and will have first choice at the vicarage stall.'

Michael left, less than thrilled at the prospect of buying some of the second-hand donations. Harley trotted at his heels in the hope of a titbit or two.

Helen flipped open the lid of the top box in the pile. 'Just a few bits and pieces from last year in here.'

She dived into another box. 'Bunting,' she muttered, 'banners, balloons – the job's already half done.'

Imogen said, 'How many are we expecting this morning?'

'Good point. I have a list. It's in one of the boxes.' Helen frowned. 'But, which one?'

After rummaging for a few tense moments, she abandoned the effort, sank into a chair, and took a deep breath. Catching sight of the plate in the centre of the long table, she clapped her hands. 'Cakes,' she exclaimed. 'Imogen, you are cruel. Once again, you tempt me with brownies, when you know I give up chocolate for Lent every year, and it only began last week. There is a long time to go until Easter. However,' she looked more closely, 'I spy an almond slice. That will do. You are forgiven.'

She leaned back and closed her eyes in bliss, munching. Imogen waited for the verdict. Finally, Helen swallowed and brushed crumbs from her fingers. 'Delicious. Now, since the dratted list has gone AWOL, I must think. Our committee this year consists of me, of course – it comes with the job. I'll chair, as usual, if you like.'

The others nodded. 'Imogen, you've generously offered the hotel gardens and this delightful room, and Adam, whom I saw as I arrived, is joining us and has offered the services of his exotic chef from over the pond, to help feed us all. Barbecue for everyone, I hope. My favourite.'

She stopped in mid flow. 'Where is Adam, by the way? Has he got lost, like my list?' She stopped to chuckle at her own joke.

Imogen said, 'He was waylaid. He'll join us when he can.'

'Excellent. Now, who else?'

Steph said, 'Me?'

'Good grief, of course. Couldn't do it without you, Steph. You're our Communications Director. Vital role, vital. Now, Jenny Trevillian usually sits on the village committees, but this year, she's sending Joe. She says he's keen to get involved in the fair, since it's in aid of fixing the village hall roof. She said he'll be helpful with the heavy work of setting up the fair and he'll be able to get a few other local farmers involved.' Helen laughed again. 'I don't think he had any choice in the matter. Still, isn't that wonderful? We never have enough men organising things. It's almost as though they don't enjoy village fairs. Imagine.'

'Joe Trevillian?' Imogen repeated, thoughtfully. Joe seemed to actively dislike Adam. She had no idea why, but he seemed to seize on the slightest opportunity to sneer at 'the village's new explod'. Putting them together on the committee was – well – courageous.

There was a wicked gleam in Helen's eyes. 'He'll be with us once the morning milk's been collected, or a fence mended, or something. Always on the go, is Joe. Never a dull moment when he's around.'

She continued to tick off the committee members on her fingers. 'Edwina Topsham can't be here this morning as she's in the shop, but she sends her regards and wants to help. She's bagged the cake stall unless anyone objects. Now, is that all?'

Imogen hardly dared ask. 'Maria Rostropova?' she murmured.

The force of Helen's shout of laughter made the coffee cups rattle. 'How could I forget? And, if I'm not mistaken, I think she's on the way.'

Sure enough, Maria's perfume preceded her into the room. 'My dear Mrs Pickles,' she gushed. 'I hope I'm not late. I wouldn't want you all to wait for me.'

Imogen said, 'You're not the last, but we're very pleased to see you. Have a cake.'

Maria's eyes opened in horror. 'My darling, I cannot eat cake. My poor figure...' She smoothed her tight skirt and lowered herself gracefully into a vacant chair at the table, shifting it back a little so she could cross her legs to show off her expensive shoes. Four inch heels. How could she even walk?

Steph said, 'I'd like to propose we co-opt Daniel Freeman to the committee.'

Heat rose from Imogen's feet, all the way up her spine, to settle uncomfortably at the back of her neck. What was Steph up to?

When the three of them had met for the first time in thirty years, at a school reunion, Imogen had thought Steph was in a relationship with Dan. At the time, Imogen had been preoccupied, trying with Adam to prove her innocence of her husband's murder. Since then, she'd spent a lot of time with Dan and he'd denied any special bond with Steph, but the idea still rankled.

'Don't look so puzzled,' Steph said. 'I thought we could persuade him to do a painting of the fair. He's already offered to donate one to sell. He's very generous with his work.'

Maria's face lit up. 'Daniel Freeman – that handsome man I see with you sometimes, Imogen. He's rather Byronic, I think. Dramatic. Such a good idea to have him on our little committee.'

She'd better not attempt to get her claws into Dan. Imogen pushed the savage thought away.

Triumphant, Helen thumped the table. 'Agreed, then. Just as well, because I already asked him and he'll be here any minute now.'

That would be the day. Dan had almost no sense of time.

'So, let's begin,' Helen beamed.

* * *

Imogen sneaked a glance at her watch. The meeting had been going on for almost an hour and they hadn't decided anything beyond the committee membership. This was going to take some time.

As she topped up coffee cups, Joe Trevillian arrived. He

stopped in the doorway. 'Morning, ladies. I hear you need some help...?' His gaze fell on Maria. Her dress revealed more than a hint of cleavage, and his voice tailed away.

'Darling,' said Maria. 'How wonderful to have a strong man helping us out. Things always go better when men are involved, don't you think, Imogen?'

Before Imogen had time to respond to this slur on the sister-hood, Adam arrived, having seen Diane Sandford safely off the premises. 'So sorry, got held up.'

Joe, choosing a chair directly opposite Maria where he could enjoy the full benefit of her embonpoint, glared at Adam. 'Might have known you'd be involved, Hennessy. Good place to catch villains, you think, the village fete?'

Adam, unruffled, nodded to everyone, sat down and helped himself to a brownie.

'Actually,' Steph said, 'it's a Spring Fair.'

Joe's upper lip twisted and he adopted a high-pitched, refined voice. 'Oh, yes. So much nicer. Don't want the common workers cluttering up the place.'

Helen said, 'Now then, Joe. The fair's for everyone, as you know, it's in aid of the village hall roof, and we'll all benefit from that. We don't want the playgroup being washed away, do we? I know your little one loves it there, so don't tease.'

'Well, that's as maybe,' Joe said, in his normal voice, 'whatever we call it, we're sure of a good turn-out. Nothing folk like more than the chance to poke around the gardens where a murder happened.'

A shocked hush fell at the enormous gaffe. Most of the committee would die rather than mention what had happened to Imogen's husband. Imogen longed to crawl under the table, out of sight.

Adam said, mildly, 'Absolutely. There's no end to ill-informed, vindictive curiosity, is there, Joe? Especially about family tragedies.'

Helen joined in. 'And Imogen's brave enough to put that terrible time behind her for the sake of the village. Heroic, I call it.'

'And,' Steph said, with the sweetest of smiles at Joe, 'at least none of her workers has sued her for negligence.'

Joe's jaw dropped. 'What are you talking about?'

His cheeks collapsed like two burst balloons. He reddened. 'That was years ago—'

'It was. Ten years and five months, to be exact. Still, the hospital managed to reattach Mr Hanson's finger and thumb, and I'm sure your equipment has fully functioning guards in place now, doesn't it?'

Imogen blessed her friend's lively curiosity and encyclopaedic knowledge of local affairs.

Joe stood up. 'I don't have to listen to this,' he snapped. 'You can stick your committee, and your posh Spring Fair, where the sun—'

Maria interrupted. 'Oh, Joe, I only agreed to help because I heard you'd be here. We need people who know how things work. Someone like you. You've run the most successful farm in the county for years. Don't desert us, please.'

Her eyes shining as though with unshed tears, she gazed up at him, her shoulders thrust back, showing off her chest to its best advantage.

Joe was lost. He sank back into his seat.

Adam said, 'I think the past should stay there, don't you? Everyone has unfortunate or embarrassing moments in their dim and distant. It's all part of the human condition.'

'And we can all be forgiven,' Helen said, fingering her white clerical collar.

Joe blinked. He rarely set foot in church, but his wife, Jenny, was an eager, if untalented, choir member. He cleared his throat. 'No offence,' he grunted.

'And none taken.' Imogen said.

* * *

Adam, watching the interplay among the committee members, inwardly congratulated Helen on her cleverness. Bringing Joe onto the committee meant he couldn't snipe from the outside about the fair. She was quite the politician.

Helen moved on to the next item on her agenda, the budget available for the fair's expenses. 'Minimal,' she said, 'as always. We want every penny we can spare to go towards the village hall.'

As the committee argued over various suggestions for persuading local businesses to contribute, or, as Joe put it, 'screwing money out of the local bigwigs,' Adam was distracted by a spate of excited barking outside.

Imogen's head bobbed up. 'That's Harley,' she said. 'What's he up to now? I thought he was here, with us.'

Steph said, 'He followed Michael downstairs.'

As one, the committee rose and scrambled to reach the window. Down below, a series of jumps were scattered over a stretch of grass and Harley, under Michael's instructions, was galloping and leaping, soaring higher at each fence, and barking furiously.

A small crowd of guests had gathered to watch, applauding each jump.

Imogen clapped a hand to her forehead. 'I don't know which is worse, Harley or Michael. Look at the grass – Oswald will have a fit.'

Adam turned at a sudden, unfamiliar sound, like a creaking wheel.

It was Joe, laughing. 'Will you look at that animal...' he chuckled.

As they watched, Harley turned, skidded on the grass, gathered himself, accelerated and leapt, clean as a whistle over the tallest fence, a construction of planks balanced on towers of bins.

'I think Oswald's in on it,' Imogen said. 'Those bins come from the potting shed. They're full of seeds.'

Harley trotted indoors, tail aloft, for a reward while Michael dismantled the jumps.

In the Hawthorn Room, Helen called the committee to order, a suspiciously self-satisfied smirk on her face. Under cover of the general movement back to the table, Adam whispered in her ear. 'Did you know that little show was about to happen?'

She winked. Her plot, designed with Michael's cooperation to defuse Joe's antagonism, had worked perfectly. 'Joe's crazy about dogs. I thought he'd enjoy it,' she hissed.

From that moment on, Joe couldn't be helpful enough. At regular intervals, a grin spread across his heavy features and he chuckled. 'Quite a dog, that one.'

With hardly any more argument, the list of stalls for the fair was agreed and the committee members assigned to every task Helen could devise, from running the barbecue to serving in the beer tent. She even persuaded Joe to liaise with the head teacher at the local primary school. He had clout there, for the six Trevillian children, ranging in age from twenty to two years, had helped keep the school numbers high enough to see off the threat of government cuts.

Steph agreed to write to the local papers. 'Although, they'll all be full of this affair at the racecourse.'

At that, the meeting, on the verge of breaking up, became electric with interest.

'My Jenny told me the girl who did it stayed here at your hotel, Mrs Bishop.' Joe made it sound as though Imogen was responsible.

Before anyone could respond, he was on his feet. 'But I can't stay around here all morning, gossiping. I have work to do.'

'I have to go home, too. I have so much on my plate...' Maria followed him out.

Steph watched them go. 'Am I imagining things, or—'

Imogen started to laugh. 'I do believe those two are up to something.'

'Nonsense,' Helen said, sternly. 'Pure coincidence. Maria's a busy woman and Joe would never dare stray. Jenny would have something to say about that.'

Adam leaned back in his chair, considering. When he'd first arrived in the village, Maria had cast some kind of spell over him. He would have done anything she asked. But now, the enchantment was broken. A weight shifted from his shoulders as he looked around the table at his three trusted female friends. What more could a man want?

Even as he asked himself the question, he knew the answer. A simple friendship with Steph, although a privilege, would never be quite enough for him.

'I hate to gossip,' Steph was saying, 'but I've spent my whole working life chasing stories and I'm dying to know more about the death at the racecourse.'

A little shamefaced, she pulled her collection of newspapers out of her bag, and spread them across the table. 'Imogen, since you had some of the racegoers staying in your hotel, I'm hoping for plenty of inside info. So, come on, what are the facts?'

'Sorry to disappoint,' Imogen said. 'But I know little more

than the writers of these columns. In fact, they seem to know several details that I don't.'

Steph laughed. 'Don't take their accounts as gospel. They have word counts to meet, you know.' She leaned forward and spoke in a stage whisper. 'They make things up.'

'Well,' Imogen said, 'the police were here on Saturday, talking to Belinda Sandford—'

Adam said, 'And the woman that collared me just now is her mother.'

Just then, Imogen's phone rang. 'It's Dan.' Tactfully, the others looked away as she fumbled with the phone.

'Dan. Why aren't you here?' she asked.

'Sorry,' he said. 'I'm running late. Forgot the time. Am I still welcome?'

8

PLANS

Daniel Freeman arrived in the Hawthorn Room, flushed, his hair standing on end, a canvas clutched under one arm. Harley followed, tail wagging furiously. Dan – Adam supposed he should call him that, to be friendly – would look good if he'd just fallen in the river. Even Harley had a special soft spot for him.

'I'm sorry, Helen,' Dan said. 'I promised I'd come and help with this fete.'

'Spring Fair,' Steph and Imogen corrected, in unison.

Dan looked from one to the other. 'Exactly. Is the meeting over?'

Steph said, 'You missed quite a show, but don't worry. We've come up with plenty for you to do.'

'Well, I brought this as a peace offering.' Dan unwrapped the brown paper from his painting – a sunset view of Ham Hill – and leaned it against the wall. 'I thought you might like to raffle it.'

Helen, Imogen and Steph gathered around, exclaiming, as Adam scratched behind Harley's ear.

Helen straightened up. 'Dan, I will forgive you anything. This is such a generous donation. I think we might have a special event – what do you call them, when people bid for things.'

'An auction,' Adam suggested.

'Exactly.'

Dan scratched his head. 'That would be great – but I'm no auctioneer.'

The women all turned to look at Adam.

'Oh, no—' he said, a hand raised in protest.

'Great idea,' said Dan. Was that a malicious twinkle in those big brown eyes? Adam ground his teeth.

Helen said, 'You'd be perfect for the job. Do say you will.'

'Go on, Adam,' Imogen grinned.

'Absolutely,' said Steph. 'We're counting on you.'

Adam gave in. Wonderful, he thought. Now I have to big Dan up in front of the whole village. Serves me right, I suppose. I'd like the man if only he were slightly less handsome, or a bit less talented.

Helen had to dash off, blaming another meeting. 'This one's with the Bishop, and it's about plans for the Easter services, so I'd better not be late. Thank you all for your help. This year's Spring Fair will be the best ever.'

Imogen rang down for more coffee, and as the four of them waited for Michael to bring it, Imogen divided up the last brownie.

As he arrived, Imogen said, 'I see you've been training Harley.'

Michael blushed and stammered, 'I didn't think you'd mind, Mrs Bishop...'

She laughed. 'Of course I don't mind. You've done a good job. Well done.'

Michael left, crimson with pleasure. Steph swallowed the last crumbs of cake and licked her fingers. 'Now, what did Diane Sandford want with you, Adam, that kept you so long?'

Adam hesitated. Should he tell them Diane's business?

Imogen nodded, encouragingly. 'We'll agree not to spread rumours. There were more than enough of those when my husband died.'

Steph said slowly, 'I imagine she wanted to talk to you about her daughter and this death at the racecourse. The press are already calling it a murder.'

Adam half rose, about to object, as Steph went on hurriedly. 'All right, I know there's no evidence but the speculation's already started and Belinda's name has risen straight to the top of the papers' suspect lists. So, if you're thinking of doing a spot of investigating on behalf of her mother, maybe I can add something. I'm a journalist, and journalist equals nosy parker.'

Imogen agreed. 'Come on, Adam. Trust us to help. If two heads are better than one, look how useful four will be. I bet policemen don't operate all alone; not even Columbo. We can be your back-up team.'

'Actually,' Adam pointed out, 'Columbo's a TV detective, not a real one.'

'Exactly,' Steph exclaimed, illogically. 'You need a team.'

Adam was tempted. Alex Deacon's death might be murder, in which case the killer must be found and punished for her sake. If it were an accident or suicide, no harm would be done by a little gentle probing. Besides, how could he resist the temptation of working closely with Steph?

His face must have given him away, because Imogen nudged him. 'Good. I'll vouch for Dan. You know he never chats, much, anyway. Do you, Dan?'

Dan laughed. 'I suppose not. I don't know what I can add, though. I've never done any sleuthing, if that's what you're planning. But I do know how to keep my mouth shut.'

Adam sighed and gave in, recounting the hour he'd spent

with Diane, listening to her fears for her daughter. 'She seems on the verge of hysteria, but I suppose that's normal. She's worried about her daughter, and it's not long since her husband died.'

Imogen thought about that. 'Maybe she's not convinced Belinda is innocent. That would terrify a mother. She'd want to hide it from herself.'

Steph shuddered. 'I should say so. Imagine discovering your child's done something really terrible. A crime, I mean. I've written about crime victims, and about the perpetrators, but the criminal's family usually stay safely in the background.'

Dan said, 'Not surprising. Who would want to be known as a killer's father or brother?'

'Or even worse,' Steph said, 'their mother.' She gave a small shiver.

By common consent, they turned to the newspapers, poring over details, soon realising that, thanks to the police visit to the hotel and Diane's plea to Adam, they already knew more than any of the journalists did.

'Look at this one.' Dan jabbed a finger at the byline of the paper he was reading. A line of blue paint showed on the edge of his sweater, as though it had brushed against one of his paintings.

He flipped his paper round on the table so that Imogen could read it.

John Harris.

The name meant nothing. 'This is a pretty damning description of the race,' Dan said. 'According to this chap, who seems to be a racing journalist and self-styled expert, Belinda Sandford was riding dangerously and was only let off the hook through sympathy from the stewards for an inept beginner. Here, this is what he says.

To discover poor Alex dead, later this same day, is a tragedy. No doubt the police will get to the bottom of this unfortunate death of an accomplished rider with a wonderful future ahead of her.'

He read on,

Did Belinda Sandford nurture animosity towards the up-and-coming Alex Deacon, a welcome addition to the small group of highly talented women on the racing circuit? Was her disappointing performance in her first race the final straw?

Steph shook her head. 'It's almost an accusation, although he's keeping on the right side of the law.'

Dan said, 'Look at the photo.'

The camera had caught the two jockeys face to face. Alex had her back slightly turned to the camera but Belinda was caught full face. Fury had distorted her features into ugliness and she gripped her whip at shoulder height, as though about to use it on her rival.

Steph said, 'Clever camera work. It makes Belinda look terrible doesn't it?' She smiled grimly. 'I'd love to talk to this John Harris character. He seems to have already decided Belinda killed Alex. I wonder why.'

Dan was nodding. 'Could you arrange a meeting with him? After all, you're both in the business. It sounds like he'd love the opportunity to dig his knife even further into poor Belinda.'

Adam shook his head. 'Hold on a minute,' he said, 'let's slow down. There'll be an autopsy soon and James, my old pathologist friend, will let me know what they find. Or I could even talk to DCI Andrews. Imogen and I got to know him over her husband's murder.'

'He doesn't think much of me,' Imogen pointed out, with a

wry grin, 'but I bet he'd listen to you. You were a detective chief inspector yourself.'

'Exactly,' Steph said, 'and I don't see any harm in nosing around a little. Besides, I can't resist a story and you never know, maybe I'll write it up and make a fortune. True crime's popular these days, and it would save me the trouble of working out my own plot.'

Imogen said, 'Then, we're agreed, are we?'

Adam looked at each face in turn. He'd seen enthusiasm like theirs in newly arrived detective constables. It could be infectious. 'So long as we're careful,' he said.

Steph punched the air. 'Let's get started, then.'

Dan said. 'I can't imagine I'd be much good at interviewing. But if you're interested in Leo Murphy's racing yard, where Belinda works, I might be able to add something, because, as it happens, I'm in the middle of a commission for Leo. He asked me to paint some of the horses in his yard. That famous one, Pink Gin, who won the Gold Cup at Cheltenham last year, and a couple of the young and up-and-coming yearlings – or two-year-olds – or something like that. Leo saw a painting of my donkeys, Smash and Grab, and he seemed to like it.'

Steph said, 'Dan, that's a brilliant idea. You can visit the yard and go on painting or taking photos or whatever, while you keep your eyes and ears open. You'll hear the rumours – what the stable hands think about Alex's death – that kind of thing. They probably all knew her. You can find out what sort of person she was.'

She turned to Adam. 'That can't do any harm, can it?'

Adam said, reluctantly, 'It's worth a try.'

His arms were folded and he was frowning even as he nodded. 'Just take care, everyone. If this is murder, there'll be a killer out there. And they won't want us finding them.'

* * *

Dan and Steph left with the light of battle in their eyes, excited by the prospect of taking action. Adam and Imogen remained in the room, sitting across the table from one another.

Imogen said, 'I think I should put a locking filing cabinet in here. One would fit in the corner. We don't want any information we may gather getting into the hands of guests.'

Adam took a breath. 'Let's not get carried away.' The arrangement bothered him. The others were just amateurs, setting themselves up to solve a real crime, and even he was no longer a police officer. He decided to contact Andrews, the local Detective Chief Inspector, and drop a hint in his ears, just to let him know they wanted to help the police if they could.

'I'm not sure the others are taking this seriously,' he said. 'I know Steph is excited. She's a journalist so she can't help it, but at least she's worked on crime stories before.'

He swallowed. He needed to tread delicately, 'But Dan's an artist, with no background in crime. He could easily get himself into trouble.'

Imogen's eyes flashed. 'I don't know why you're so set against Dan. He's very intelligent, he's willing to help and he's much nicer than you think. Anyway, all we're going to do is gather information.'

Adam sighed. 'I know.' The truth was, he was afraid Dan would break Imogen's heart. She'd told him about their past; they'd met at school, but had somehow never got together. Then, after uni, while still a young struggling painter, Dan had been engaged by her father, Councillor Jones, to paint the hotel's gardens. Imogen had spent many hours with him as he painted, but just as they realised they had real feelings for each other, Imogen's father had fired him.

Hurt and embarrassed, unaware of the true reason he'd been sacked – because his painting revealed some of the Councillor's illegal activities – Dan had disappeared without a word and stayed away, eventually marrying and living in France.

Could he be trusted not to hurt Imogen again? Adam loved her like the sister he'd never had. Let Dan put one foot out of place...

Imogen reached across the table and put her hand on his. Her fierce expression had softened. 'I'll talk to Dan, make sure he doesn't rush into anything.' Her cheeks were quite pink.

'Tell him to be careful,' Adam said. That was the best he could do.

'Trust me,' Imogen smiled. 'Anyway, you once told me most murders are domestic affairs. This one – if it is a murder – looks no more complicated than a fight over boyfriends or girlfriends that went too far. I bet the culprit is one of the stable hands who lost his temper in the heat of the moment, and it will all be over in a couple of weeks. Of course, it could be Belinda, losing her temper over the race. She looked furious in that photo...'

Adam nodded, unconvinced. 'I hope you're right,' he said, but responsibility weighed heavily on his shoulders. He'd keep an eye on things, try to make sure none of the quartet did anything too foolish. Especially Dan.

9

JAMES

On Tuesday, Adam spent an hour coaching Wyatt on how to calculate the supplies needed for the next week's food.

When Wyatt said, finally, 'Got it, boss. Can do,' Adam was in dire need of a lungful of two of fresh air.

He nipped over the road to borrow Harley. 'Not up to a run, today?' Imogen asked.

'Too late. I might be seen. I only run before people are around and I don't fancy making myself Joe Trevillian's laughing stock.'

'He's a horrid man, isn't he, very aggressive? Steph did a good job of keeping him in his place, yesterday.'

'Nothing like a journalist for digging up the past. She gave him quite a shock.' Adam replayed the look on Joe's face when Steph had confronted him. 'I think he's harmless, though. Jenny seems to be the boss in their house, despite Joe's bluster.'

The dog by his side, Adam set off around the village. Wyatt could serve the lunches unsupervised. He'd already mixed up some tempting spices for the borrowed beef. It was only arithmetic – or math, as he called it – that caused him problems.

Rex was in charge behind the bar, helped by a local farmer's son. Adam knew he could be trusted, so long as Joe didn't come in and wind him up.

Today's walk kept Adam away from the tempting lunch on offer in his pub and assuaged his guilt for not having his run this morning. He was already behind schedule with the fitness programme. 'I'll catch up another day,' he told Harley, who couldn't have cared less.

He thought about the dead jockey, Alex Deacon. If Adam were in charge of the case, he'd be gathering as much information about the victim as possible, but he was no longer an officer. He wasn't entitled to read pathologist's reports or interview Alex's parents. The police would look after them, advising them not to talk to anyone else. Steph planned to use some old contacts to find out about, and if possible attend, any press briefings, but as they knew, official information was likely to be kept deliberately scarce.

His friend James's contacts, on the other hand, were more promising.

He leaned on a gate, letting Harley run through the deserted field, and called James. He caught him eating lunch in a noisy pub somewhere in Birmingham. James agreed to pass on any information he could glean from his fellow pathologists. 'I knew you'd be all over this business at the racecourse,' he said. 'Regretting leaving the force, are you?'

Adam took barely a second to consider that. 'No, actually. There's plenty about being a policeman I never want to do again – the meetings, the jostling for power and promotions, the endless paperwork...'

James groaned. 'Tell me about it. I spend twice as much time writing reports as I do dissecting my cadavers. And then there are the court appearances. That's what I'll be doing this afternoon.'

He sounded depressed.

'Got problems?' Adam asked.

'Just juggling a few things; fixing the wife's mother's broken TV, keeping an eye on our two girls and their endless love lives with the wrong types of guy, fighting with a new Chief Executive at the Trust I work for, who's a bigger prat even than the last one, and toiling through a tricky drugs court case where the defence are trying to call me a liar and querying my qualifications.' He drew a breath. 'But I'm not downhearted. Just counting the time to retirement, when I can swan around in the countryside like you. A bit of sleuthing on your behalf will cheer me up a treat.'

'I'm grateful. Not to mention smug, as I'm enjoying Somerset while you slowly choke in smoggy Birmingham.'

James's usual sense of humour bounced back. 'Treat me to dinner in The Plough and I'll forgive you. I've taken quite a fancy to Wyatt's fried chicken, not to mention that Maria who borrows money off you. She's a cracker. Now, got to go and listen to this barrister droning on about how "substance abuse disorder" is a valid excuse for robbery with violence. Heigh-ho.'

Adam slid his phone back into his pocket. He'd never known James so downbeat. Maybe he'd find out why when they had dinner.

Meanwhile, he'd keep away from Alex Deacon's family and leave them to the police. He'd concentrate instead on Belinda Sandford.

He gave his approach some thought. If her temperament was anything like her mother's, she must be in a state. No one feels good after an interview with the police, no matter how sensitively handled the interview or how innocent they may be.

Was young Belinda as squeaky clean as her mother assumed? Adam longed to find out.

Diane had given him Belinda's details, so he could phone her to introduce himself. No, that would give her the chance to refuse to meet him. Another disadvantage of his amateur status. Instead, he should take her by surprise.

Harley returned at that moment, a stick in his mouth for Adam to throw, and Adam had an idea.

Belinda was a horse lover, and he'd never met a horsey person who didn't also adore dogs. He would use Harley to break the ice. 'Fancy an outing, tomorrow, old fellow?' he asked.

Harley dropped the stick, reared on his hind legs and did his best to lick Adam's face. Neither Imogen nor Adam had managed to break him of that habit. 'Funnily enough,' Imogen was fond of saying, 'He never jumps up at anyone else. Just you.'

Adam complained, but deep down a flicker of pride warmed his heart. He didn't understand dogs. He'd made that perfectly clear. Harley was best off staying with Imogen. But it was good to know he'd forgiven Adam for giving him away.

'Get down, you idiot.' Harley subsided long enough for Adam to fit his lead in place on his collar. He led him back to The Plough, looked in to check lunch was in full swing and watched Rex cheerfully trotting to and fro with huge plates of beef. Happy that the bar was in good hands, he took Harley back home, and begged Imogen to take him out tomorrow, before devoting a long afternoon to the boring but necessary administration involved in keeping a business afloat. A country pub was never going to make Adam rich, but all he asked was to do slightly better than breaking even.

The hours of paperwork made his head ache, but he persevered, until he could flip his laptop shut with a clear conscience. After so long spent dealing with budgets, forward planning and VAT returns, he could hardly wait for a day of investigation in Harley's company.

10

BELINDA

Next morning, Adam loaded Harley into his ancient car, bribed him with dog biscuits to lie quietly on the back seat, and drove out towards the row of ex-farmworkers' cottages near Leo Murphy's racing stables, planning to catch Belinda at home in the tiny house she shared with two other stable hands.

He had no idea whether or not she was likely to be there. Did stable hands ever get a day off or were they like farmers, responsible for making sure the animals ate every day? But it was worth a try.

He drew to a halt outside Belinda's small house, pulled on the handbrake, let Harley jump out and followed him along a short path to the house.

He knocked on the door, and caught sight of the flick of an upstairs curtain. Belinda must be taking care not to speak to reporters, but at last she opened the door. She was a small, neat girl, slim but strongly built. She wore jeans, a chunky jumper and a gilet, a pair of hefty boots, a scarf wound two or three times around her neck, a woolly hat and a pair of strong leather gloves.

'Belinda?'

She blinked, hesitant, maybe thinking about shutting the door in his face. 'Who are you?'

Her eyes slid to Harley. As Adam had hoped, Harley put on a show of bright-eyed delight at the sight of a new human being, his body a-squirm with enthusiasm.

Unable to resist his charms, Belinda leaned down and offered her fingers. Harley sniffed, she tickled him behind the ears, and his tail thrashed with joy.

She straightened up, looked at Adam, and her smile faded.

Telltale bags underscored her eyes. No wonder. Innocent or guilty, sleepless nights must be guaranteed after the past few days.

'What do you want? I've nothing to say.' Her voice was flat.

'I'm not the press,' he said, trying to look unthreatening, blinking behind his spectacles. 'Your mother gave me your address.'

Belinda nodded, her face impassive. 'Adam Hennessy?'

'That's me.'

'The ex-detective. My mother said you'd be coming. I suppose I'd better let you in.'

She bent over to pat Harley. 'You come in too. I'm sure we can find you a biscuit or two.'

Adam hoped he might be offered a biscuit. Well, at least she'd let him into the house. He stood, awkwardly, just inside the door which opened into a tiny living room.

She said, 'I was on my way out. I have to get back to the stables soon, but I can talk for a few minutes.'

'Your mother tells me you're innocent of anything to do with Alex Deacon's death.'

'Of course I am,' she sighed. 'I just wish the newspapers didn't keep pointing the finger at me. Mum says not to read them, but I can't seem to help it.'

She looked exhausted, and tightly wound.

She waved a hand towards one of three shabby corduroy covered chairs grouped around a wooden table. The surface was cluttered with newspapers, magazines – he spotted a copy of *Horse & Hound* – and used coffee mugs. Belinda gathered the mugs into one hand.

Adam sat, keeping his coat on. The room was almost as cold as the weather outside. Stable hands, he supposed, earned very little and were hardy creatures, not bothering with central heating. 'I gather you share with two other people?'

'Simon and Jane are out this morning. We all work at the yard. This house is cheap – we don't earn much – and the three of us can split the costs. Living together means we can share lifts and things, and we can talk about horses.'

For a moment, her face lit up. Horse mad, Adam realised.

She offered him tea and encouraged Harley to follow her into the kitchen. Cups clattered, a kettle boiled loudly and she returned bearing two different mugs, each containing a teabag on a piece of string with the milk already added. She clutched a packet of custard creams under one elbow and dumped a mug in front of Adam. 'Sorry, we don't have sugar.'

'Don't need it, thanks.' The tea looked disgusting, even to Adam, who wasn't fussy. He hated what James called 'pseuds' teas, and stuck to dark brown English Breakfast. But even he drew the line at adding the milk before removing the teabag.

Belinda pushed a small upturned lid towards him. 'For the bag.'

With a grimace, Adam picked up the string between finger and thumb, removed the teabag from the pale grey liquid, let it drip a while in the hope that the tea would turn brown, realised that was not going to happen, and laid it on the lid.

He sipped. The tea was terrible. Like a police station brew. 'At least it's warm and wet,' his sergeant would have said.

Meanwhile, Belinda sat on the worn, saggy chair by his side, unwound her scarf, pulled off her hat and gloves and crossed her legs. 'Fire away, then,' she said.

She was far more composed and in control than her mother had been. She looked at Adam without flinching. 'I suppose you're expecting me to tell you I didn't kill Alex?'

'Well, I hope you didn't, or I'll have some explaining to do to your mother.' Adam's joke fell flat. He thrust his hands in his pockets, wishing he'd brought his gloves from the car. The tiny house must be at least ten degrees colder than The Plough.

Belinda heaved a sigh. 'She's such a fusspot. Dad used to keep her under control, but now she's like a nervous horse that's eaten too many oats. She twitches at the slightest sound, worries about me all the time, and would wrap me up in cotton wool if she could and only let me out where she could see me.'

'That's perfectly normal for a widow and her only child,' Adam said, irritated. He'd expect more loyalty to a widowed mother. 'It's not long since your father died, is it?'

Belinda looked away, towards Harley. He'd crunched the biscuit she gave him within seconds, and was now lapping noisily and messily at the bowl of water in the corner of the room.

She turned back to Adam. Her eyes gleamed, too bright. She'd taken his rebuke to heart. The cool exterior was an act, then, an attempt at self-defence.

'Saturday,' she said quietly, 'was meant to be the most exciting day of my life. I thought if I could win that race and prove myself, it would stop Mum worrying about me.' Her lip quivered.

Adam said, more kindly, 'If you tell me exactly what happened I may be able to help.'

She gave a deep sigh. 'Haven't you read it in the paper? Seen that photograph that made me look like an axe murderer about to strike?'

'Of course, but photos don't always tell the real story. The journalist made his opinion clear, but what does he know? I'd like to hear it from you. And I'd prefer the truth. It saves time.'

The noise she made was half laugh, half sob. 'The journalist who wrote that piece and took the photo is Alex's uncle.'

'So not entirely unbiased, then?'

She sniffed, leaned back in her chair and crossed her legs. She was trying to look relaxed, but her hands were busy, plucking at the edge of her sweater where a thread had come loose.

'Everything was going so well during the race. I hadn't expected to win, but I had a plan – I'd talked it over with Leo, the trainer, so many times. I stayed near the back, went over the jumps carefully, and gradually moved up the field until the final hurdle. Then I let Butterfly Charm go. She was so keen. Everything was going perfectly, but I suppose I got overexcited when we passed Alex's horse.' She looked Adam in the eye. 'I'm convinced Butterfly Charm only moved a centimetre or two before I got her back in line.'

She screwed her face up, looking like a child who's discovered that life isn't fair. 'Alex made the most of it, and I'm sure she checked Season's Greetings deliberately. That didn't really show in the video, of course.'

Adam nodded. Her account matched everything he'd heard. 'And afterwards?'

'Alex and I had words. She's such a snobby—' Belinda gave a little gasp. 'I'm sorry, I shouldn't speak ill of her, should I? I sort of forgot she's dead.' Her voice broke a little on the last word.

Adam said, 'I want you to be honest. I won't hold your feelings against you. I'm not the police any more, and I won't judge you.

But in order to help, I need all the facts in as much detail as you can remember.'

'Well, she said I'd made a rookie mistake, so I asked her if she'd held her horse back deliberately, and she didn't deny it. In fact, she laughed. I was so angry, and then her uncle took that photo—'

She bit her lip, but couldn't prevent it from trembling. 'I don't think I can tell you anything else. I didn't see Alex again, after that photo. To be honest, I was so angry, I could have punched her, but I didn't.'

Adam said, 'Are you sure you didn't see her at the – what do you call them – the stalls at the racecourse? If you did, was she with anyone else? Try to think back.'

She closed her eyes. Adam watched, letting the silence draw on. In her mind, she was reliving the afternoon of the race.

She kept her eyes closed. 'No, after I talked to Alex, Leo found me. He was very kind. It surprised me – you know he's often quite gruff. But he said not to worry, we'd talk about the race tomorrow and I hadn't committed a crime. I felt a bit better, then. I'd thought he would be furious. I went back to the jockeys' area to make sure Andy – that's the lad acting as Butterfly Charm's groom that day – had rubbed her down and given her water and so on, ready to load her back into the horsebox for the drive home.'

She gave a little nod, as if confirming her movements to herself. 'Then, I found my mother drinking coffee in the Owners & Trainers bar and she drove us back to the hotel. I didn't see Alex again, although there were plenty of other people milling around when I left.'

Adam would ask DCI Andrews who'd been at the races – his officers would have all the names and addresses.

Belinda opened her eyes and blinked, as though returning to reality. 'That's truly all I remember. To be honest, I couldn't think of anything except the race, and how disappointed Mum would be, and how I'd let Dad down.' Her voice shook.

Adam said, 'Do you have any theories of your own about who might have attacked Alex?'

She shrugged. 'No idea. I mean, she wasn't my favourite person, and she often upset people. She thought a lot of herself. Like, she was the best up-and-coming jockey, and the rest of us were rubbish. But being a pain doesn't normally get people killed, does it?'

'Not usually,' Adam agreed. He paused, watching Harley as the dog wandered across and collapsed on his back at Belinda's feet. She leaned over to scratch his stomach. Adam said, 'Tell me about Alex's private life. Did she have a boyfriend?'

She kept her eyes on Harley. 'You mean, was I jealous of her because boys liked her?'

'Were you?'

Belinda nodded to herself, as though considering her answer. 'I would be lying if I didn't admit I envied her in some ways. Her looks, for one thing. She's – she was – good-looking. But, once people get to know her, they find she's not as nice as she looks – looked. Sorry.'

Adam said, 'Go on. Be honest. It's just you and me.'

'She could be a b—' Belinda stopped. 'She didn't mind who she upset. Boys, I mean. Ask any of them at her stables. She's been through them all.'

'She doesn't work in the same yard as you, then?'

'No, she's with Ann Clarkson. Ann's one of a handful of women trainers in the country and one of the best in the area. She took over the yard when it was losing money and she's made a real go of it. She has some great up-and-coming horses, now.'

Belinda's focus had soon returned to horses, stables, and racing.

'These boyfriends?' he reminded her.

This time she was quiet for a long time. At last, she seemed to make up her mind. 'I suppose there's no point in lying to you. Anyone will tell you that Alex's boyfriend – or, one of them – used to go around with me.'

Her cheeks were scarlet. Harley, as if in sympathy, sat up, laid his head on her knee and gazed soulfully into her face.

Adam took the boyfriend's name and address. 'Tim Booth,' he repeated.

'He's one of the lads at Ann Clarkson's yard. He and I were really just friends. No – well – no spark, I suppose. We're more like brother and sister.' She heaved a sigh. 'I don't expect you to believe me, but maybe Tim will back me up...'

'Back you up, how?'

'That there was nothing serious between us. You see, Alex thought there was. She went out of her way to take Tim from me.'

Adam scratched his head. 'How did she do that, exactly?'

She gave a short laugh. 'It happened a few weeks ago, at Exeter. I didn't have a ride. I was there with one of the other horses, but Tim rode. He came in third on one of Ann's older horses, one not really expected to do well. He was so pleased.'

She grinned. 'After he'd weighed in, he and I were chatting and Alex came along. She stood right in front of Tim, between him and me. You know, with her back to me? She gushed all over him. How that was one of the best rides she'd ever seen, how she wished she could ride like that...'

Belinda giggled at the memory. 'It was so blatant. Poor Tim isn't used to that kind of thing. He's a bit on the small side, and thin, and not really much to look at. Alex only wanted him because she thought he liked me.'

Adam sat in silence for a few moments, thinking this through. The racing world was small, but these two girls' apprenticeships involved them in travel round the country to race meetings. They must know dozens of people – everyone at the races, all the staff at different yards. The racing world must be teeming with young people, all with complicated relationships, jealousies and love affairs. Maybe Imogen was right, and Alex's murder was the direct consequence of someone's broken heart.

Belinda twitched, gasped and leapt to her feet. 'I'm horribly late. I need to get back to the yard now. I had the morning off, but I should be there by now.'

She wound the scarf around her neck, jammed her woolly hat on her head and made for the door. 'I'll have to throw you out, I'm afraid, before my housemates get back. They'll have a fit if they arrive home and find you here alone. They'll be calling the police. Everyone's on edge at the moment.'

'I've never been to a racing yard,' Adam stated, hopefully.

She grinned. 'You mean you'd like to come with me?'

'Don't forget, I'm on your side.'

'It's tricky. We're not supposed to have visitors in the yard. But, maybe this once...'

Adam said, 'I've no intention of telling lies to your boss. I'll introduce myself and explain why I want to get a feel for his – er – yard. If he's a reasonable man, there should be no problem.'

She shrugged. 'Very well, then. Just don't touch anything. Especially the horses. They can be sensitive.'

Adam held his hands up. 'I shall keep as far away from them as possible, I promise you. What about Harley?'

'Probably better left in the car. No, that's not fair. Put him on the lead at the yard and I'll ask Leo. He's crazy about dogs. So long as Harley behaves, it should be fine.'

* * *

Just then, a rattling of keys, a shuffling and stamping, heralded the arrival of her two housemates, who tumbled through the door, shouting, 'Sandford, if you don't get your butt down to the yard pronto, you'll be in trouble. Leo's on the warpath 'cause Callum was late for work, and your name's already mud down there. Oh—'

The small wiry youth caught sight of Adam.

'It's okay, Simon,' Belinda said. 'Mr Hennessy is – um – a friend of mine. I'm going to show him round the yard.'

Simon sucked his teeth like a man twice his age. 'Take it carefully. Leo wants everything perfect today, because he's showing some of the Butterfly Charm syndicate around. Not your Mum, though, Sandford. I think Leo wants to cheer them up after Wincanton. Not that they need cheering up, from what I saw. That barrister fellow, Henry Oxon, is as keen as mustard, and his wife's a looker, and no mistake.'

Adam raised his eyebrows. The lad had the grace to blush. 'Wait until you see her.

'Nice dog, by the way. Me and Jane are starving. Any food in the house?'

He wandered through into the kitchen in stockinged feet, one large toe peeking through a hole. Presumably, the commotion Adam had heard at the door had been him shedding his work boots.

The other housemate, a girl just a few years older than Belinda, had a plain face but startlingly brilliant green eyes. She shot a glance at Adam, immediately looked away, and followed Simon in silence.

Belinda whispered, 'She's very shy.'

Adam and Harley followed her out of the house. 'Want a lift?' Adam suggested, but she shook her head. 'No, the yard's only half a mile away. I like to run. It's part of my fitness training. Tell you what, give me ten minutes to get there before you and I can lay the groundwork. Make sure Leo's happy. It sounds like he's on edge today.'

With a wave she jogged down the lane and disappeared around the corner.

'Well, Harley,' Adam murmured. 'It looks like we've got a quarter of an hour or so to kill. How about a stroll to work off some of your energy? Can't have you nipping at the heels of these valuable racehorses. It seems to me they're pampered like rock stars.'

11

RACING YARD

The cold air made Adam shiver. He pulled his padded jacket closer and led Harley down the lane, away from the direction of the yard. They were only a couple of miles from Lower Hembrow and he was curious to explore.

But after a ten minute walk along lanes lined with hazel, beech and brambles, and lit by the sun sloping through bare branches, he'd discovered only one lone farmhouse, set well back from the road.

He squinted through the gate that divided the farmland from the public road, but there seemed to be no activity. The fields were empty, presumably because any livestock – cattle perhaps– were indoors for the winter, living the high life on hay and silage.

Adam flapped his arms to keep warm. This must be the most expensive time of the year for a farmer, keeping the animals going while the grass lay dormant and the winter fodder supply dwindled; worrying about feed costs leaping up and animal prices dropping. He'd heard the locals in The Plough on the subject, many times.

He leaned on the gate, Harley scrabbling through the hedge

hopefully, although the noise he made would have scared away any nearby rabbits, mice or shrews.

He pulled out his phone and called the police station, planning to request an interview with DCI Andrews. A young lad took his call. 'DCI Andrews left a note for me to call you. He says please would you make an appointment to meet him.'

Not, Adam supposed, because he was a suspect, which meant Phil Andrews must want to pick his brain. Great minds think alike, he reflected, relieved to know he was no longer going behind the DCI's back. As he was making an appointment, a huge four-by-four SUV shot past, far cleaner and shinier than any of the farm vehicles around Lower Hembrow. Wheels squealing, it rounded the corner and disappeared, racing in the direction Adam had been heading – travelling too fast for him to do more than register the fact that there was a single person at the wheel.

'I'm losing my touch,' Adam said to Harley. 'I didn't get the number. I wonder if it came from the racing stables? There don't seem to be that many other places around here. Let's put in our appearance at the yard and find out. I'm hoping it's warmer there.' But he doubted it. Judging from Belinda's house, horsey folk were tougher than pub owners. 'Time to go. You're on your best behaviour, now.'

Harley turned and trotted back up the lane towards the car parked outside Belinda's cottage.

They drove up the lane and soon arrived at the racing yard.

Everything about the place shouted of horses and purposeful activity; the distant clatter of hooves, the bawled commands, the sweet, meaty smell of horses, manure and hay, and the subdued dog-barking. Adam had a distant view of a string of horses setting off up the hill behind the stables, in single file, watched by a short man in a flat cap. The man raised a pair of binoculars to his face as the horses broke into a steady gallop.

Belinda was waiting, grinning with pride.

'They make it look easy, don't they?' Adam remarked. 'Is it all right for me to be here?'

'Leo agreed.'

'Is that him?' Adam jerked his head towards the watcher.

'No, that's the head man, who runs the yard. Leo's over there.' She pointed to a burly man. 'He's agreed to see you, because the syndicate's here and I asked if I could bring a friend, also keen to own a part of a horse – that's you by the way, sorry.'

Clever girl, Adam thought. Maybe a touch devious?

'Anyway,' she said, 'Leo says you're very welcome, and you can bring Harley, but he'll have to stay in one of the kennels.'

'Hear that, Harley? I'm about to buy part of a horse, apparently.'

Belinda led the way to the source of the barking. Harley's ears pricked up and his tail whipped from side to side as they drew near to a row of low buildings.

'Harley looks as though this is his spiritual home,' Belinda remarked.

'He's a fine fellow, he loves other animals, people, gardens – everything really. He doesn't like being cooped up for long.' Adam winced at the memory of the mess Harley had made when left alone for an hour or two at The Plough. This was a dog who needed company and space, and as much of both as possible.

'He'll be fine. He can talk to the others. Everyone at the yard keeps dogs, but Leo won't let them all near the horses. Some of the young ones are easily spooked.'

With Harley installed in the kennels and happily nosing through the partition at a delicate-featured Dalmatian, Adam followed Belinda through a brick archway into the yard. A row of horses' heads, hanging over the stable doors, regarded him with a mix of suspicion, curiosity and boredom. He mirrored the suspicion; at least they were all safely locked away. He mused on a series of jokes about bolting stable doors, and decided now was not the time. Belinda would have heard them all, anyway.

At the end of the row of stables, a small group of human beings wearing expensive wellies and jackets clustered in front of a handsome grey horse. 'That, presumably, is Butterfly Charm?' Adam asked. Belinda nodded and Adam took a deep breath, smiled broadly and joined the group, wondering how long he could conceal his total lack of horse knowledge. He wasn't used to going undercover.

Leo Murphy was a broad, strong-looking Irishman, with vein-threaded cheeks and cauliflower ears from more than one heavy fall.

He shook Adam's hand, enveloped it in fingers as fat as sausages, and dismissed Belinda with a curt nod. Maybe he hadn't quite forgotten Saturday's racing blunder. She rolled her eyes at Adam as she left.

Leo introduced him to the three syndicate members: two women and a large, beefy man in a well-worn Barbour coat and green wellies. Adam felt uncomfortably aware that his own boots, quite sturdy enough for walking around the village, were woefully inadequate for navigating steaming manure mountains.

With a silent groan, he concentrated on the syndicate. Leo introduced Henry Oxon, who exclaimed, 'Good man, good man,' and grasped Adam's hand in a grip that threatened to crunch the bones to a pulp. Adam recognised the voice. He'd heard it boom loudly from the dining room at the hotel on Saturday evening. This was the barrister, a long-term friend of Diane and her late husband.

'Meet the wife.' Henry threw an arm around the smaller of the two women and squeezed. Elegantly, she detached herself and shook hands with Adam, her hand encased in the softest of tan leather gloves.

'This is Ling,' Henry announced. 'Don't be fooled by appearances. She looks like a lotus flower but she was the sharpest barrister in the chambers.'

He thumped her on the back and laughed.

He was right, though. She was lovely, her black hair neatly caught into a chignon at the base of her neck, with not a wisp out of place. She smiled at Adam, her lips bow-shaped, her teeth small and white. Her eyes were dark, almost black. It would be hard to know what she was thinking.

Clearly used to her husband's heartiness, she said, 'Butterfly Charm expects a treat from every visitor. Here.' She dipped a hand into her pocket and brought out a carrot.

Adam gulped. She expected him to offer it to the horse. He feared for his fingers.

Ling said, 'Hold out your hand, like this. And keep your thumb out of the way or Butterfly Charm will think it's the carrot and bite it off.'

Less than convinced, he copied her, his thumb stretched backwards so far it hurt. The horse snuffled his hand gently and took the carrot. The lips were warm and soft against his bare skin.

The other woman in the party, the elegant blonde – Laura Wilson, Adam deduced – said, 'You're not used to horses?'

Adam sighed. It had taken less than five minutes to give himself away. No point now in trying to pretend.

He chuckled, and the woman beamed, a smile crinkling the skin around warm brown eyes. She held out a slim hand, bare of gloves, one finger sporting a diamond ring that glittered like frost in the still air. 'The trophy wife,' Imogen had called her.

'Don't worry,' Laura said. 'You don't have to ride the horses you own. Henry's never been on a horse in his life, so don't let

him fool you. He and Ling come for the thrill of the racing.'
Henry laughed, unperturbed.

'I'm Laura, by the way. I do, in fact, come for the horses. I've ridden
all my life. It's very good to meet you and you'll soon fall in love with
racing. My husband, Magnus, did and now he's as keen as I am. I'm
sorry you've missed him. He's been called away. He's an anaesthetist
at Yeovil District Hospital and at the mercy of his phone.'

'I think I saw him leaving,' Adam said. 'Range Rover?'

Henry's laugh, of which Adam was already weary, drowned
out Laura's reply. 'Practically a uniform, out here, a Range Rover,'
he said. 'And not one of those namby-pamby Chelsea taxi affairs
folks drive in London. Magnus has a Sport. I'm waiting for
delivery of my latest – like to keep up with the newest version
every couple of years, don't you know?'

Adam kept a straight face, mentally dubbing Ling's husband
Hooray Henry. Public school and wealthy parents. Nice life as a
barrister. Adam had better keep him away from James Barton,
who had no time for people he called 'rich prats'.

Adam smiled at Ling, hoping for something more from this
morning than a conversation about whose car was best.

'We've all had a shock,' she said, with a slight wave of the
hand, as though dismissing her husband's behaviour. 'I see you
know Belinda.' There was no change in Ling's tone, but she shot
Adam a sharp glance. Definitely the bright one in that family, he
decided. 'I expect she told you about Saturday's race. Not really
Butterfly's fault, that problem at the end. Just a spot of bad luck,
impeding the other horse by mistake. I'm sorry Diane didn't feel
up to coming here today. She was so upset about Belinda's race.'

Adam wondered if anyone would mention Alex Deacon's
death. They seemed far more interested in that race.

Leo described it in detail, his Irish accent stronger as he

became more animated. 'Tons of potential in this horse. Just a touch of inexperience on Belinda's part, so there is. My mistake, perhaps, letting her ride a young one.'

His face softened as he offered the grey a carrot and stroked her nose. 'Will you look at her now,' he said. 'She's a real lady, is Butterfly. No wonder Belinda begged to be allowed to ride her. Was it Butterfly you were interested in, now?'

Put on the spot, Adam thought fast. 'I'm just a beginner,' he said. 'A townie for most of my life. I've only lived in Somerset for a couple of years, at The Plough in Lower Hembrow, but my locals keep telling me Somerset has the best racing stables in the country, and I heard this is one of the premier yards.'

Nothing beat a spot of flattery.

Leo beamed. 'We're proud of our success, to be sure, here in the south-west. You can keep your Newmarkets. We've taken over a hundred thousand pounds in prize money so far this season,' he added. 'We have fifty boxes here.' He talked on, listing Butterfly Charm's parentage and throwing in facts and figures about the yard's successes that meant very little to Adam, but sounded impressive.

As Adam nodded seriously, he glanced up and met Laura's eyes. Her mouth twitched. She really was a most attractive woman. Lucky man, this absent Magnus.

'It's a cold old day today,' Leo said at last. 'Let's get in the warm and have some lunch. You'll join us, will you, Mr Hennessy? We've plenty of food, now Magnus has been called away.'

He led the way out of the other end of the yard, nodding to the elderly, wizened little man who'd been watching the exercise string ride out on the hill.

'This is Pat, my head man,' Leo said. 'He runs the yard, has done for years. If you've any questions about the horses and I'm not around, Pat'll give you the nod.'

Pat, short, wiry, his battered flat cap moulded to his head as though he'd worn it his whole life, nodded at the men, twinkled at the two women and gave a barely-concealed sigh as he looked Adam up and down, taking in his inadequate jeans, sweater and waterproof jacket.

Nothing got past these horsey people. Adam's cover was flimsy and they'd seen straight through it. He followed the others inside, wondering whether any of the group realised they could be suspects in a murder. So far, they'd behaved as though Alex Deacon's death had never happened.

12

SYNDICATE

Lunch was a convivial affair. Leo, a hard-living, hard-working, hard-drinking kind of Irishman, swallowed vast amounts of wine and whisky with no obvious ill effects. But no one, Adam thought, has seen his liver. He stuck to water with his own lunch.

Adam seized the opportunity for a chat with Laura, who sat by his side. She was around thirty-five, he judged. Her hair was blonde, but the sun had caught it while out in the yard, glinting on strands of red. Strawberry blonde, he decided, with no dark roots. Either she was a genuine blonde or she kept a hairdresser on weekly standby. He grinned to himself. Hair and make-up were a mystery to him.

Her clothes were figure-hugging, beautifully cut, perfectly fitting, but low-key; a cashmere sweater and designer jeans. Her voice was beautifully modulated, with just a hint of a local West Country burr.

Like all well-brought-up girls, she seemed far more interested in talking about Adam than about herself. 'The Plough' she smiled. 'I think I've been there. A lovely old place, although it was a little run-down, at one point. I expect it's doing well, now.'

'It keeps me busy. Are you a local girl?'

'I am. Born and bred in Somerset. My parents have a farm, and had five children.'

'But, you're not a farmer yourself.'

The smile played on her lips. 'Sadly, no. Just a few chickens at our place near South Petherton.'

Adam shot a glance at Laura's fingernails. Imogen often told him you could recognise someone who works on the land by their ruined hands. Laura's, though, were immaculate.

She'd turned the conversation again. 'Belinda tells me you brought the most delightful dog with you today.'

'Not mine. He belongs to the hotel across the road.'

Laura's laugh was deep and sounded genuine. 'That's right. I met him at The Streamside, when we had dinner on Saturday after – you know, after the races.' She swallowed, apparently not keen to talk about that day. Adam pondered. Was that important? Laura didn't know he was investigating. Maybe she was just too well-brought-up to gossip. If so, she had more self-control than anyone in Lower Hembrow.

'Who would have thought a hotel and a pub would work so successfully, just across the road from each other?' she said. It seemed she knew Lower Hembrow well. She went on, 'I gather the new owner of the hotel is something of a celebrity gardener. The owner of Haselbury House is full of praise for her skills. She remodelled the grounds there. He's very excited about the number of visitors he's expecting this year as a result.'

'Imogen's very talented. She's working on the hotel garden, and planning to open it soon, although she's a bit worried that the Spring Fair in the hotel grounds might ruin the lawns.'

'Ah, the Lower Hembrow Spring Fair. In May, isn't it? I've been going to it for years, and they're usually lucky with the weather. Magnus and I will make sure to be there – although,' her face fell,

'Magnus is so busy. He's often called back to the hospital. I've stopped giving dinner parties, because I end up hosting alone. Not,' she leaned closer, as though sharing a secret, 'not that I like dinner parties, anyway. Magnus enjoys them more than I do. He likes to invite the other members of the syndicate, and he's wonderful company.'

Adam said, 'Rupert Sandford was another member of the syndicate, wasn't he? You must all miss him?'

Laura's face fell. 'Dreadfully. I knew Rupert well – he was a lovely man. I worked in the same chambers before I married Magnus. Nothing intellectual, I'm afraid. I was admin only, unlike Ling and Henry. Rupert was quite brilliant, of course.'

Henry's braying voice cut across their conversation. 'Expecting any winners in the next few weeks, Leo? Where should we put our money? Any tips?'

He dominated the conversation for the rest of the meal, talking almost exclusively to Leo and Adam, leaving Ling and Laura to talk quietly to each other. Adam caught the odd word. They chatted a little about Ling's son, currently taking A levels before going to university. Then at last, they turned to Alex Deacon's death. They, at least, were thinking about the poor girl who'd died. Adam hoped for a few titbits of information. He tried to listen covertly.

'Diane's in pieces,' Ling said, 'and Belinda's terrified she'll be blamed, because of that bust-up after the enquiry.'

'Imagine,' Laura said with a shudder. 'Drowned in a water trough. Dreadful. It might have been an accident, I suppose.'

'Let's hope so, but I can't see how.'

Every time Adam tried to speak to either woman, Henry, ever the barrister, interrupted with a question. How long had Adam been at The Plough? Was it a going concern? Why did he want to join a syndicate?

He made no mention of the tragedy.

By the time they reached dessert, Adam was frustrated to boiling point by the talk of betting odds, the cost of fodder and Butterfly Charm's chances for the rest of the season. Did these racing men not care about the death of a jockey?

He could bear it no longer. He opened his mouth to ask a question about Alex Deacon, but at that moment all conversation died, drowned out by shouting. The syndicate stopped eating. Henry's mouth hung half open.

'Don't you dare.' A woman's voice. Belinda's? Something clattered on stone. Adam could hear the telltale sounds of a scuffle.

He half-rose from his seat, but Leo held up a hand and he subsided. He wasn't a policeman nowadays, and this was Leo's yard. His nerves twitched.

Leo drained the last drop of whisky from his glass, rose calmly to his feet, excused himself and left the room, closing the door firmly. The diners pretended not to listen and began a polite, half-hearted discussion about the merits of Wincanton Racecourse as compared with Exeter and Taunton, none of which Adam had ever visited.

Someone screamed.

Adam threw good manners to the winds and ran outside, and the others followed.

Leo and Belinda faced each other in the yard. With one hand, Leo gripped Belinda's arm. In the other, he grasped a small knife. Belinda's, Adam guessed.

'You try anything like that again, young lady, and you'll be out of my yard for good,' Leo hissed.

Belinda struggled to pull her arm free. 'I wasn't doing anything,' she shouted. Her face was brick-red, screwed into ugliness. 'He called me a murderer.'

'She tried to stab me.' A boy of about Belinda's age, face flushed, stood full-square in front of her, arms folded.

'I never did,' she shrieked.

'Pipe down,' Leo said. 'There are guests here.' He gave her arm a shake. 'And what were you doing with the knife?'

'Opening a bag of oats. I just – he had a go at me about the race. I just turned round and he screamed out that I was attacking him.'

The boy's face was brick red. 'I thought you were going to knife me. Kill me – like Alex.'

'Are you accusing me?'

The air turned several degrees colder. In the silence behind Adam, one of the syndicate gasped.

Leo growled, 'No one's accusing you of anything. Calm down, both of you. Andy, watch your mouth. Don't go around accusing people, and you, young lady, learn to keep your temper.'

He gave her arm a shake, and let her go. Both Andy and Belinda stared at their feet.

Looking from one to the other, Leo seemed satisfied. 'Now, get out of my sight for the rest of the day and I'll decide what to do with you later. Pat!' he shouted. 'Sort these kids out before I fire them both.'

Pat grabbed the teenagers by the arm and marched them both out of the yard.

Leo turned to his guests. 'I'm so sorry,' he said, smoothly. 'The kids in the yard can be more trouble than the horses, and of course they're upset about young Alex. Let's finish our meal.' A vein pulsed at his temple.

Henry said, 'No problem at all. This business with the dead girl's bound to cause a bit of trouble in the yard.'

And with this massive understatement, Leo's guests returned to their meal.

* * *

They'd all lost their appetites. Ice cream gently melted in their bowls.

'We're not used to such excitement here,' Henry said.

Laura said, 'Poor things. They're just children, really, and they knew the girl that died. Of course they're upset.'

Leo sighed. 'Such a tragedy, Alex Deacon dying like that,' he said. 'She was an up-and-coming star of the future. She rode one of my horses once, earlier in the season. Ann Clarkson asked me to give her a ride when one of her horses went lame.'

Leo and Ann Clarkson must be on good terms, if she was willing to share a jockey. Leo said, 'She came in a good third, and with a bit more experience, she might have won. Ann wouldn't let me borrow her, since then. Still, Belinda's shaping up well enough.'

Henry said, 'She'll be top of the heap, now.' The others glared. 'What?' he asked. 'I'm only saying what everyone's thinking.'

Ling tapped his wrist. 'Sometimes, it's best not to, darling. You're not in court, now.'

Adam ventured, 'Do the stable boys and girls from different yards all know each other?'

Laura nodded. 'Yes, they bump into each other all the time. You see, the grooms look after individual horses and accompany them to the races. They groom them and tack them up, and lead them around the parade ring before the start. There's quite a bit of rivalry as you can imagine. There's usually a prize for the best turned-out mount.'

'Do all the grooms become jockeys?' Adam asked.

'If they show signs of enough ability. They attend courses run by the British Racing School. I believe Alex and Belinda were on the same one recently. They're taught for a few weeks and they come away with a certificate that allows them to ride as a conditional jockey. They don't have to carry so much weight, you see, as the professionals do. That's why those two were competing on Saturday. Their trainer supervises them before and after the race, to make sure they weigh out and in again properly, and so on.'

'And then, if they're successful, they go on to become professionals?' Adam asked. 'How close is young Belinda to that?'

'She's got a little way to go. This was her first ride as a conditional.'

Ling said, 'That's why she was so upset at the Stewards' Enquiry. It would have been a real feather in her cap if she'd won that race.'

'That's the way it goes,' Leo said. 'I think she has a future. I'm giving her another ride in a few weeks. I don't want her to lose her nerve.'

Henry was looking at his watch. 'Time for us to be getting back, old thing,' he announced, taking Ling's arm. His words were slurring a little. His wife had been drinking only water.

'Thanks for your hospitality, Leo,' he said. 'Looking forward to seeing Butterfly run again in – what is it? Three weeks?'

'That's right. If you want to come and watch her one morning on the gallops, just let me know. And Belinda will be schooling her over the jumps, once Butterfly's rested a little – if she behaves herself and I decide not to kick her out on her ear.'

His laugh was relaxed. Maybe his bark was worse than his bite. 'Have to give a young horse time to recover after each race. Don't want to wear them out too soon.'

Henry snorted. 'Racehorses. They're like actors. Always on the edge.'

Adam said, 'It's been fascinating meeting you all,' he said. 'I can see why you love the racing world. Maybe a few shares in a horse will be a great investment.'

'The best in the world,' said Henry. 'Tell you what, why don't we get together one day soon. I'm looking for shares in a different horse at this yard. Maybe you and I could find one together.'

'That would be perfect.' Adam was keen to know Henry better. Gregarious, friendly enough if overbearing, he didn't seem a likely candidate as a murderer, but Adam wondered about his interest in racing. He seemed to be in it for the money. Was it a way to get rich quick? And could a young jockey like Alex Deacon have managed to get in his way? Adam thought a successful barrister and hard drinker like Henry might be ruthless, if crossed.

As Adam started the car for the drive home, Harley heaved a huge sigh of contentment, sending a gust of doggy breath in Adam's face as he curled up on the back seat and slept, snoring loudly, for the entire drive.

13

JOURNALIST

While Adam spent the day dipping his poorly clad toes into the choppy waters of racing yard culture, Imogen and Steph were cooking up a plan to talk to John Harris, the journalist who'd written the article about Butterfly Charm's race.

Imogen said. 'We need to remember he'll be upset about his niece's murder.'

Steph smiled, rather sadly. 'He's a journalist. Like me. I'm afraid we develop a thick skin when it comes to news stories. He'll put aside his personal feelings, especially if he thinks there's an opportunity for collaborating on a book. Something about female jockeys, or racing accidents or murders. His article suggests Belinda killed her rival, so I bet he'd jump at that idea.'

Imogen looked closely at her friend. 'Steph, are you planning to dangle that in front of him, as a way of getting him to agree to talk to us?'

'You bet. But, I'm putting nothing in writing. I don't want him suing me for anything I publish.'

'Is that quite – ethical?'

Steph blushed. Her 'tough journalist' stance was an act developed over years in a challenging world.

'Of course it is. The newspaper business is incredibly litigious. I'll offer John Harris an unofficial collaboration, and he can write what he chooses as a result. He's already treading a fine line in his article. He practically accuses Belinda of killing her rival, which is pretty unethical and unfair. I think there's almost a case for libel there, although he probably consulted lawyers about that.'

Imogen nodded. 'We'll try your offer of collaboration first, then, and see where we get. How do we start?'

'I suggest we do a bit of background research on both him and Alex. The first thing I learned in the school of hard knocks they call journalism, was to do your homework thoroughly first, before talking to anyone. And that's much easier these days, when everything's online.'

So the two women spent the afternoon in the Hawthorn Room.

Steph rested a brown case on the table, sliding from it a thick notebook and an iPad. 'I don't know how we all managed before these machines.'

Imogen opened her own laptop and they sat in silence, drinking coffee and making notes, both pairs of eyes on the World Wide Web as they searched for information on racing, jockeys and, especially, John Harris.

It didn't take long.

'I've got him,' Steph exclaimed. 'I'll send you the link to his website.'

Imogen rose and stretched. 'I need a break. This man is racing mad, and he talks about people in the business as though they're all personal friends. I've discovered more than I ever thought I needed to know about movers and shakers in the racing world.'

Steph said. 'It's harder to dig out the personal information about our Mr Harris himself. But here are a few titbits. He's not quite as closely related to Alex as we thought at first. It's through his ex-wife, the sister of Alex's mother.'

She rubbed her eyes and frowned at the screen. 'He appears to work mostly as a freelancer, sending articles to various racing papers, with the odd piece in national newspapers. He's doing quite well. No books to his name yet, I see. That's good. I'll contact a few of the papers he writes for and see if we can winkle out where he might be. If he's not at a racecourse, he might even be at home, writing.'

'Do we have his address?'

'No, but I bet I can get his phone number out of one of the publications, and I'll take it from there.

* * *

'Well, fancy that,' Steph looked up from a series of text messages with her newspaper contacts. 'John Harris lives in Somerset, not far from Wincanton, and I have a phone number.'

She grinned, cleared her throat and tapped in the number. It was answered in moments. She introduced herself. 'I've been reading some of your work, Mr Harris.' Her voice oozed admiration. 'I won't waste your time with flattery, but I'm looking to write a book about true crime in the racing world.'

She winked at Imogen and put the phone on speaker. A suspicious baritone voice said, 'Who are you, now? And why would I be interested in your book?'

'I'm offering you the chance to collaborate.'

'Oh, yes. That's a likely story. I can write my own books, you know.'

'I thought it would be more fun to work together. Combine

your knowledge of racing with my experience in criminal journalism.'

Steph laid out her qualifications. Imogen hadn't known half of the work she'd done. She'd been published in newspapers and magazines from *The Sunday Times* to *True Crime*. She had specialised in the psychology of some celebrated murderers.

She referred to Harris's articles in the *Racing Post*. 'I thought my experience and yours, as a racing expert—' Imogen grinned at the flattery.

Steph went on, 'If you'd be willing to meet for lunch, in Lower Hembrow...'

As they talked, Imogen left to organise more coffee. She returned, carrying a tray piled with chocolate biscuits, to find Steph chuckling to herself. 'Success,' Steph said. 'No journalist worth his salt refuses a free meal. It's practically written into the code of conduct.'

She helped herself to a chocolate digestive. 'I told him what a great pub we have in The Plough. I said I'd meet him there at twelve thirty on Friday and I'd bring along my collaborator, an investigator. Do you know what he asked?'

Imogen shook her head.

'He wanted to know if the collaborator would be male or female.'

Imogen rolled her eyes. The man would be hoping the assistant would be young and nubile. She was already beginning to dislike Mr Harris.

14

HARRIS

The Plough was quiet on Friday when Imogen and Steph arrived for the meeting with John Harris. Wyatt was off duty for the day and Adam, dividing his time between manning the bar with Rex and serving food, greeted them with the offer of a free drink and gave them a menu.

'Just things with chips, today,' he apologised.

Imogen knew that was all Wyatt would let Adam cook. 'You're a great guy, Adam, but you're no chef,' he'd said. 'Your food'll poison the neighbourhood. Just flip the burgers, right?'

For the strapping young farmers in The Plough, burgers, sausages, and chips were perfect – and the more generous the portions, the better.

A clatter of nails on wood heralded the arrival of John Harris, preceded by a sturdy bulldog with a bitten ear. Imogen murmured, 'It's Bill Sykes. He's escaped from Oliver.'

John Harris was stocky, not unlike Oliver Reed in build, with the telltale bulbous drinker's nose but considerably less hair. In his mid-forties, he wore a typical off-duty uniform of cords, jacket and checked shirt. Two farm workers at their favourite table in the corner looked up at his entrance, grinned as the dog sniffed at their legs, and went back to their food. John Harris fitted in perfectly at the country pub.

'Steph.' Harris grinned and held out his hand. 'Good to meet you.'

He'd picked her out at once. Imogen wasn't surprised to find he'd done his own research before meeting this possible collaborator.

He turned his attention to Imogen. A smug smile spread across his coarse-featured face. 'You're Imogen Bishop,' he said. 'I know you from your photo in the paper when your husband died. Quite a story, that. I've read all about it.' Imogen sighed, inwardly cursing the internet. Her face would be linked to her husband's murder for ever.

Rex came from behind the bar, took their orders and returned with their drinks; Imogen's Coke, an alcohol-free beer for Steph and a large red wine for Harris.

Harris turned to Steph. 'That story about The Streamside Hotel murders likely to turn up in this book we might collaborate on?' Imogen had to control a shudder.

Steph answered, calmly, 'No, I think we should stick to racing.'

Harris's eyes were small and set closely together, but they were sharp and alert. He was no one's fool, and not about to throw information around for free. Still, he was here, and that was the first step.

Imogen said, 'We're very sorry for your loss.' He looked puzzled.

She raised her eyebrows. 'Alex Deacon. Your niece?'

Harris's cocky grin faded, replaced by a solemn, unconvincing frown. 'A very sad day, that was.' he said, 'Very disturbing, but an open-and-shut case.' He shook his head. 'Those teenage hormones at work. Belinda Sandford should have learned to control her jealousy.'

Steph said, 'Why are you so sure she killed Alex? Or that Alex was murdered, for that matter. The police haven't called it that.'

He gave an exaggerated snort of derision. Imogen's hackles rose, but before she could say anything, Adam arrived with three plates balanced on his arms, piled high with chicken and chips.

Harris smirked. 'I know who you are, too. Adam Hennessy, isn't it? Ex-detective, righter of wrongs, and master sleuth, I believe. Also involved in solving the murder at The Streamside Hotel. I congratulate you.'

He looked around the trio and waved at the table's remaining empty chair. 'This is quite a team of investigators you have here. Won't you join us, now you've got me here? You won't want to miss our discussion.'

Adam smiled but his nose twitched. He liked to hide his feelings behind his thick specs and broad smile, but Imogen knew him well enough to recognise when he was on edge. He hadn't taken to John Harris any more than she had.

He distributed the plates neatly around the table and said cheerfully, 'You've done your homework, I see. And you're right. Once a detective always a nosy parker, that's what I say.'

Harris laughed, but his eyes glittered.

Adam smiled again, 'I'll listen in for a minute or two while things are quiet.'

'I take it I'm not a suspect,' John Harris said, with an unconvincing laugh. He wasn't quite as confident as he pretended. Adam's presence unsettled him.

'Not so far.' Adam's friendly smile never wavered.

Breaking into the rising tension between the two men, Imogen said, 'You were just about to tell us why you think Belinda Sandford killed Alex Deacon.'

'I was, was I? Well, stands to reason, doesn't it? Two girls, rivals on the racetrack, each hoping to make the grade. They're highly strung, these young jockeys. As bad as the horses. Apprentices see the world stretching before them. They dream of winning the Cheltenham Gold Cup and the Grand National and they'll do anything to get a ride and climb the ladder. Young Belinda found winning wasn't so easy on Saturday. You saw the photo. She cheated, she was found out, and she couldn't cope with it. That's why she killed Alex.'

Adam said, 'That photo of yours, though. It looked like a set-up to me. Your niece knew you'd be there, and she goaded Belinda Sandford so you could get a good shot. Of course Belinda was upset. It was her first race and she'd thought she'd won, but losing a horse race is no reason to murder someone. Do you seriously think a normal woman would kill someone because they lost a single race?' Imogen looked at her plate to hide a smile at the sarcasm in Adam's voice.

Harris coloured a little. 'Well, besides that, there's sex in the mix. Professional jealousy is one thing, but Belinda Sandford had also lost her boyfriend to Alex, who would have easily beat her in the race if the Sandford girl hadn't cheated – well that's enough to spur any girl into rash behaviour. It's easy to see what happened. The two of them quarrel after the race, Belinda goes off in disgrace and probably takes a rocket from Leo. Then she bumps into Alex near the horseboxes. Maybe they had more words.' Harris had thought this through, Imogen decided.

'In any case,' he went on, 'Belinda could have come up behind poor Alex and stuffed her face into the trough. It doesn't take that much force to hold someone's head under water, and young Belinda's a strong little thing. Have to be, if you're a jockey. Think of the muscles she's gained controlling thoroughbred horses.'

He forked a mound of chicken into his mouth and said, voice

muffled by the food, 'It's an open and shut case, if you ask me.'

He waved the fork in Adam's direction. 'Nice chicken, by the way, and not a bad pub. I'd stick to serving if I were you. Keep your nose out of other people's business.' The small eyes flashed. The sudden venom in his tone shocked Imogen.

Steph said, 'Tell us more about this so-called boyfriend.'

She leaned on the table, her eyes on Harris. He smiled at her.

A shiver tracked up Imogen's back. She and Steph had thought they'd be interviewing Harris, but he'd been keen to meet because he had his own agenda. He had no intention of collaborating with Steph. Why would he? He was a rival. He was hoping to raise hackles and trap the trio into telling him more about Belinda – information he'd be using for his own purposes.

One of the young farmers was looking around for service. With a grimace at Imogen, Adam left the table.

Imogen went on puzzling. Why had Harris mentioned Alex's boyfriend? He wouldn't give away information with no reason. Could it be an attempt at misdirection, to guide the conversation away from the race itself?

Adam rejoined them, bearing a new bottle of wine.

Harris helped himself, liberally, topping his glass up to the brim.

Steph said, 'It sounds as though your niece was quite a rising star. That must have been useful to you.'

For a second, Harris paused, his glass at his lips. 'How do you mean?' The small eyes narrowed.

Steph smiled. 'She must have been a great source of gossip. You know, which horses are under the weather, jockeys falling out, trainers in competition with each other and trying to poach new owners. That kind of thing.'

Harris took a long draught of wine and laughed. His nose was growing pinker by the moment. 'One or two titbits, maybe. A few short cuts, hints. Human interest. All above board. Every journalist has contacts, don't they, Steph? That's how we make our living. Remember when journalists spent most of the afternoon in the pub with useful sources? Those were the days. We used to drive home half-cut. Good job you're not a serving policeman, by the way, Hennessy.'

'Maybe not,' Adam said, 'but I can't let you leave here while you're over the drink-drive limit. You're welcome to stay around, though, until you sober up.'

Harris, unfazed, made a thumbs up gesture. 'Good idea. Maybe I can take a walk over the road and inspect your gardens, Mrs Bishop. They've been all over the news. As a matter of fact I've been to your other project at Haselbury House. The owner's a mate of mine.'

He raised his glass to Steph. 'Let's have another bottle, and I'll tell you all about Ann Clarkson and Leo Murphy.'

* * *

Harris sat, drinking steadily, as The Plough slowly emptied. He'd passed on very little information, just hints that the two trainers had more than a professional relationship. He claimed to have seen them together at the races. Adam wondered whether the hint at a relationship between Leo Murphy and Ann Clarkson was based on any truth. Was Harris simply trying to impress Steph with his inside knowledge? Maybe he'd taken a fancy to her.

A twinge of jealousy caught Adam by surprise. He tried to ignore it. Steph had too much sense to admire a man like Harris. But then, he was a journalist, like her. They had plenty in common.

Adam poured himself a large glass of wine.

At last, the wine bottle empty, Harris tore himself away and followed Imogen across the road to the hotel. He staggered a little as he walked, the bulldog at his heels.

Adam watched them go, wondering what Harley would make of Harris's pet.

Steph remained at their table, twirling a glass between her fingers. She refused Adam's offer of another drink but showed no sign of leaving.

She grinned. 'I wanted to make sure I'm not muscling in on this business. I know Imogen's keen to help young Belinda, and it's right up your street, but I'd hate you to think I'm just hoping to get a book out of it.'

'Like Harris, you mean?'

'Definitely not. Not his kind of book, anyway. There's a limit to the tittle-tattle I want to write about. Judging by that hint he let slip, about the relationship between Leo and the rival trainer, I'm glad I'm not Mrs Murphy. I'm almost tempted to warn her.'

Adam whistled softly. 'Stay out of other people's marriages, that's my advice. You'll end up hated by both parties.'

'And with my reputation for serious journalism gone for ever.'

She grinned at him, brown eyes twinkling.

He swallowed, suddenly as tongue-tied as a teenager.

He removed his glasses, pulled a handkerchief from his pocket, breathed on the lenses and rubbed at them enthusiastically. Without them, he could hardly see Steph's face. It was just a blur. He almost preferred that. He hoped he wasn't blushing.

His phone rang.

With a sigh and an apologetic glance at Steph, he replaced his glasses, read the name and answered the call. James. His pathologist mate and provider of useful information.

'Hey James, fancy hearing from you today. What can I do for you?'

'More what I can do for you, mate,' James boomed, in his loud North London accent. He sounded jauntier than during their last conversation – almost back to his old self. 'This possible murder on your patch. Even supposing none of your immediate friends and family is in the frame for it this time, I thought you might be planning a spot of extracurricular poking around.'

Adam laughed. 'Have to admit, it's tempting.'

'Well, being a nosy old bloke like you, I talked to a colleague of mine. I don't think you know Mike, the forensic pathologist in your neck of the woods. He had a look at that unfortunate jockey and I thought you'd be interested in what he found.'

'Yes?'

'Well, it seems that it was just what it appeared to be at first sight – a nice straightforward dunk and drown, though not sadly in the proverbial butt of Malmsey, like a royal after a bad night.'

'Go on then,' Adam said. 'What's the twist?'

'Well, you know how you expect horses to be nobbled in a race?'

'Come on, stop leading me down the garden path.'

'Well, it seems our young victim was also on something. Mike isn't sure, yet, what it was, or whether she'd taken it before the race or after, but it seems young Alex had a hefty dose of stimulants in her body when she died.'

'Interesting.' Adam let the thought sink in to his brain.

'Thought you'd want to know,' James said. 'I'll tell you if I hear any more.'

'Thanks,' said Adam. 'So, she was drowned, just as it appeared. Not strangled or smothered.'

'I'll leave it with you,' James said. 'I've got a couple of unfortunates to deal with myself now. When will these kids stop swallowing every tablet they're offered at a party? You owe me that meal, by the way. Or two. Any chance of meeting up soon?'

'Sure.' It sounded as though James had something to share. It must be something personal, unconnected to the case. 'Tomorrow? Here in The Plough?'

'I'll text you.' James rang off.

Steph was wriggling in her seat. 'Come on, what did he say?'

Adam relayed the gist of the call. 'The plot thickens,' he said. 'Drugs in the victim's system. What do you think of that?'

'Really? Don't they test jockeys for drugs before letting them ride? And, probably, afterwards. When they weigh them, or something?'

'Good question,' said Adam. 'I suppose they concentrate more on the horse for drugs. In any case, a young jockey, especially one with a conditional licence like Alex, would be under minute observation by their trainer. Like other athletes, I imagine they give samples from time to time. I wouldn't have thought it worth one of these ambitious riders risking everything by taking drugs at the beginning of their career.'

Steph laughed. 'I'm afraid, these days it's very common for young people to have a sniff of something, or swallow a tab at the weekend. Maybe the poor girl took something after the race to celebrate. To young people, taking drugs is no worse than drinking champagne and no one would object if she'd had a celebratory glass or two of that.'

Adam sighed. 'You're right.' Like James, he hated drugs. They'd both seen their effects over the years. 'I wonder where she got it from.'

'It's not difficult,' Steph said. 'Even Rose, my daughter, tells me she knows where to get stuff although, of course, she swears she never would. And as she's an adult, I have to believe her. Or, at least, I can't stop her. Worrying, isn't it?'

Adam was silent. How he'd have loved a child in his life to worry about.

15

MARIA

Dragging his thoughts back to Alex Deacon's death, Adam said, 'What we need is a proper timeline. We know the race ended at three forty-five. The Stewards' Enquiry took about twenty minutes, plus time to set up and watch the recording of the race. It must have finished about four thirty, I would guess.'

Steph said, 'We can verify that, from the time of the tannoy announcement.'

'So we can,' he agreed. 'Could we check with John Harris to be sure exactly when he took his photo of the two girls arguing, which I would guess happened between four thirty and five o'clock?'

'I'll ring him later, when Imogen's sobered him up. The time will be on the photograph. I might need some information to trade, though.'

'I don't think—'

She grinned, and waved a hand in the air. 'Don't worry. I won't tell him anything about the case, but I know a publisher who'd be interested in a trashy 'true confessions' kind of book. An old acquaintance of mine owes me a favour, from way back when I caught her 'in flagrante' with her boss's husband and let her off the hook. She owes me one as a result, so I can persuade her to look at ideas for this imaginary racing crime book. I think Harris was interested in working on it. His writing's good, by the way.'

Adam grunted. He was still thinking through the timings. 'Alex's body was found at seven. That's good news for Belinda. It shortens the window when she might have been with Alex, unobserved.'

Steph nodded slowly. 'Could Alex have died earlier? I mean, surely there were people in and out of the boxes where the horses were being prepared for their journeys home. I don't see how a body could have been left there for more than a minute or two without being seen. In fact, I don't understand how anyone at a race meeting could have the sort of fight that ended in one of them drowning, without anyone knowing. The places are teeming.'

'You're absolutely right,' Adam murmured. 'I don't think this was a fight. I think it's more likely that someone saw Alex by the trough, and seized the moment.'

He shook his head. 'A real spur-of-the moment killing. If it was a killing. Whoever did it took a big chance. Maybe they'd been lying in wait? Or too angry to think straight. But we still come back to wondering why? Killing someone over a single race? That doesn't make sense, but I think if this really was murder, and not an accident, it's the motive that will untangle it.'

At that moment, Adam heard a familiar husky voice calling, in an Eastern European accent he would recognise anywhere. 'Adam, my darling, what are you doing in a gloomy bar when the sun's shining on such a beautiful day.' Adam looked up to see Maria Rostropova silhouetted in the doorway, as lovely as ever, like an operatic countess.

Steph and Maria eyed each other. They reminded Adam of

Harley when he met an unfriendly dog in the village, but without the sniffing.

Steph said, 'Maria. How lovely to see you. Will you be at the next committee meeting?'

'I wouldn't miss it for the world.'

Adam stepped in. 'What can I do for you?' he asked. Maria always needed some little favour.

'Darling,' she gushed. 'Of course I haven't come to ask anything of you at all. I haven't seen you for days. I wanted to make sure you were well.'

'As you see, I'm in the most robust health.'

Maria frowned. 'Well, that's wonderful. You're so lucky. I'm a little anxious at the moment – oh, nothing's wrong, of course, but...'

Here it comes. Adam waited.

'On behalf of the Musical Society...'

He closed his eyes and suppressed a shudder. Last summer, she'd demanded the use of his paddock for an outdoor concert. After a great deal of time, effort and organisation on Adam's part, the concert had been moved to The Streamside Hotel, and Adam had vowed never to be taken in by Maria's pleas again.

'Yes?' he said, trying to sound forbidding, while knowing he never could. He wasn't built for it.

'I need someone to help with our craft stall at the Spring Fair. The music society is running it.'

'What did you have in mind?' Adam was guarded. He'd never heard of Maria dabbling in knitting or sewing.

'Why, willow baskets, of course. You see, I am learning how to make them, using Somerset willow. What could be more English?'

'Maria, I'm sorry. I really have no skills in that direction—'

She cut him off with a tinkling laugh. 'No, no, dear Adam. I am weaving the baskets. But, I need more raw materials. Willow is not cheap.'

Adam relaxed. As usual, she needed money. Really, the woman had no shame.

'Sorry,' he began, but Steph interrupted.

'I'll join in with you, if you like. I've made baskets before and I have a friend who lives on the Somerset Levels. He'll let us have some supplies at cost, if it's for charity.'

'Wonderful. Then come with me, and I'll show you what I've made so far.'

Adam watched Steph leave with Maria. He felt suddenly alone. No, it was more than that; he felt abandoned and bereft.

Where had that neediness sprung from? Until now, he'd been perfectly happy living on his own, running The Plough.

Until he'd met Steph. That was the problem. When he'd met her, his whole world, previously so carefully managed, had been turned upside down.

Steph was beautiful, clever, kind and independent. Adam should stop fooling himself. He'd only once in his life had what he'd imagined – mistakenly, as it had turned out – to be a proper, grown-up relationship with a woman. Once she'd cleared out his bank account and left the country, he'd taken a good long look at himself in the mirror and resolved never again to behave like a fool.

His jaw ached. He'd been grinding his teeth. He dragged his thoughts back to Maria's plans and thought fast. He'd have to watch her. Last year, she'd been planning to top-slice the proceeds of the summer concert to pay off her own debts. But then, this time Steph was on the case. He could leave her to deal with Maria.

* * *

His appointment with DCI Andrews took place late that afternoon. The police officer greeted him with unusual enthusiasm. 'Come in, Adam, come in.' He waved Adam to sit in front of his desk. Several piles of folders rested on its walnut surface. 'Just finishing up for the weekend. Going away with the wife for a couple of days. Another birthday.'

'Yours, or hers?' Adam had never met Mrs Andrews. He imagined a cheerful soul, striving to keep the DCI from sinking into the depression his hangdog expression suggested.

'Mine.' He sounded gloomy. 'She's booked some activity weekend.' His bushy eyebrows came together in a frown, almost meeting over his nose. 'Line dancing or some such.' He heaved a sigh.

Adam kept a straight face, trying to imagine Andrews, a heavyweight of over six and a half feet, dancing. 'That'll make a nice change.'

Andrews' eyes narrowed. 'Good fun, line dancing, she tells me.' He made it sound like torture.

'Well, Happy Birthday.'

'Thank you. I wanted to finish up this Wincanton races business before I go.' He opened the top folder. 'I thought you'd want to know, we have no evidence of murder.' He waved a printed page at Adam. '"Light bruises in various places on the body," the pathology chap told us. Nothing he hasn't seen on any horse rider. I can't think why folk ride horses, to be honest. Too likely to fall off – and it's a long way to the ground, I reckon. Still, they will do it.' Another world-weary sigh. 'Anyway,' he went on, his eyes suddenly alert. 'The verdict so far is it was probably an accident. The girl had water in her lungs and cocaine in her system – silly young thing, but not unusual, these days. Must have snorted a line for kicks, probably celebrating her win. We can't know where she got it. Probably from one of her friends.'

He paused for breath. Adam asked, 'What of Belinda Sandford? Is she in the clear, if there's no evidence of murder?'

Andrews shrugged. 'No more evidence against her than anyone else. Any jockey, trainer, stable hand or owner could have been around their horses after the race. It must have been like Piccadilly Circus. If it wasn't an accident, and someone gave Alex a shove and held her head under the water, they were either very lucky to find her alone, or they'd planned very carefully in advance.

'If it was a spur-of-the-moment argument, there would likely have been a fight, shouting, maybe a punch to the face leaving a nice big bruise, and some bruised knuckles, but there was none of that – Belinda's hands were work-worn, of course, not surprising, given her job, but the knuckles were fine. No sign she'd punched anyone.'

He turned a page of print. 'No, we can't see Belinda as a spur-of-the-moment attacker, despite that photo in the press. And did she plan it carefully in advance, before the race, maybe trick young Alex into meeting her there? No. If she had murder planned, she wouldn't have had a public spat with her victim.'

He closed the folder with a sigh. 'Nothing adds up to murder. Unless something else comes to light, I reckon we can let your client, Belinda, off the hook, along with everyone else.'

Adam said, 'Not my client.'

'Not being paid then?' The eyebrows rose sky-high. 'Missed a trick, there, didn't you?'

Adam shook his head. 'I'm not going into business as a private investigator, if that's what you mean. I'm just doing Belinda's mother a favour.'

Andrews rolled his eyes. Adam laughed. 'So, there's no murder and no suspect?' he said.

'None. No good motive, and no evidence. No one saw the

young lady fall into the trough, and the CCTV doesn't help. Why do these things always happen just outside its range? The most likely explanation is that Alex was excited and high, lost control, fell and maybe hit her head on the side of the trough.'

'Nothing suspicious, then?' Adam asked.

'Not enough to go on. Her parents and brother don't know of any reason she might be killed. They seem like a nice enough family. Live up near Weston-super-Mare. The brother says she might have snorted cocaine once, but didn't do it often because she didn't want to lose her job. Everyone at the yard where she worked and a couple of flatmates said the same. An ambitious girl, a bit pushy, but a good laugh and a talented rider. Not a bad epitaph, maybe, and no indication at all of foul play. So, that's that, unless the coroner disagrees.'

Adam wasn't sure. 'You're closing the case?'

Andrews tapped the folder. 'We're leaving it open until after the coroner's inquest, of course, but to be honest with you – and I say this because you used to be one of us – I don't hold out much hope of finding evidence of murder. If there'd been a nice big bump on the back of the young lady's head, now it'd be a different story, but as things are, we're looking at an accidental death outcome.'

Adam nodded, thoughtfully. There was something in Andrews' voice...

'Unless,' the DCI went on, almost under his breath, 'unless there's something we're missing. How busy are you, these days, what with your pub and all?'

The question sounded innocent and Adam nodded soberly, but he could hardly keep the grin off his face. Andrews was giving him a signal. The police wouldn't be spending much time on the case unless more evidence came to light, but Andrews wasn't happy. He didn't want to leave it there, but his hands were tied.

Adam rose to his feet. 'I'll keep an eye out,' he said.

As he left, he glanced back at the DCI. He was almost sure Andrews winked at him.

As he drove back to The Plough, Adam wondered whether he should let Diane and Belinda know what the police thought. Would he be raising their hopes too much? There was no official decision, but it seemed unfair to leave the two women hanging, believing Belinda was likely to be accused of murder.

Adam decided it was his duty to pass on the news. Diane was emotionally fragile. The police thought Belinda was innocent but they wouldn't tell her or her mother until they were sure. Adam wasn't bound by the same rules. He could put them out of their misery.

Once back home, he called Diane.

'Are you sure?' she gasped. 'Oh, that's wonderful. I'm so relieved. I was worried about Belinda, she's much more sensitive than she shows. She took it all so much to heart – thinking she was under suspicion. I knew she was innocent, of course, we all did, but the worry of it all.' Her voice cracked. 'Oh, I'm sorry. How silly of me, to cry now, when it's all over.'

'Well, it's not over until the coroner's decision,' Adam warned, but Diane seemed not to hear.

'You must send me your bill,' she said.

'No, no. That's kind, but this wasn't a business arrangement. I can't possibly accept. I'm just glad you're happy.'

'Well, I'll call her right away and tell her the good news...' Diane talked and talked, as though a dam had burst and a flood of relief overflowed. Adam thanked his lucky stars he need no longer feel responsible for such a vulnerable woman.

Finally, he managed to extract himself from her gratitude by pretending he had to serve a customer and, with relief, slipped his phone back into his pocket.

16

VILLAGE SHOP

As Imogen had expected, local journalists soon cottoned onto the fact that a member of the Butterfly Charm syndicate had been staying at The Streamside Hotel in Lower Hembrow when Alex Deacon died, so while reporting in the nationals had been focused on Alex – her youth, the promise in her career, and the exciting racing background – and had died away after a few days, the local weekly paper had carried on gathering quotes from neighbours.

'Well, I never did,' an anonymous local resident told the *Gazette*. 'And we live in such a quiet part of the world. Who would have thought it?'

Imogen suspected the journalist had restricted his research to a quick visit to Edwina Topsham's shop, for very few of the quotes were attributed to named people. The locals always had opinions, and loved to share them, but they wouldn't want to see their names in the papers. In a village like Lower Hembrow, you could find yourself ostracised for months if you were seen as a troublemaker.

The journalist who'd written the piece had little information to add, apart from the news that Belinda Sandford was a local girl, her mother had been Diane Webber, and several of Butterfly Charm's syndicate members had also spent their formative years in Somerset.

Adam had phoned to tell Imogen about his interview with DCI Andrews. 'There's precious little evidence, but it seems Andrews' sixth sense is telling him there might be something sinister in Alex's death.'

'So,' Imogen said, 'we can go on investigating, but we're doing it for Diane and Belinda?'

'Exactly. Andrews thinks we might be right to be suspicious. Of course, he couldn't say that, but he didn't warn us off.'

'If anyone asks, we believe it was an accident?'

'Exactly.'

As a result of this conversation, Imogen made one of her regular trips to the village shop, the source of all local knowledge. Harley was delighted. He'd learned that a visit to Edwina's emporium was likely to lead to a supply of biscuits and a few tummy tickles.

As it was a school day, Alfie Croft, Harley's main admirer, was absent, but Edwina was on full, bouncing form. 'So, you've had some excitement up at the hotel, m'dear,' she said. 'It's almost as though you're a magnet for murder.'

Imogen shot her a sideways look. She was never sure whether or not Edwina was joking.

'Now don't you go spreading that around, or our bookings will plummet.'

Edwina chuckled, her chins wobbling merrily. 'Don't you believe it. That last business didn't cause you too much trouble, did it? Not so far as the hotel was concerned anyway.' She blushed and her voice tailed away, for 'that last business' had included the death of not only Imogen's husband but also her father.

She laid a warm, motherly hand on Imogen's arm. 'Now, don't you take any notice. My mouth runs away with me, I'm afraid, but I don't mean any harm. We like having you up there at the big hotel, and I know you send your guests down to pop into the shop.'

She treated Imogen to a conspiratorial grin.

Imogen said, 'Plenty of the guests come down from the city, and there's nothing they like more than dropping into a proper corner shop. Especially since you started serving all those old-fashioned sweets.' She pointed at the long neat row of jars lined up on shelves behind the counter. 'I find little bowls full of them everywhere in the hotel. The staff are as bad as the guests.'

Edwina chuckled. 'That's right, folk remember those sweeties from when they were little. Why, back along when I were a lass, I used to buy a quarter of milk bottles every week.' She nodded towards a jar half full of the small, rubbery, milk bottle-shaped sweets. 'Unless, now and then, I'd have those sherbet pips. Not that my mother liked me eating those. Not since my little sister stuck some up her nose. Had to take her to the doctor, we did, to find out why she wasn't talking properly. The doctor poked around, looking up her nose, and she gave a great big sneeze. The sherbet pip popped out, just missed the doctor and shot right across the room. That's what my Mum said, anyway.'

Imogen laughed. 'Well, since I'm here, I'll have some of your bonbons, please, but only if you'll weigh them out on your proper brass scales.'

The two women traded grins. Imogen felt a surge of affection for Edwina. She meant well, and she was highly influential in Lower Hembrow.

As bonbons rattled into the scales, Imogen said, 'The paper

tells me that one of our guests eating in the hotel the other weekend was a local girl. Laura Wilson. Does the name mean much to you?'

'Laura Wilson?' Edwina nodded. 'She used to be Laura Collins before she married that stuck-up doctor of hers. The Collins family have a farm over towards Haselbury Plucknett. Five daughters in that family, can you imagine? As bad as the Trevillians. Must be something in the water, I reckon.'

Still shaking with mirth, she went on, 'Martha Collins, their mother, said her husband wanted to keep going until they had a boy, but after Laura was born, she told him that if he wanted a boy, he'd have to get a divorce and remarry, because she'd had enough of the whole business. And who can blame her?'

She transferred the bonbons into a white paper bag. 'But you were asking about Laura, m'dear, weren't you? She was the youngest of the girls. She didn't want to stay buried down here on her parents' farm and off she went to the city for a while. Mind you, she came back. Married Magnus Wilson, and they live in South Petherton. You can take a girl out of Somerset but...'

Imogen nodded. 'You can't take Somerset out of the girl. Very true, I'd say. Look at me, back here after all these years. I don't remember any of the Collins girls. Younger than me, of course, and I didn't ride.'

Edwina paused, her face screwed up in thought. 'The beauty of the family was Laura. She looked like an angel, but there was nothing stuck-up about her. A good, down-to-earth Somerset girl, she was, but my goodness me she had a mouth on her could turn a pig blue. She would outswear any of the boys working on the farm, and didn't they love it? Like flies around a honeypot, those lads.'

To Imogen's disappointment, Jenny Trevillian's arrival with two of her children put paid to any more revelations. Imogen held the door open as Jenny guided a toddler in a stroller inside, another child, of about four in age, in tow. 'Just come from the playschool,' Jenny said. 'Jack does enjoy it so, but he gets tired and fights with his little sister for the rest of the day. So, I said he could come and choose something for his lunch.'

Edwina turned her attention to Jack. His coat was wet through and his trousers muddy from the knees down. There was a scab on his nose and scratches down the side of his face. 'You look like you've been in the wars, young man. What do you fancy for lunch. Sausages?'

Jack made a face. 'Pizza,' he lisped, and grabbed one of Harley's ears. Harley grunted and heaved a resigned sigh.

Edwina bustled about, collecting different types of pizza for Jack's inspection. 'And what did you do to your face, young man?'

'Tree,' said Jack. He pointed at an ancient oak across the road, in the grounds of the village hall. The playgroup operated in the hall, three days a week, the adults forced to set buckets on the floor when it rained to catch water from the ailing roof. Many generations of village children had climbed that tree and swung from the rope swing attached to its sturdy branches. Jack was far from the first to fall.

As Jack's mother paid for the pizza, Imogen seized the opportunity. 'Are your children friendly with the Collins family?'

'Laura used to babysit for us,' Jenny said, 'and she got my eldest interested in riding. The Collinses were always mad about horses, and all their girls spent most of their lives down at the pony club.'

Jack's sister, up until now sleeping peacefully in the pushchair, suddenly woke and set about gaining her mother's attention. Her wails could probably be heard inside Imogen's hotel.

'Oh, and she's off. She needs her lunch,' Jenny Trevillian

thrust the pizza in her bag, grabbed Jack's hand, shouldered the door open, and set off up the hill at a cracking pace towards the village's only car park.

Edwina swung the paper bag full of Imogen's bonbons energetically over and over, holding the corners until they stuck out like cat's ears. 'How she copes with all those children and a farm as well, I'll never know.'

'There's Joe to help.'

Edwina snorted. 'Much help that one is. Like having another child around the place, Jenny says. He's been in trouble with the police, more than once, for fly-tipping and what-not.'

No wonder Joe had a grudge against Adam, an ex-police officer.

Imogen took the package, paid, and left, Harley trotting happily at her heels.

17

FARM

Back at the hotel, Imogen sucked bonbons and took a shower. Her stomach churned. She was going with Dan to Leo Murphy's yard, to discuss the commissioned painting of the trainer's top horses.

Her pulse raced with all the confusion, anxiety, and excitement of her tentative, unsuccessful relationship with Dan, that began and ended over thirty years ago.

They'd seen a lot of each other lately, but a quick peck on the cheek after lunch or an evening meal in The Plough was the nearest they'd come to any kind of physical intimacy. They were like magnets with their poles together, preventing them from drawing close.

Imogen knew the fault was largely hers. Since her marriage went sour, she'd been terrified of commitment.

Newly independent, she'd tried to convince herself she was satisfied by the challenge of the hotel and its gardens. She needed no kind of dependent partnership. Harley was a more reliable, warm-hearted, and non-judgmental companion than any man.

But in her heart she knew their problem was confusion and,

perhaps, fear of the unknown. What did Dan want from her? Just friendship? Was he the perfectly behaved, old-fashioned soul he seemed, too polite to press her for more, or had he lost interest?

She told herself she would be happy with a simple companionship, like the one she shared with Adam. And yet, and yet...

The prospect of time with Dan knotted her stomach. She spent ten minutes coaxing her hair into a French pleat, viewing it from all angles and employing a chipped hand mirror to get a close-up of the back.

Impatient, and desperate to avoid appearing to try too hard, she tugged out the pins, replaced them with a simple elastic band at the nape of her neck, and twisted the ponytail into a loose bun. That was better. Casual. As though she hadn't thought much about it.

A dollop of tinted moisturiser failed, as always, to conceal the crow's feet around her eyes, or those two pesky parallel, vertical indents that had taken up residence between her eyebrows.

A smudge of blusher – what Emily insisted on calling 'a pop of colour' –brightened her face a little. She tried a new mascara that, as expected, failed, as so many other mascaras had done, to make her sparse lashes appear long, thick, and glamorous.

She spent a ridiculous amount of time wondering what to wear.

This was a trip to a racing stables. What was appropriate? Trousers, of course, but perhaps not those old brown cords she used for gardening. No, something newer, tighter fitting, that showed off the length of her legs, her secret vanity.

Finally, she chose a moss green cashmere jumper that she hoped combined restrained glamour with robust warmth –that was how it had been advertised in the catalogue, anyway. She hid a warm thermal vest underneath the cashmere, slipped a suede jacket on top, and zipped on a pair of her sturdiest boots, a kind of cross between wellies and Doc Martens.

She left the hotel, after putting her head round the door of the office to warn Emily she'd be away for the afternoon.

She felt, smugly, that Emily had betrayed her interest in Wyatt when The Plough needed to borrow beef, but she said nothing. She just hoped Wyatt wouldn't let Emily down. Imogen didn't want to lose her.

While Imogen was out, Harley would stay at The Streamside. There was no shortage of staff or guests for him to entertain.

* * *

The route to Leo Murphy's yard took Imogen past the farmhouse Edwina had described as the one occupied by Martha and Ed Collins, Laura Wilson's parents. Nervous restlessness at the prospect of being with Dan had brought Imogen out far too early for their meeting. She had half an hour to spare.

Giving in to curiosity, she drove through the open gate, up the winding track through fields bounded by hedges and fences, past a coppice of woodland. A network of branches, mostly bare but showing early traces of the year's green buds, left visible gaps where ancient elm trees had died and been removed.

She pulled up in a neat yard. As she got out of the car, the sights, sounds and smells of a busy farm surrounded her. Over to one side was a barn full of cattle, who lowed contentedly through mouthfuls of hay. On the opposite side of the yard was another brick building. As Imogen watched, the door flew open and a woman emerged, carrying a bundle in her arms. Surprised, Imogen recognised Laura Wilson from dinner on the evening of Alex Deacon's death.

Laura trotted past Imogen. 'Sorry, can't stop, got to get this little fellow in the warm.'

Through the open door of the barn, Imogen heard sheep. The barn door swung shut, cutting off the plaintive noise, and Imogen followed the younger woman towards the long, low stone-built farmhouse.

Laura, her hair invisible under a woolly hat, her bare hands red with cold, glanced behind her. 'Come inside, in the warm. I'll be with you in a minute.'

Imogen looked around the cosy farmhouse kitchen. A huge table almost filled the room, its surface white from many years of scrubbing.

As Laura opened the door of the Aga, heat spilled out, wrapping itself luxuriously around Imogen. She moved closer as Laura lowered her burden into a cardboard box lined with sheepskin. A puny, bedraggled lamb lay limply in the box. It kicked out weakly with one leg.

'This little fellow's been rejected by his mum. We haven't got a foster mother for him at the moment – we've only lambed one or two ewes so far – but I thought I'd try him in here. My father's out in the barn with the others.'

Laura, now warming a milk bottle in a bowl of hot water , smiled again, showing perfect teeth with the white gleam that suggested professional polishing.

'I know you,' she said. 'You're from the hotel.' Her brow creased with effort. 'Sorry, I can't remember...'

'Imogen Bishop.'

Laura wiped her hand on her jeans and extended it towards Imogen. 'Of course. I've come back to help my parents out with the lambing for a week or two. They're getting on a bit now and it's all too much for them.'

She lifted the tiny lamb onto her lap and used the dropper to get milk into its mouth. 'I remember your father, the Councillor. He was quite the celebrity around here.'

Imogen smiled and nodded at the lamb. 'Can I help?' Once or twice, as a schoolgirl, she'd helped out at local farms during lambing, although she'd never known the Collinses.

With a grin, Laura handed over the bundle. 'Dad tells me I'm wasting my time with the weakest lambs. We try to put them in with a foster mother who's lost her own baby, if we can, but this one's too weak to suckle. He needs a lot more TLC.'

She raised her well-groomed eyebrows at Imogen, who remembered she hadn't given an explanation yet for her unannounced arrival, and hadn't thought to construct one.

While she racked her brains for a good excuse, Laura said, 'I expect you've come about that terrible business at the racecourse. Was it me you were looking for?'

Her directness took Imogen by surprise. 'Well, this morning, in the local shop, they said they thought you were around.' She was stammering. She never could tell lies. She ploughed on. 'You see, I'm worried about Belinda. Her mother's convinced she's going to be accused of killing Alex Deacon.' That was true, at least.

'And you thought you'd like to help.'

Was that a hint of sarcasm in the other woman's voice? Imogen decided to take the words at face value. 'That's right. Belinda Sandford seems to be the newspapers' favourite suspect, and her mother's desperate, as I expect you know.'

Laura smiled. 'Diane's very fragile, since her husband died. That was a terrible time. We all tried to help out – Ling was especially kind. Magnus and I visited whenever we could. Now Belinda's all Diane has left. So if I can help, I will.'

Imogen thought she caught the gleam of unshed tears in

Laura's eyes. Despite her wealth and beauty, and her reputation as a trophy wife, it seemed she had a soft heart.

At that moment, the lamb latched on to the bottle in Imogen's hands and set about sucking vigorously. Laura smiled. 'If he gets that down he'll be doing well. It's colostrum, you see. The first ewe's milk, full of all sorts of great stuff. We keep some handy during lambing.'

Imogen felt a warm glow, as though she'd single-handedly saved the lamb's life. It must have shown in her face, for Laura chuckled. 'That feeling never fades,' she said. 'Wonderful, isn't it?'

Suddenly, the door burst open with a crash. Startled, the lamb jerked violently. Imogen clutched him to her chest just in time to stop him falling from her arms.

An elderly woman stood in the doorway, her eyes wide. 'Laura, come quick. it's your father. I don't know what – I mean, I think – he's – come with me—'

Without another word to Imogen, Laura dashed after her mother. 'What is it? Wait? What's happened?'

Imogen left the lamb in its box and followed them across the yard to the lambing shed.

'I found him like that,' Mrs Collins was gasping for breath, clinging on to one of the lambing pens for support.

Laura and Imogen knelt on either side of the elderly man who lay curled in the hay, one hand limp against his chest. Laura felt for a pulse. She shook her head at Imogen, turned her father on his back, loosened his scarf and leaned over his face. 'Call an ambulance,' she said, and set about alternately breathing into his mouth and thumping his chest.

Imogen called 999, while Laura worked on her father. The minutes ticked by, seeming like hours, and still he lay, not breathing.

Mrs Collins paced up and down, unable to stand still,

opening and closing her hands, her expression agonised. 'I told him to rest,' she muttered, over and over again. 'He's had a bad heart for years, but he wouldn't listen.'

Imogen, feeling helpless, dragged a blanket from a railing and wrapped it around the woman's shoulders. She seemed not to notice. 'He's been off colour for days,' she muttered, shivering. 'He won't stop work, you see. He was out all night. It's too much for a man of his age with a weak heart. I told him, too much. He's hardly had any sleep.'

At last, when Imogen had begun to despair, an ambulance arrived and a paramedic took over. Laura staggered back, white as a sheet.

Imogen suspected there was little to be done to help Mr Collins.

The paramedics slid him onto a stretcher and carried him into the ambulance, Mrs Collins trailing behind them.

Imogen stood outside with Laura. Laura heaved a deep sigh. 'He won't make it,' she said. 'It's obvious. They won't be certain until they get to the hospital, I suppose, but anyone can see it. He's over seventy, you know.'

'Come inside,' Imogen suggested.

Laura's eyes were wild, unfocused. 'I'm expecting a couple of the ewes to lamb, any minute.'

'Is there someone who can come and help?'

Laura frowned, as though answering this simple question took every ounce of her concentration.

'I'll ring Eric. He's due in tonight, but I know he'll come earlier. I'll stay with the ewes until he comes. Could you – I know it's a cheek, but could you look after the lamb in the farmhouse?'

To Imogen's relief, the new arrival still lay, sleeping peacefully, in his cosy corner near the Aga. She touched his body and felt the little heart pumping through the wool of his chest.

She was suddenly close to tears. Just as one life had gone, a new one had sprung into being. Wiping her eyes, she made a pot of tea in the huge brown teapot that the Collins family had undoubtedly used for years. Imogen's grandmother had insisted on keeping just such a pot, refusing to put it in the dishwasher. 'Spoils the taste, me duck,' she'd said, straining dark brown, tannic tea into china cups.

Brushing off the desire for comfort, Imogen sent a text to Dan.

Can't meet you at yard – emergency at the Collins farm.

Her phone rang, and she heard Dan's voice. 'I'm at the yard. Shall I come over?'

Imogen's tears threatened again. 'Can you?' Briefly, she explained.

'I'll be there in ten minutes,' he said. She took a deep breath. Everything would be all right. Dan was on the way. With renewed energy, she poured the tea.

She was in the barn when he arrived, with Laura, sipping from a mug. The warm barn full of ewes was comforting. One was circling, restless. Laura said, 'She'll be next.'

Eric arrived. An elderly man with a lined and wrinkled face, he took one look at Laura and jabbed his thumb towards the house. 'Now you get along inside. I'll be fine here and my boy will come after he finishes work. You do what you need to do, Missy.'

As Laura, Dan and Imogen sat in the cosy kitchen, the phone rang. Laura answered, her hand shaking as she picked it up. 'It's Mum,' she mouthed.

She listened, eyes glistening with tears. She turned to Imogen. 'He's gone.'

* * *

The next hour or so was a blur, as Laura struggled to contact her four sisters.

Dan busied himself making endless rounds of toast as they ran through the dull, painful business of death. Imogen knew the rituals only too well; the paperwork and the sad, bureaucratic arrangements that must be made.

At last, there was nothing else to do except wait, and they fell into conversation.

Laura's hands still shook, but she seemed to take comfort in talking. 'What a week. I mean, it's no surprise about Dad. A shock, but we'd all seen it coming. He thought he could go on forever, but then, we all think that, don't we? But so soon after that – that horrible death at the races.' She blew, hard, into a tissue.

Dan said, 'Is there anything else we can do? I mean, we can stay, if you like, but we don't want to get in your way.'

Imogen said, 'Would you like us to contact your husband?'

Laura made a noise halfway between a grunt and a laugh. 'No, I don't want to drag him away from the hospital. He's needed there and he can't bring Dad back. Sick patients have to come first.'

Imogen bit back a start of surprise. Maybe all doctors had to put their patients before their families. That didn't seem fair. Dan said, 'Did you know Alex Deacon?' Imogen gave him a warning look. Surely Laura was too distraught to talk about anything except her father.

But Laura seemed relieved to think about something else. 'Not lately. I knew her years ago, when she joined the pony club. I used to help out with the younger ones there. She's been working at Ann Clarkson's stables recently, of course. There's tension between them and Leo Murphy's yard, where Belinda works, but it's never been more than a friendly rivalry. No hint of real trouble between the two establishments. I wouldn't put it past some of the stable hands to try and nobble riders from the other place, but it's hard to do and I'm not suggesting anything like that really happens.' She thought for a moment. 'I did meet Alex, recently. It was at Exeter, I think. Yes, that's right, it was her second ride. Butterfly Charm wasn't running that day, but Magnus was interested in joining a second syndicate. He's been involved in racing for a while now. He loves the atmosphere, the long lunches, the excitement of winning a few bob.'

'And you don't?'

Laura laughed. 'I'm just a country girl at heart. I like racing for the horses. I'd rather be in the stables, grooming and filling up the hay nets. Of course, we're not allowed to do that on race days, but when we visit Leo's yard on open days he lets me play at being one of the stable hands.'

She waved her hands in a gesture encompassing the farm. 'Dad would have liked me to take over this place with my husband, but it's not Magnus's thing.' There was a hard edge to her voice. Had there been quarrels with Magnus?

'How did you meet your husband?' Imogen asked, half expecting Laura to tell her to mind her own business.

'At the races, many years ago. I'd been down on the farm, helping out with lambing during the university holidays. I went down to Wincanton to watch an old family friend ride in one of the races, bumped into Magnus and spilt a cup of coffee over him. I thought he was the most glamorous person I'd ever met. He's a few years older than me, you know.'

'Any children?' Dan asked. Imogen gulped. She had to admire his direct style.

Laura seemed perfectly happy to keep talking. 'Two. Boys, both at boarding school. Oh dear,' she sniffed, the tears suddenly spilling over onto her cheeks. 'They were going to come here for Easter. They love to follow Dad around the farm.'

The door opened. Mrs Collins was there, with an older, plainer version of Laura. One of her sisters. Mrs Collins hardly noticed Imogen and Dan, who made quiet excuses and left.

Outside, Dan went to his car and Imogen to hers. He said, 'Let's go somewhere for dinner tonight. You look like you could do with cheering up.'

'We arranged to meet Adam and Steph for dinner this evening.'

Dan's face fell. 'So we did. I'd forgotten,' he said. 'But maybe it's a good thing. There's plenty to talk about. I learned a thing or two from Leo Murphy, but I'm going to make you wait. We can talk over dinner.'

With a broad grin and a wink he jumped into his car and drove away.

18

DINNER

Imogen had reserved her favourite table for four in the hotel, neatly tucked in a little alcove in one corner of the room.

Adam was first to arrive, to Harley's delight. Unfortunately, the dog had just spent a happy half-hour in the garden where he'd found the muddiest spot close to the stream and rolled enthusiastically in the sludge.

Adam held Harley at arm's length in the foyer until Emily rescued him. She took Harley by the collar and led him away. 'I'll get Michael to give him a bath,' she said.

Adam brushed mud from his best trousers. That served him right. He'd dressed up, telling himself it was out of respect for the elegance of The Streamside Hotel's dining room, such a contrast from the casual atmosphere of the Plough, although he knew it was for Steph.

Imogen grinned. 'Nice shirt,' she said.

'This old thing?' Adam mocked. 'I've had it for years. Isn't that what you're supposed to say?'

'Can't fool me. It's new, and I'm sure...' she twinkled, 'I'm sure Steph will be looking lovely, as always.'

Adam snorted with laughter. 'And what will Dan be wearing tonight, do you think?' he teased.

'Painter's smock?' Imogen suggested.

'And a beret, of course. Did he paint in a garret in Paris?'

'Well, at the art school, anyway.'

'Maybe a string of onions, then.'

'And that, Mr Hennessy, shows your age. I bet you can remember when onion sellers came from Brittany to sell their wares from their bicycles.'

Adam threw up his hands. 'Not quite, but I learned about it at my mother's knee.'

They were still giggling like children when Dan arrived, soon followed by Steph. They made their way towards the restaurant.

Steph's dark curly hair had mostly withstood the fading of time, except for a white streak at her temples. This evening, her purple paisley shirt and orange scarf lit up the dining room. Adam swallowed hard, suddenly short of breath.

He caught sight of himself in a mirror and snorted quietly at the contrast. There was no point in kidding himself. 'Smartly dressed' was the best he'd ever achieve. He'd been born with genes that had stopped him growing taller than five foot six, but seemed to have no such scruples when it came to sideways growth. Once or twice he'd tried a diet, but the truth was, he loved the good things of life.

He hadn't been out for a run since Saturday morning.

Still, friends, good food and good wine mattered more to him than his figure. He'd never lasted more than three days on any diet. At least he looked the part as the host of The Plough.

He really should get back to that fitness plan, though. He was eating far too many restaurant meals these days. He'd treated James Barton to dinner here at The Streamside a couple of days ago, thinking his friend needed more than the pub meal he'd originally promised. It had been his thank you to James for feeding him information on Alex Deacon's death, and was designed to bring him up to date on Adam's meeting with DCI Andrews. At least, that was the excuse, but really he'd been hoping to find out why his old friend seemed depressed. James had been close-lipped. He'd given little away, except to say he was counting the days to retirement. 'The wife's sick of Birmingham,' he said. 'I'm hoping she'll cheer up once the weather warms up.' Despite Adam's hints, he'd said nothing more.

This evening, though, Adam put the nagging worry about his old mate to the back of his mind. Dan had arrived, and Imogen seemed to have a kind of inner glow. Adam loved to see her face light up like that. He'd keep an eye on her, make sure Dan did nothing to hurt her.

The four of them chose their meal with care, agreeing on a 2018 Camel Valley Pinot Noir Rose Brut from Cornwall to enjoy with the smoked salmon starter and duck main course suggested by the young waiter. The newest member of staff in the dining room, he hovered a few metres away, topping up their glasses of water with painfully obsequious care.

Dan murmured, 'He reminds me of Uriah Heep.'

Imogen beckoned the young man over. 'We've got business to talk through, Thomas, so please will you make sure everyone leaves us alone until we give you a signal?'

Thomas blushed brick-red at the responsibility and for the rest of their meal watched from a respectful distance whenever he wasn't actively engaged in serving other customers.

Steph smiled, 'Your staff are very loyal.'

'I'm so proud of them,' Imogen said. 'They've made me welcome here, ever since I arrived. I wasn't sure I'd keep the hotel at first, but Emily and her team run it so smoothly that I hardly have to do a thing, except the garden.'

Dan said, 'When will you be opening it to the public?'

'In the spring. It used to be such a feature of the hotel, and people like to spend a day walking round gardens. Oswald, of course, is against us opening the whole area. He doesn't want what he calls "lazy gardeners" trampling over the grass and pinching bits of plants for their own gardens, although he's letting us use it for the Spring Fair. He says that's traditional.'

Once the smoked salmon arrived, they picked up knives and forks, and silence fell while they ate their starters.

As he laid his fork down, Adam said, 'It seemed a good idea for us to meet this evening to talk through Alex Deacon's murder. I have to say, though, this wonderful food and wine is a problem. It's going to be hard to keep our minds on the job.'

Dan agreed. 'Maybe we should take coffee up to your Hawthorn Room, Imogen, when we've eaten. We might concentrate better.'

Imogen nodded. 'I've had a small filing cabinet moved in there, so we can keep notes and things secure.'

Steph laughed. 'Wow, it's starting to sound like a police incident room, isn't it, Adam?'

'Absolutely, but without the chipped cups, crumbs in keyboards, and weird smell from somebody's microwaved lunch.'

'You could be talking about the newsroom at the local paper, except there'd also be someone shouting down a phone, or an intern sulking because the subeditor's blue-pencilled most of her article.'

'I had an interesting time at Leo Murphy's yard,' Dan said, frowning earnestly. The man might look like a pop star, Adam thought, but he took life very seriously.

'I didn't take to the head man, Pat,' Dan said. 'He walked me round the yard, and seemed very keen for me to include two female apprentices, as well as the horses, in my painting.'

Adam raised an eyebrow. 'Any idea why?'

Dan grimaced. 'Rivalry with Ann Clarkson's training yard where Alex worked, I reckon. Pat's fiercely loyal to Leo. I think he's trying to show his devotion to equality – you know, plenty of women working here, we're more right-on than other yards where there are so many men and boys. Somehow he made me feel a little suspicious.'

Adam nodded, 'I know what you mean, but too much political correctness can't be a motive for killing Alex.'

'I suppose not,' Dan sounded grudging, 'but something he said rankled. "Having a few women around pulls in the punters". It grated on me, that did.'

A short silence followed while they digested this remark. Was it innocent? Just an old-fashioned tough man's so-called humour, or something less acceptable?

'I wonder,' Imogen said, 'how many others in the yard hold a similar opinion?'

As they ate, they continued to share the information they'd gathered so far.

'At least,' Adam said, after Imogen recounted her stressful afternoon, 'DCI Andrews has given us his blessing. He's not happy with an accidental death decision, but his hands are tied without evidence. So, it's up to us to find some.'

He leaned back in his chair, 'Laura Wilson sounds a thoroughly likable woman, helping out her parents, and dealing with a family tragedy.'

Steph said, 'But we haven't seen much of this doctor husband of hers. Not at the yard when you were there, Adam, and not at the family farm with his wife. I think we need to get to know him better.'

Dinner over, plates cleared and stomachs pleasantly full, they made their way to the Hawthorn Room.

There was a whiteboard on the wall, used when business meetings took place there, and Imogen acted as scribe while the others listed the suspects. She put Alex's name in the middle of the board, and surrounded it with other names, linking them with arrows to show their relationships.

From Leo's yard they listed Belinda, Leo himself, and Pat the head man, followed by the members of the syndicate.

Imogen said, 'Then, there are Alex's fellow workers at the other yard. Ann Clarkson is the trainer, and Tim, this lad that went around with Belinda and then with Alex. He works there.'

She drew arrows from Leo to Ann. 'There was something about Leo's relationship with Ann. Closer than rivalry, I think that was the suggestion. We need to know more about them. We said we'd leave them to the police...'

Adam shook his head, 'The police didn't find anything unusual there. They talked to Alex's friends and family, and to Ann Clarkson, but they drew a blank. Everyone at the yard's shocked and upset, of course, although it seems Alex wasn't especially well liked. The police picked up a sense that she'd happily step on anyone who stood in the way of her climb to the top of her profession, but that's not too unusual in a competitive field like racing.'

Steph said, 'My money's on the syndicate members and that race.'

She held up one hand as the others' voices rose in protest. 'I know it's just a hunch, but hear me out. Let's assume Alex's death was murder. All the likely suspects had to be at the races that day. The syndicate members are a close-knit group, rallying round when Belinda's father died and persuading her mother to stay in the syndicate, even though Diane's not a horse-lover. They know each other well. They were all at Wincanton, that day, with plenty of free time, plus access to the Owners and Trainers areas, and they all have an interest in the horse that lost the race, Butterfly Charm. They've said they don't care much about the prize money, but is that true? If Butterfly Charm wins big, she'll grow more valuable which could bring in big bucks in a sale.'

Adam grinned. 'I have an open invitation from Henry and Ling to visit them at home and talk more about buying shares in a horse, and I plan to take them up on it. I agree that we need to know more about them.'

Imogen had been sitting quietly, listening. 'There's one more person we need to consider.'

They all turned to look at her, puzzled. She grinned. 'John Harris. He's Alex's uncle – well, almost – he's in the racing world, and he was very keen to meet Steph and me to talk about Alex's death. He didn't believe the story about writing a book, and he'd taken care to find out all about us before we met.'

She took a pen, wrote his name on the board and underlined it. 'He was also keen to hint that something more than business was going on between Ann Clarkson and Leo Murphy. Let's find out more about him, shall we?'

19

THE PLOUGH

Adam spent the next morning at The Plough. Rex Croft had come in early, to fill him in on business from the night before.

'That Maria Rostropova came in last night,' Rex's grin split his face from ear to ear. 'Not bad for her age, that one.'

Adam opened his mouth to warn him off. Maria had an unusual moral code. She'd love a short dalliance with Rex but Adam would hate to see her break the young lad's heart.

Rex had read his expression. 'Don't worry, Mr Hennessy.' Always polite, he never used Adam's first name. 'She's not my type. She wanted to get me involved with some basket weaving.' He snorted loudly. 'I passed her on to Belinda. I thought she needed cheering up.'

'Was Belinda here?'

Rex blushed. 'She drops in for a drink, from time to time.'

Adam gave a non-committal nod, hiding a twinge of anxiety. What if Rex was serious about Belinda and she turned out to be a killer? She was still a suspect, if Alex had been murdered.

He sighed. Detection was more complicated when you lived close to those involved.

'Are you okay, Mr Hennessy?' Rex asked.

Adam said, 'You like Belinda?'

'She's okay. We get on fine. She's in a state at the moment, thinking the police have her down for Alex's death.' He tossed his head. 'Stupid cops. Can't see beyond their noses. But she said you're on the case, doing a spot of off-the-books detective work. Her mother arranged it.'

Adam didn't try to deny it. 'She's worried about Belinda, of course, but the police have no evidence of foul play, so far as I know.'

'Well, that's a relief. She's a typical fussy mother, that Diane. Always in a proper state. Doesn't think I'm good enough for her daughter. So, don't you go telling her we're seeing each other—'

'You know me better than that.'

'True. You listen, don't you, but you don't give much away? Like in the evenings, in here. The locals have a pint or two, and start telling you their life story. I reckon that's why you bought The Plough – for the information.'

Adam laughed. 'There's something in that. Just don't tell anyone. And, while we're on the subject, did you also know Alex Deacon?'

'Not really. At least, I know Tim, Alex's boyfriend, he was, at one time. He used to be with Belinda before that. He works for Ann Clarkson, at her yard.'

'I don't want to talk to him in his workplace. I'm planning to catch him at home. Does he live with friends, like Belinda?'

'No, with his parents. They're both a bit the worse for wear. His father has early onset dementia and his mother was diagnosed with cancer a few months ago.'

'Poor lad. That's quite a burden.'

'Anyway,' Rex said, 'here's his address.'

* * *

Adam called in on Imogen, partly to thank her for the meal in the hotel but mostly to see Harley. 'Great food, as ever,' he said.

They were in the reception area. Imogen smiled, 'Glad to see you're none the worse. I always worry when my friends eat here. I know hygiene in the kitchen is as good as it gets, but even so, I get nervous. I couldn't bear to find we'd given anyone indigestion, let alone any kind of—' she leaned in and whispered, 'food poisoning.' She put her finger to her lips. 'We never say that aloud. It's our worst nightmare.'

Harley greeted Adam in the usual way, like a puppy instead of the middle-aged fellow he was.

Despite their best intentions, Adam and Imogen had never discovered where he'd come from. It seemed he was a genuine stray, with no chip. Adam wondered if he'd escaped from a dog farm, but as Imogen said, 'Who would want to breed from a mutt like Harley? He's lovely, but there must be a dozen different doggy types in his family tree.'

'It's hybrid vigour,' Adam remarked, 'no inbreeding. It's a good thing.'

He threw Harley's rabbit for the dog to chase.

Imogen said, 'I'm about to spend an hour or two in the garden. Oswald and a couple of lads from the village are planting trees where the orangery used to be.'

She avoided Adam's gaze. They'd found her husband, Greg's, body there.

'I think you were right to pull the building down,' Adam said. 'Trees will be a much better memorial.'

'I thought I might put a tiny plaque on one. Greg would like that, I think.'

As Imogen shrugged into a warm coat, she met Adam's eye. 'You know, I'm starting to remember the good things about Greg. Our marriage was a mess towards the end, but we did have fun together once, even though he wasn't the perfect husband. But I wasn't the perfect wife, either. It takes two to make a marriage, doesn't it?'

Adam chuckled. 'Don't ask for marriage guidance tips from me. That's one road I've never travelled.'

They walked through the gardens to the clearing where the orangery had once stood, while Harley chased to the river and back, searching for sticks.

Every trace of the building had disappeared, and Oswald's boys were busy digging planting holes. 'I thought I'd stick to old English woodland trees,' Imogen said. She pointed to the row of hawthorns lining the stream. 'I want them to merge with those old thorns, and look as though they've always been here.'

Oswald stopped work and stretched, watching Harley snuffling through the undergrowth. He looked far too old and frail to be out in the wind and rain, but he found the indoor life unbearable and his wife encouraged him to spend his days outside, leaving her to potter happily in her kitchen, baking bread and cakes.

'Beech,' he said to Imogen. 'We should plant beech, hazel, and willow here. Native trees. What do you think, Mr Hennessy, sir?' His Somerset accent refused to acknowledge the letter S, replacing it with a buzzing Z.

'Sounds wonderful,' Adam said.

Buds were visible on the hawthorns, blurring their outlines and promising spring.

Adam pointed. 'Look at the daffodils over there. Quite a sight, aren't they?'

'Ah,' Oswald grinned, showing a set of well-worn dentures,

'They're nearly over now. They're always the first out. Every year, no matter what. It gives you hope, doesn't it?'

He pushed his cap back on his head and leaned on his spade. 'Talking of which, I saw that James Barton that comes into The Plough was having dinner here with you, t'other night. He's a good man, is James, for a Londoner.'

'I owed him a meal.'

'Funny though. His wife came for dinner a few weeks ago. With another man.'

Oswald grinned at Adam's shock. 'Thought that would surprise you. She's been here before. I reckon your friend needs to keep an eye on his missus.'

Adam's head reeled. 'Are you sure it was James's wife?' he asked, but he knew the answer. Oswald was a regular at The Plough, and James sometimes drove over during the summer with his wife and daughters for a pint in the beer garden, watching the sun go down over Ham Hill. It was Elinor, his wife, who'd suggested Adam could expand his own courtyard garden to give himself a bit more privacy.

Of course the gardener recognised her. You couldn't drink in The Plough more than once without Oswald knowing all about you.

Oswald chuckled. 'When you get to my age, you notice these things.'

Adam's spirits fell. Was James's marriage in danger? He and Elinor had always seemed happy. But it would explain his recent change of mood.

Oswald had returned to his saplings, but Imogen held up a warning finger. 'I know what you're thinking, Adam, but don't you dare tell James. He must work things out for himself.'

She was right, of course. Instead, Adam would distract himself with the racing murder case. He wanted to find out more about the syndicate members, Henry and Ling Oxon, before he met them again.

Putting James' troubles out of his mind, he decided to start, reluctantly, with the internet. He hated sitting at a computer. When he'd been a DCI, he'd delegated online research to detective constables who enjoyed nothing better than a quiet morning at the desk.

These days, he had no team to instruct. He would have to do the grunt work himself.

'Why don't you get Steph to help?' Imogen suggested. 'She's easily the best of us at online research.'

Adam pictured Steph sitting with him in his living room at The Plough drinking coffee and eating pastries, while they trawled through the internet together.

Imogen said, 'Come on, you know you want to. Shall I suggest it to her?'

'I can manage,' he said.

'Well, I suggest you phone her, and then she can't see you blush.'

Adam raised his eyebrows. 'And are you seeing Dan today?'

She grinned. 'We're just a pair of overgrown teenagers, aren't we?'

They worked in companionable silence for a while. Imogen selected a sturdy-looking silver birch and held it in an enormous hole, while Adam shovelled earth around it. 'I feel like Prince William, planting commemorative trees,' he said.

Imogen grinned. 'It's good to have you around, Adam. I don't know what I would have done without you.'

He felt a blush creeping up his neck, but Harley arrived to save his embarrassment, stick in mouth, ready for a tug of war. Adam grabbed one end. 'We make a decent team, don't we?'

20

HENRY AND LING

It was the day of Adam's lunch with Henry and Ling Oxon at their house in Wedmore. He'd spent a morning of research with Steph, drinking in the sight of her head as she peered over reading glasses at her computer, two small frown lines between her eyes. He'd never seen a lovelier sight.

They'd stuck strictly to business. Maybe that was best. No embarrassing declarations, no chance of Steph turning him down.

When she'd left, The Plough seemed cold and unfriendly, only the daily arrival of the young farmers livening the place up.

At least, today, he would be out of Lower Hembrow. He reviewed the information Steph had found on the Oxons. There was little of interest beyond birthdates, lists of Facebook friends, a few self-important papers written on obscure points of law and many photographs of Henry, posing thoughtfully.

As Adam drove through Wedmore, he spotted the Oxons' sparkling Range Rover. He drew to a halt outside their home, a luxurious sprawling building on the outskirts of the village, the front garden laid out neatly, conventionally, with well-trimmed evergreen bushes, and perfectly manicured lawns.

Ling had seen him arrive and the door was already open. She wore an embroidered jacket and slim pink silk trousers. Her slippers, too, were beautifully embroidered.

Adam instinctively liked women who were smaller than he was, and Ling's smile was warm. 'Come inside, it's cold today.' She gave a little shiver. 'I thought we were into spring weather at last, but I was wrong. Still, at least we're in March. January and February are so dark in England, and they seem to last for ever. I don't know how we'd get through without the racing to cheer us up.'

Adam followed her through into a huge room with a wall of glass that looked out over more immaculate gardens and on, towards open fields. The sun shone through the glass, warming the room.

An oval oak table was laid simply, with bowls and chopsticks.

Ling said, 'I like to serve Thai food. Henry laughs at me, because it's not what he likes. He's a meat and two veg man, but I'm afraid of forgetting how to cook my native dishes, so I use my guests to practice.'

Henry arrived, casual in an open-neck shirt, crew-neck sweater and cords. 'Sorry, I was on the phone to a client.'

He held out a giant paw and enclosed Adam's hand in a wince-inducing grasp, ushering him into a huge, soft armchair angled to give the best view of the garden.

'Great to have you here, Adam,' Henry said. 'Leo wants me to persuade you to join one of his syndicates, but I don't want to put pressure on you. Now, before we get down to business, what are you drinking?'

Adam indicated his car outside. 'Low alcohol beer?' he suggested. 'If you have it? Or maybe tonic water?'

Henry's face fell. He hesitated, as though about to protest, finally nodding reluctantly. 'Good choice.' He was being polite. He clearly preferred a 'proper' drink. He disappeared, returning with glasses and two bottles of beer. 'Ling says we have ten minutes until lunch. Will that do for you?'

'Perfect,' Adam said.

Adam wondered whether Henry believed his cover story of investing in racehorses. The man was sharp – very bright, and probably not easily fooled – but he gestured to a pile of glossy brochures on a side table. 'You're welcome to take these away with you,' he said. 'There are dozens of horses on offer and you can choose to invest in almost any number of shares. They start out at about three hundred pounds a share, or you can pay up to thousands. Of course, the younger the horse and the more untried, the bigger gamble it all becomes. But, for those of us who've been doing this for a while, the rewards are definitely not financial.'

He poured his beer into a glass and took a long swig. 'Okay, you get a portion of the prize money for your horse, but the fun's in the feeling of ownership. The owners' boxes, the special events, the trips to the yard, like the one we had. That one was a bit unfortunate, though, wasn't it? What a kerfuffle that was. Good job Diane wasn't there to see it. Let's hope Belinda's calmed down.'

Adam picked up the top brochure and flipped through it. 'The horses look fit,' he commented.

Henry said, 'I truly believe they're some of the most beautiful creatures on earth. Far better than we humans. I've met the worst of humanity in my line of work. Fraud, money laundering, identity theft – and they're at the lower end of the scale. Once you get into violent crime, rape and murder, you get to see some of the worst people in society.'

He took a gulp of his beer. 'Having said that, many people in court are foolish, weak, and often simply vulnerable. Most of them don't set out to be bad.' He put the glass down on a marble coaster. 'But you know all this, don't you, Adam? As an ex-police-man, I mean.'

Adam gave a slow nod. The internet, again. Of course, Henry had looked him up.

Ling returned, placing bowls of steaming, wonderfully scented food in the middle of the table, and the two men settled at their places. Adam's stomach growled. 'Ling, did you really cook this wonderful feast yourself?'

'Oh yes. All Thai girls learn how to cook this way.'

Henry said, 'I was blown away the first time Ling cooked a meal for me. It made me ashamed of my love of steak and kidney pudding.'

'But, darling, there are times when a steak and kidney pudding is perfect,' Ling soothed. 'At the end of a race day, when it's drizzled for hours and your horse has struggled at the back of the field, you need good, hearty English food.'

Henry smiled at Adam. 'Ling,' he said, 'has an appetite as enormous as Butterfly Charm's, though you'd never believe it to look at her.'

'Now, then.' He waved chopsticks at Adam, 'about young Alex Deacon's death. It strikes me that Belinda could do with some representation. I've recommended a solicitor who deals in most of the crime at our practice. Just in case it turns out to be murder, and the local plod try to pin it on Belinda.'

Adam said, 'I expect Diane told you she's spoken to me and I'm undertaking a spot of detective work on her behalf. She was worried that Belinda might get the blame, and mightily relieved to hear the police view that Alex's death was probably an acci-dent.' No need to tell the Oxons about DCI Andrew's doubts.

'But you're not so sure?' Henry peered into Adam's face.

Adam smiled, gently. 'Not yet, and I want to be certain. No harm in that.'

Henry acknowledged this with a nod. 'No smoke without fire, you mean. So, you have no official status in this?'

'None at all,' Adam said. 'I'm a private citizen. But Diane asked for my help and I was willing to give it.'

'Good man, good man,' Henry murmured. 'Best we all pull together, get this cleared up as soon as possible, put an end to any stupid gossip about Belinda. What have you found out?'

As though, Adam thought, they were in some kind of partnership, on the same side and sharing information.

With an innocent smile, Adam said, 'Just in case it turns out not to be an accident after all, I'm hoping you can help. You know the racing world in this part of the country.'

A faint smile crossed Ling's face, as though she was enjoying the way Adam handled her husband. Or, was there another reason for her enigmatic expression? She might be slight, but Adam was willing to bet she could have held Alex under water – especially while the jockey was high on drugs.

Henry paused, as though considering how much information to share. His lawyer's instincts would warn him to say as little as possible, but if he were innocent, he'd want to help Adam find the truth. Unless, of course, he was covering for Belinda or Ling, or another of his friends.

Henry finished his beer, replaced the glass on the table at his elbow and steepled his fingers together. 'I don't think I can help much. There's a culture within the racing yards of folk looking after each other. You'll get the most information from Belinda and Alex's circle, but they may find it hard to talk frankly.'

He nodded. Enjoying his own performance, Adam thought.

'It's a world of its own, racing,' Henry went on. 'Like a closed society. Neither Ling nor I can tell you much about the individuals who work in it, but I expect you're keen to know about our friends in the syndicate. I might be able to help you, there. And, no doubt, you'll be talking to them about us.'

With a grin, he reached for his empty glass and raised it in a salute. 'Fancy another beer?'

* * *

As Henry brought more bottles from the kitchen, Adam said, 'I've been wondering about the comings and goings at the racecourse on the day Alex Deacon died. You see, I would have thought the place was heaving. The stands, where the public mill around, might have thinned out at the end of the day, but behind the scenes it must have been busy; in the parade ring, the owners' areas, jockeys' locker rooms, showers and so on. Now, once the Stewards' Enquiry was over, the horses and their jockeys, trainers and whatnot would get home as soon as possible, I imagine. There must be quite a melee – people everywhere, getting packed up ready to leave. I'm wondering how Alex could be attacked with no one knowing.'

Henry nodded, thoughtfully. 'A good point. Either there was some kind of incident that at least one other person must have witnessed but isn't talking about, or Alex was killed by someone seizing the moment.'

'Exactly,' said Adam. 'So, for the sake of dotting i's and crossing t's, where were you and the other members of the syndicate between the end of the Stewards' Enquiry at four thirty and dinner at eight thirty in the hotel?'

Ling spoke first. 'Laura, Diane and I hung around with everyone else, during the inquiry. When the result was announced just after half past four, Diane was upset, of course.

It's hardly surprising. She's very fragile and it's less than two years since Rupert died. She was so excited about seeing this race, Belinda's first as a professional.'

'Did you see Alex Deacon at all?'

Ling wrinkled her nose. 'She was in the winner's enclosure after the stewards' announcement of the result, thrilled to bits with her win, of course. I don't remember seeing her after that.'

Ling frowned. 'It was all very hard on Belinda. She went back to the stables after the result, making sure Butterfly Charm was ready to go home. The jockeys and stable staff love those horses like their own children. Diane, Laura and I went to the owners' bar. After a while, Diane went to find Belinda and bring her back to see us. They were both pretty emotional, although at least Butterfly Charm hadn't been disqualified. Belinda will get over the race, of course, and the experience won't do her any harm in the long run. Second place isn't at all bad for a 25-1 runner, but she didn't see it like that. There were a few tears.'

'And then?'

'Belinda calmed down while she was talking to Laura and to me – we're all good friends, even though she's younger.'

She smiled. 'I'm rambling a bit. Sorry. Where was I? Belinda and Diane went back to the hotel to change – they were staying overnight. I expect the staff there will vouch for the time of their arrival. Laura and I went to find our husbands.'

'Where were they?'

'Sharing a drop of the hard stuff,' Henry admitted. 'Magnus and I have known each other for years. We've owned parts of several horses and we've learned to celebrate whether they win or lose. As I said, a syndicate's not about the prize money. It's a different matter for the trainers. Their prestige, and the funding to keep their business going – training horses is an incredibly expensive business –matters a great deal to them.'

He laid down his chopsticks. 'I wouldn't mind betting Leo had a few private words with Belinda. He would have taken her off somewhere quiet. In fact, thinking it over, I can't see that Belinda had many chances to attack her friend, or, to be honest, any reason to.'

21

DAN

Around the time Adam left Henry and Ling Oxon, Imogen was driving to Dan's studio.

'It's not a date,' she told herself, sternly. 'We're going to talk over the case, and the Spring Fair.'

She concentrated on her driving, watching the signs of spring peeping out in the countryside. She even caught sight of a few ewes with their lambs in the shelter of the hedgerow. Before long, the field would be full of the cacophony of new-born lambs losing and searching for their mothers.

It was time to stop letting Harley run through the fields. Delightful as he was, Imogen could never trust him around livestock.

She arrived at the narrow, steep, permanently muddy lane that twisted downhill towards the studio – Dan's home. His two donkeys, Smash and Grab, hung their heads over the fence, hoping this new arrival would offer at least a pat on the head and maybe something to eat.

Imogen produced two apples. 'You're getting fat,' she told

Grab, recognising him from the dark patch on his flank. He was always first at the feeding trough.

Dan, was, as usual, working in his studio.

She'd let him finish whatever he was doing before announcing herself. His attention on his painting was fierce, and she liked to watch him in silence, his hair flopping over his forehead, eyes narrowed in concentration. Once or twice, she'd taken him by surprise and he'd almost jumped out of his skin.

Today, though, he had no brush in his hand. Instead, he had a pile of small, square photos on the table and was examining each one minutely.

She joined him. He glanced up at her but his mind was very clearly still on his work. 'I've taken a few Polaroids of the horses Leo wants me to feature in the painting. The trouble is, one horse looks very much like another to me, apart from the colour. I don't say that to him, though. I'm trying to find some sort of composition that won't just look like three horses standing in a field.'

'And hello to you too,' she said.

He put the photos back on the table. 'Sorry, didn't mean to be rude.'

'It's okay.' But it wasn't, not really. She was about to move on, let it go, when she stopped. For years, she'd let Greg get away with putting her down and she wasn't going to take it from Dan. 'Actually,' she corrected herself, 'It's not okay. I've driven a long way to see you—'

'And I've been selfish and horrible. I'm really, truly sorry. I get too wrapped up in my work. It's not an excuse, I know. Erica, my ex-wife, called me obsessive. That's—' he broke off.

'One of the reasons you split up?' Imogen suggested.

He smiled. Imogen's stomach always turned over when she saw that crooked grin. 'One of the reasons she left me. And quite right too. I deserved it.' He frowned, earnestly, like a small boy caught scrumping apples.

'How can I make it up to you?'

'You can make some coffee,' she said.

As he fiddled with mugs and a cafetière, she went on, 'You were about to tell me more about Leo's yard.'

'That's right,' Dan turned. 'I was. Interesting place—' He broke off. 'Why haven't I drawn you?' he murmured. 'That face...'

'Don't even think it,' Imogen said.

'Seriously, you have the most amazing bone structure.'

'And you're making me uncomfortable.' She buried her face in the mug of coffee he put in front of her and took a sip. 'Tell me what you know about the racing stables,' she insisted.

'I've been there two or three times now, although I only met Leo himself the first time. I'm not sure I'd want to work for him. He's got a sharp tongue, not to mention an eagle eye. The grooms seem to like him okay, but I heard him give a right roasting to one lad, who'd forgotten to fill a hay net or something.'

She nodded, and he went on, 'The young people seem to be well-supervised, and not just by Leo. In fact, he probably spends less time in the yard than the head man. So far as I can see, Pat's the mover and shaker around the horses. He's a little fellow, wiry, fit as a flea, almost completely bald, and his language would turn your hair grey.'

Dan picked up the photos he'd been examining when Imogen arrived and shuffled through them, then laid them out neatly for her to see. 'Here we are,' he said, triumphant. 'Here's Pat leading Butterfly Charm out of the stall.'

He pointed to another photo. 'Here are some of the other grooms. Look, this photo has Belinda in the background, and,' he peered more closely, 'would you believe it, that groom next to her has his arm around her shoulders. I hadn't noticed that before. I was too busy looking at the horse.'

Imogen leaned in. 'Interesting,' she said. 'I wonder – is that the boyfriend she lost to Alex, or a new conquest?'

'There should be a date on the photo,' Dan said. 'Yes, there it is. December, just before Christmas – of course it is, you can see the garland above the box.'

Imogen said, 'That means it may be a new boyfriend. Who can we ask?'

'Doesn't Belinda share a house with another couple? We should ask them. Oh—'

He fell silent.

Imogen stared at him, puzzled. 'Are you okay?'

'Sorry, I've had a thought.' His face broke into a broad grin. 'Maybe I should forget about painting the horses standing still. I'll never be Gainsborough, but I could show them as part of a working yard. You know, Butterfly Charm being led, just like this, and Pink Gin behind, perhaps with one of the jockeys. I gather he's been ridden by some of the best. I wonder if Leo would be able to persuade them to be in the picture...'

Imogen blinked, stunned. How could Dan forget about the case so easily? Almost in mid-sentence. It was infuriating. She said, 'Can't you even—' but she stopped talking, realising the truth. The poor man couldn't help it. His work was everything to him. It was almost like an illness, and she couldn't compete with it. She liked Dan – even, she admitted to herself, stood possibly on the verge of more than liking – but she wouldn't be able to change him.

Did that matter? Could she put up with his absorption in his work, letting it take first place in his life?

But, she reasoned, she felt like that about her garden. She took a long look at his puzzled face and started to laugh.

'What is it?' he asked, looking at her as though she was the crazy one. Then, his own lips twitched. 'I'm doing it again, aren't I?' he said. 'Obsessing about work. Sorry.'

Imogen took a long breath. This was Dan. She must either take him as he was or forget about forging a closer relationship.

She explained, 'I thought you were about to come out with some insight into who killed Alex, but you were thinking about the painting.'

'I'm not much help in this inquiry, am I?' He thrust his hands through his hair until it stood on end. Imogen looked at the photos on the table. 'Why do you use Polaroids instead of taking photos on your phone?'

He thought a moment, his eyebrows working. 'Habit, I suppose. I use the phone sometimes, but I like to have the photos printed out so I can move them around and think about them. It's a fuss to do that with digital photos. I just wish they made the Polaroids a bit bigger.'

Imogen picked up the photo of Belinda. 'I'd like to know more about this stable hand. Belinda told Adam about her previous boyfriend, Tim, the one Alex took from her, but he was young, like Belinda. This man's much older. I don't think it's Tim. Don't you think that's odd? I mean, the 'jealousy over Alex pinching Tim' motive doesn't hold water if Belinda's already over him, does it? And she looks pretty keen on this one, judging by the photo. I want to know more about this man.'

'We were going to go for a long walk in the countryside,' Dan objected. 'I'm wearing my walking boots and everything.'

'But this might be important.'

'Now who's being obsessive? I'll tell you what, let's nip over to the yard now and I'll introduce you to some of the workers. Mrs Hammond, who cleans for me, will cycle over later this afternoon and I like to be out when she's here – don't have to stop and chat, you know. She's a good soul, but my word, she can talk for England.'

He collected the photos together, slipped them into an envelope and transferred them to his pocket. 'Leo said I can come and go at the yard as I like, so long as I check in with Pat when I arrive.'

He took one of Imogen's hands in his. She felt a jolt, like electricity, as their fingers touched. She gasped, and Dan smiled, 'Then, we could go somewhere quiet for a spot of dinner. I will stop thinking about painting and concentrate on you, as you deserve. Will you forgive me for being so rude when you arrived, if we do that?'

* * *

Imogen and Dan arrived at the yard, where Pat welcomed them with a nod and a frank stare at Imogen. 'Come to take more photos, have you, Dan? Thought you were a painter. Haven't seen you with a brush yet.'

Imogen glanced at Dan, but he seemed happy to let the sarcasm float over his head. 'I wanted to show you one of these.' He tugged the photograph that showed Belinda from his pocket. 'Who's that with Belinda?'

Pat peered at it, his head only reaching as high as Dan's chest. He sucked his teeth loudly. 'Now, what do they think they're up to, during working hours? I'll have a word or two with our Belinda. Hasn't exactly covered herself with glory recently, has she?'

Imogen said, 'I was wondering about the man in the picture. Is he Belinda's boyfriend?'

'Nah. Look, you can see, she was having one of her meltdowns. Inclined to be weepy, that one. Some of the younger girls are like that, haven't grown up yet. I guess he was just giving her a hug. You know, to cheer her up or whatever.'

Judging from his tone, and his comment about working hours, Pat disapproved of comforting hugs in a racing yard.

Dan said, 'Women a problem in the yard, are they?'

Pat pushed his cap back on his head, and scratched his bald pate. His eyes darted from left to right. 'Now, we don't say things like that these days but between you and me and the gatepost, and saving present company of course, ma'am,' he nodded at Imogen, but his eyes were cold, 'life was much easier back in the day when we were all lads together. You have to watch your language, these days. Can't even say women are weaker than men.'

He glanced around again. 'You mark my words, some of these girls aren't up to the job. One thing goes wrong and they burst into tears and expect the lads to help them out. Then again, some of the young boys don't have the sense they're born with. They see a pretty face like young Belinda's, and they're taken right in.'

Imogen heard Dan's angry intake of breath. She kept her hands in her pockets, fists clenched. They weren't here to tell Pat what they thought of him. She wondered if Leo knew about the man's attitude to women – that their only use was decorative. The yard would be in trouble if one of the girls complained about sexist comments.

Pat was still talking. 'This fellow in the photo, Callum, he's been with us for years. He'll stay a groom. He don't have what it takes to be a jockey, but he's popular. Especially among the girls. He's a nice shoulder to cry on, that's our Callum.'

He looked at his watch. 'I need to get on. Don't go in any of the boxes without the grooms, and no flashbulbs. And, let me know when you leave.'

He turned away, then, catching sight of a groom coming out of the next box, shouted, 'Oi. Come over here. Our artist wants a word with you,' and left, going about his business elsewhere.

Callum was instantly recognisable from the photograph. A full head taller than Pat, he was older than most of the lads, about thirty, with a turned up nose, straw-coloured hair, and light eyes prematurely surrounded by crows' feet, as though he'd spent many hours gazing into the sun.

He smiled at Imogen, hardly glancing at Dan. 'Can I help you?' His voice was soft and pleasant. Imogen couldn't imagine him ever shouting across the yard like Pat.

Dan showed him the Polaroid. 'Is this you, with Belinda Sandford?'

He took it, and grinned. 'That's right. I remember. She'd had a fall, that day, and twisted her ankle. She'd been pretending it was all right, but she was tired by the time you took this photo. Had a bit of a cry.'

'Pat thinks the girls are less tough than the rest of you.' There was ice in Imogen's voice.

'That's just Pat's way,' Callum said. 'He doesn't mean anything by it. He treats us all the same – yells at us all, girls and boys. You should have heard him lay into me the other day when I dropped a bucket of oats just as some of the owners arrived. Almost had me in tears.' His grin spread widely across his face. Imogen found herself smiling back.

'In any case,' he said, 'he hides it well, but I reckon Pat has a soft spot for Belinda. He suggested Leo give her the ride on Butterfly Charm. We were all surprised at that. Still, he was right. She did a good job.'

Imogen said, 'Despite the Stewards' Enquiry?'

'Anyone can get a bit overexcited, especially in their first race. That's why we don't expect them to win first time out. Besides, that Alex did a job on Belinda. What a performance – she should have been on the stage. You could steer a barge between the two horses. Still, you had to hand it to Alex, she made it look good.'

He took a breath. 'Poor Alex...' he added hastily.

Dan said, 'So, you and Belinda. Are you an item?'

Callum scratched his head. 'No chance. She's a nice enough girl, but not for me. Anyway, Leo's banned liaisons in the yard. Mates, that's all we are.'

22

STUDIO

That evening, Dan and Imogen ate dinner in a quiet country pub. Dan was painfully attentive, taking her coat, holding her chair while she sat down, and agreeing with everything she said. He was on his best behaviour and it made Imogen nervous.

'You don't have to treat me like a piece of fine porcelain,' she pointed out. 'Let's just be normal, shall we?'

With a sheepish grin, Dan relaxed back in his chair. 'Sorry, just trying to be a better date.'

'Well,' she turned the conversation to their visit to Leo's yard. 'What did you think about that story we heard. The one about Belinda hurting her foot and Callum comforting her. It all sounded a bit odd to me. What did you think?'

'I agree,' Dan said. 'I'm wondering if there's a bullying problem in the yard. It could be Pat upsetting the women, perhaps. Callum might have been telling the truth but I wonder what Belinda's tears were really about. By the way, I think I left that photo at the yard. I can't find it in my pocket. Do you think it matters?'

Imogen laughed. 'Not really. It's not as though we were going to tell tales to Leo.'

The earlier tension between them had lifted, and they turned to more personal matters, easier to broach in this quiet pub, tucked away several miles from The Streamside and The Plough. It was good to be free from the ever-watchful eyes of Lower Hembrow. There was only one other couple here, seated on the other side of the room, and neither Imogen nor Dan knew them.

As they tucked into gammon and pineapple, they caught up on their life stories. Imogen knew Dan had an ex-wife and son, but he rarely mentioned them. 'Tell me about Pierre,' she said. 'Does he ever come to England?'

Dan shifted in his chair. 'Hardly ever. I used to get over to France two or three times a year to see him, but I haven't been for the past year. He'll be starting university in Paris soon.'

'Why don't you ask him to come over and stay with you?' Imogen asked.

Dan thought about that for a long time. 'Not sure he'd want to do that. We didn't part on good terms last time we met. I'm afraid I was a thoroughly bad husband and father. Too self-centred, and, as you've seen, too wrapped up in my painting.'

'I'm sure he understands now he's grown up. Is he artistic, too?'

'He's keen on photography. Talented, I think, and he writes as well. He's planning to study psychology. He's a little like you. He understands people.'

Imogen's heart lifted at the unexpected compliment. 'You could ask him to come for the summer. Though the weather won't be quite up to South of France standards.'

By the time the meal ended, Imogen felt as warm and happy as if she'd drunk several glasses of champagne, although she'd swallowed no more than a single small glass of wine.

Dan drove them back to the studio, and Imogen's car. She wondered how the evening would end. What did she want from it? Coffee, of course. Wine, perhaps, and then what? If she drank more wine she wouldn't be able to drive home.

She sat back, enjoying the ride through the night, the sky clear and speckled with stars. Her thoughts were hopelessly muddled. Did she want to stay with Dan, or keep him at arm's length? She breathed in the citrus smell of his aftershave and her heart accelerated.

They rounded the last muddy corner and parked by the donkey field. She followed Dan to the door of the studio.

He stopped. 'That's funny.'

'What is?'

'The door's not shut.'

'It must be,' she said. She thought back to when they'd left the studio. She could remember Dan locking the door and dropping his keys in his pocket.

Her breath caught in her throat. 'Someone's been here,' she hissed in his ear.

'Go back to the car,' he said.

She ignored that. 'Call the police,' she whispered.

He shook his head and pushed the door gently with his elbow. Silently, it swung inwards. He took a step across the threshold and flicked on the light switch.

Imogen gasped. The room was a wreck. Pictures lay higgledy-piggledy on the floor, an easel had fallen on its side and the drawers of a cabinet had been pulled wide open and left hanging, their contents in a mess of paper on the floor.

Imogen bit her lip. Dan stood stock-still, shocked. She couldn't even hear him breathe. 'We definitely need the police.' She dialled 999.

Dan started to gather up the paintings from the floor as she talked.

As she finished the call, Imogen laid a hand on his wrist. 'Don't touch anything.'

'Are the police on the way?' Dan asked. His voice sounded odd, strangled.

'I'm afraid not. They said if the burglars aren't here any more, they'll leave it till the morning. They said we should try not to touch things.'

Dan swore once, sharply.

Imogen moved her hand to his shoulder. 'They'll come tomorrow. They said there's been a whole series of burglaries in South Somerset.'

She felt helpless. Dan's face was ashen. In two long strides he crossed the room and lifted a canvas that lay, face down, on the floor. The oil paint had been wet and it was smeared across the floor.

'Do you keep money in here?' Imogen asked. He shook his head. 'I don't have a safe, or anything. I don't own anything of great value.' He gasped. 'Except my laptop, of course.'

Imogen followed his gaze to the table. The laptop had been perched at one end.

It had gone.

'What about the rest of the house?' Imogen murmured.

Dan gave a sudden exclamation. 'The bicycle.'

'What bicycle?' asked Imogen.

Dan said, 'I saw it. On the way in, when the light came on. It didn't register, but Mrs Hammond rides a bike when she comes to clean. It must be hers.'

He was already on his way out of the door, into the darkness. The single bulb near the front door came on, as it had done when they arrived. She'd barely noticed it then. A movement sensor must turn it on.

In the sudden blaze of light, she could see the bicycle, leaning up against the wall of the studio.

'Why's it still here?' Dan murmured.

Imogen swallowed. 'Your Mrs Hammond.' She followed him back into the house. 'She must be here as well.'

Imogen felt the dull ache of dread in her stomach as she followed Dan out of the studio, through a hall into the kitchen, which was part of the large open-plan area forming much of the barn conversion.

The room was empty.

'I'll try the bedroom.'

He opened the door on the other side of the living area. Imogen had an impression of a very masculine room, with a black-and-white quilt, dark furniture, and sheepskin rugs on the floor. She looked under the bed as Dan jerked open the wardrobe and thrust aside the clothes hanging inside.

Imogen opened the door that led from the bedroom into a bathroom. 'Where on earth can she be?' The knot of anxiety grew tighter. 'Maybe she walked home?'

'Not likely,' Dan said. 'She lives in the next village. It's too far for her to walk. She's over seventy.'

Imogen swallowed. 'Maybe someone came and collected her in a car? Someone from her family?'

'She's a widow, but she lives with her brother, I think.'

'Have you got his number?'

He shook his head. 'But I've got hers, of course.'

He pulled out his phone and jabbed at the buttons.

As they listened, Mrs Hammond's phone rang and rang, finally switching to voicemail. 'Sorry, I'm not available at the moment. But, do leave a message.' The voice was rural and friendly, and Imogen imagined a rosy-cheeked, cheerful elderly lady, happy to make a few pounds with a spot of light cleaning in an artist's house.

Dan said, 'We're going to have to call the police again.'

'Wait. What's that?' Imogen had heard something. A sound, far away,

Dan's eyes met hers. They each held their breath and listened.

'Outside.' Dan ran back into the living area, and out through a door that led to the back garden. It was dark on this side of the house, with no outside light.

Imogen switched on the light on her phone and waved it in an arc. 'There she is,' she shouted, but Dan was already running along the gravel path that led along the wall of the house.

Mrs Hammond was trying to struggle to her feet, half leaning against the wall. 'Help me up, my dear.'

'Are you hurt?'

She put a hand up to her head. When she brought it down Imogen saw blood.

'Someone hit me,' Mrs Hammond said, in a surprised voice.

She made it to her feet, leaning on Dan. 'Take it easy,' he said.

'I'm quite all right,' she insisted.

Imogen rang for an ambulance, insisted on talking to the police and made sure they were on their way. Breaking and entering had turned into assault, or even grievous bodily harm, and there was no question of waiting until the next day.

Dan helped Mrs Hammond inside. She was still protesting, 'It's just a little bump, nothing to worry about. I don't need an ambulance.'

Dan lowered her gently onto the sofa. 'Now, Dan,' she said. 'I'll get blood all over your lovely white sofa.'

'I don't care about that. Can you remember what happened?'

He looked at Imogen. 'Should we give her something to drink?'

Imogen shook her head. 'I don't think so. We should wait for the ambulance.'

Mrs Hammond was feeling carefully around the back of her head. 'Not much damage done,' she said. 'It knocked me out for a few minutes, but there's only a bit of a bump there now. I don't even think it's bleeding any more.'

'We'll let the paramedics decide,' Dan said.

Mrs Hammond said, 'You asked me what happened, my dear, but I can't really remember much of it. See, I came over on my bike, like I always do.' Her eyes were half shut as she remembered. For an elderly lady, Imogen thought, she was remarkably calm.

'Then, I opened up the door at the front – the one that goes into your studio, dear, and walked through into the kitchen. I was just filling my bucket with a bit of Flash and some hot water, when I heard a noise, back in the studio.

'At first, I thought it was you, popped back to get something.' She smiled, rather weakly, at Imogen. 'He's always forgetting things, I expect you've noticed.'

Imogen laughed aloud. This lady was a tough old bird.

Mrs Hammond went on, 'Well, I was on my way to the studio when I thought about my brother, Pete. You see, Pete tells me I'm too impatient. "Think before you act, Lily," he always says. So I stopped and thought, and I could hear this banging and crashing in the studio. I thought, that's not Dan. If it was, he'd come and say hello to me. Very polite, is Dan,' she said to Imogen, with a watery smile.

'Anyway,' she went on, 'instead of going back into the studio, I went out through the doors into the garden. It was dark, so I crept along beside the house. I thought I'd take a look through the studio windows. See what was going on.'

She shook her head at Imogen. 'How he manages with bare windows and no curtains or blinds, I don't know. It would give me the chills, it would. But there, we're not all made the same, are we, and Dan is an artist after all.' She said the word 'artist' in the same hushed tone of voice she might use to say 'the Queen'.

'Anyway, I'd just about got to the window when something hit me on the back of the head. And that's all I remember, until I heard you shouting my name just now.'

Dan's face was ashen. 'If I get my hands on whoever did this, they'll be sorry...'

A hammering on the door heralded the arrival of a pair of paramedics in an ambulance and in the blink of an eye, the room was the centre of action, as one sat beside Mrs Hammond on the sofa and asked gentle questions, while another pulled out equipment from a case, taking her blood pressure, oxygen levels and temperature and peering into her eyes and ears, all the time chatting in a quiet voice as though this was the most ordinary situation in the world with no need to worry at all.

* * *

By the time the police arrived, Mrs Hammond was lying in the ambulance, still insisting there was nothing wrong with her apart from a 'little knock on my head', and that she really would rather go home.

The police took a short statement from her, along with one from Dan and another from Imogen. 'I'm afraid this is a crime scene, now,' they pointed out. 'Is there somewhere you can stay?'

'Come back to the hotel,' Imogen suggested.

One of the policemen, an older man with a haircut that, long on top and shaved at the sides, would have looked silly even on a man of half his age, peered closely at her, tapping his teeth with a pen. 'I recognise you, ma'am. Mrs Bishop, isn't it?' He glowed with self-congratulation. 'Trouble seems to follow you around.'

Imogen bit back a retort. It seemed she'd never escape the fallout from her husband's murder.

As Dan was now shut out of his home, which seethed with forensic investigators, yellow tape, white suits and gloves, she drove back to the hotel, Dan at her side.

'Finding poor Mrs Hammond like that put everything else out of my head,' she said. 'but I wonder what the burglar was after.'

'It's very odd,' Dan agreed. 'Why would they attack an old woman, just for a laptop? It's not as though there are any secrets on the machine.'

Imogen shivered and gripped the wheel tighter. 'What if you'd been at home?' she said.

He half-turned in the passenger seat. 'I'd fight them off, of course.'

She scoffed. 'A likely story.'

He gave a short laugh. 'I'd rather the burglar attacked me than Mrs Hammond, poor soul. I feel terrible about her. I hope she'll be all right.'

'At least she's in good hands, and safe in hospital.'

They drove on in silence, both lost in thought.

At last, Imogen said, 'Do you think this has anything to do with Alex Deacon's murder?'

'That's what I'm wondering,' he said. 'But I can't see any connection. I'm inclined to think my place is just a gift to burglars, stuck out in the middle of nowhere. I've been meaning to get an alarm, but I hadn't got round to it. Maybe they saw my car was gone and tried their luck.'

'But my car was parked there. I don't think it was just a spur-of-the-moment burglary. I think you were deliberately targeted.'

'But, why?'

'That's the big question. What do you have on that computer? And, why did they ransack your studio but not the rest of the house? I think your burglar knew exactly what he was looking for.'

'But I can't imagine what it was.'

They drove into the village and parked at the hotel. Dan said, 'If this burglary is linked to Alex's death, things are getting even more serious, and maybe DCI Andrews' misgivings are right and she really was murdered.'

'I think,' Imogen said, 'we need to talk to Adam as soon as possible. He's the one with experience. The rest of us, you, me and Steph – we're just amateurs bumbling about. We might be making matters worse.'

There was silence in the car. Then Dan heaved a sigh. 'You're right, of course.' A note of sarcasm crept into his voice. 'Let's ask the expert – though, don't forget, he took early retirement after a disastrous case. Maybe he's not the investigative genius everyone imagines.'

And with that, he elbowed the car door open and they made their way into the hotel. Imogen, unsettled by Dan's display of antagonism toward Adam, booked him into an empty room, on a different floor, well away from her own private rooms.

23

NEW PLANS

At eleven o'clock the next morning, Adam, Steph and Dan congregated in the Hawthorn Room, summoned by an anxious Imogen for an urgent conference.

Steph's eyes were like dark pools of horror. 'You mean,' she said to Dan, 'someone broke into your studio, stole your laptop, and attacked your cleaning lady? They mean business, don't they?'

Adam said, 'Alex Deacon's murder and Dan's burglary may be entirely unconnected, but we can't assume that. Someone is willing to stop at nothing, and that includes beating up an old lady.'

Imogen nodded, thoughtfully. 'Do we know any more about the syndicate?'

Adam said. 'So far, I haven't managed to winkle out any motives for them, and it seems to me this case is all about motive. Alex's murder – I'm willing to call it that now – seems unplanned. There were plenty of people – jockeys, stable hands, trainers, owners – all of whom had the opportunity to drown her in the trough, but it would be almost impossible for them to know when she would be unobserved. Whoever killed her seems to have acted impulsively when they found her alone. I wondered whether the drugs in her system were part of a murder set-up, but that doesn't make sense. Giving her a dose of coke wouldn't guarantee she'd fall into a water trough. It's too long a shot. No, she had a circle of young friends, any one of whom might share drugs with her. There's no evidence of anything sinister, like date-rape drugs – the cocaine in her system was probably taken after the race. While she was celebrating, I suppose.'

He shook his head. 'But I'd like to hear more about Laura Collins's father's sudden death.'

Steph gasped. 'Surely you don't think that has anything to do with this business? He was an elderly man, a farmer. He'd been fit all his life, and wouldn't accept he was getting frail. He probably pushed himself far too hard and his heart gave out. It happens all the time. What do you think, Imogen?'

Imogen traced patterns on the table with her finger. 'On the face of it, there's nothing suspicious about his death. He'd been up all night, lambing. As you say, he was in his eighties, and his wife said he'd suffered from heart problems for several years. The heart attack – and it seems likely that's what killed him – was going to happen one day. If so, the only suspicious element is the timing, because it happened so soon after Alex died.'

Dan said, 'We need to be sure of the cause of death.'

Adam grunted. 'That's not too easy. I'll call James, but the chances are Ed Collins won't have had an autopsy. If he'd seen his doctor recently and had a diagnosed condition the police wouldn't think it necessary. Budgets are too limited.'

Disappointed, they sat in silence for a while.

Imogen said, 'Maybe we ought to concentrate on Dan's laptop.

It was the only thing the burglar took. What did it have on it, Dan?'

He shrugged. 'Correspondence and social media stuff, of course; emails, Facebook, Twitter and so on. A few saved contracts for painting commissions. Photos, plenty of music and e-books which I can access on another device, so they're not lost. In fact, I can retrieve most things on my phone, which wasn't stolen. I had it in my pocket.'

Imogen said, 'The burglary doesn't sound very well thought out, does it? If it's connected at all, it seems another example of spur-of-the-moment behaviour.'

Adam looked up. 'Photos? You hadn't mentioned those before. Are they backed up somewhere else?'

'Not all of them.' Dan's forehead was wrinkled. 'I'm hopeless at keeping copies. But I can't imagine there's anything there of particular interest to anyone except me. Everything is connected to my paintings. I'd been taking pictures of the horses in the yard.'

Steph had sat quietly, listening. Now, she said, slowly, 'You've been to Leo Murphy's yard a few times. You take photos there, you talk to the staff and you've met Leo himself once or twice. Maybe you know more than you think.'

He frowned. 'Most of the photos I take at the yard are Polaroids and I had them all with me that afternoon. Imogen and I went to the yard because of the image we saw in one of them. I took a snap of a horse, but Belinda was in the background with Callum, one of the stable lads.'

He explained the relationship between the two. 'I showed it to Pat, the head man, yesterday, and I must have left it at the yard, but there are plenty of other photos.'

He spread them on the table, and the four of them leaned in.

Adam said, 'Anyone see anything of interest? Maybe in the background?'

After several minutes of disappointed head-shaking, Steph gave an exclamation. She grabbed one of the photos, squinting at it. 'There are a couple of people I recognise in this shot.'

Adam sat up straight. 'Go on?'

Her brow was wrinkled. 'It's hard to tell, because this is such a small photo, and they're in the distance, but that fellow with the hat looks very like that journalist we talked to. Alex's kind-of-uncle, John Harris.'

'Is that a connection?' Imogen said, hesitantly. 'I mean, how likely is it that Harris would be in Leo's yard?'

'Unfortunately, very likely,' Steph sighed and replaced the photo on the table. 'He's a racing journalist, so he'll know all the trainers. Leo's yard is successful, he's been doing very well this year, and it's not surprising Harris would be around, probably writing a piece about Leo.'

Dan leaned over her shoulder to get a better look. 'I took this about three weeks ago, judging by the date,' he said. 'I imagine if John Harris was writing a piece about the yard it's probably appeared somewhere by now.'

Steph considered. 'You could be right. Print articles don't appear for ages, but we may be lucky – he could be writing for a blog. I'll get online later today and scroll through all the likely places to see if I can find his article. I don't think we should ask Mr Harris himself. If there's the slightest chance he's a suspect, we don't want to alert him.'

Dan sat back in his seat. 'It's a very long shot though, isn't it? It's been several weeks since Alex Deacon died, there's been a separate burglary resulting in an elderly lady being attacked, and another death, although that one could be natural causes. But what worries me is that we may be stirring up trouble and making matters worse. This amateur detective work might be dangerous – not for us, but for other people.'

Adam looked up and the two men's eyes met. For once, neither displayed any sign of irritation. Adam nodded. 'You're right. If these events are connected, we may be getting close to the truth. If Leo Murphy's yard is at the centre of this, I want to know what's going on there. There are plenty of possible motives for murder in the racing world, I'm beginning to realise; drugs, betting, fierce competition and raging teenage hormones, to name but a few.'

Steph said, 'We can't stop now. We've come too far.'

Imogen said, 'Adam, you spent time with Henry and Ling. Did that take us any further?'

Adam shook his head. 'Not on the face of it. Our Hooray Henry's a smooth character – just what you'd expect from the head of chambers. Racing seems to be his passion. He got a bit tense, though, when we talked about the finances – seemed keen to stress that he isn't in it for the money, but that it's a hobby. I did wonder how true that is.'

Steph said, 'I read an article recently discussing the new rules for legal fees. Apparently, the law doesn't bring in too much, these days.'

'Really?' Imogen raised her eyebrows. 'I thought all lawyers were impossibly rich.'

Adam smiled. 'Not true. The money's all in corporate law. The everyday stuff – domestic violence, burglary, fraud and so on – is far less lucrative. All the barristers I know are pleading poverty.'

Imogen's head bobbed up. 'Could Henry be involved in one of those what do you call 'em – doping rings?'

'Who knows,' Dan said. 'Stranger things have happened.'

He went on, leaning forward, animated. 'I've been thinking about this, and about motives. There's the jealousy angle, both between the two female jockeys and the different yards. Then there are boyfriends; Belinda said Alex pinched her man, but she seemed to quickly find another chap, Callum, who may be a boyfriend, or may not. But none of these motives is strong enough for murder, in my opinion. Would anyone really kill for these reasons? Surely, they'd have to be unbalanced – and everyone we've met appears to be reasonably normal. A bit obsessed with horses, maybe, but not enough to commit murder.'

He sat back, his eyebrows raised.

Steph smiled her agreement. 'Perhaps we need to throw our net wider. Should we look harder at some outsiders – like John Harris? I'm not sure I would trust him as far as I could chuck him.'

Adam chuckled.

'What?' Steph said.

'You couldn't lift him, never mind throw him.'

'Don't you believe it. I may be small, but I'm strong,' she said. 'I've taken self-defence classes.'

Adam said, 'Joking apart, I think you're right. We began work on this case because Diane asked for help, and as a result, we've started with the people who know her and her daughter. We've focused on Belinda. But we've kept away from Alex, leaving her side of things to the police.'

He glanced at the others, but no one disagreed, so he went on, 'We looked at everything through Belinda's lens, hoping to prove her innocence. We've thought she's unlikely to be the killer, not because her mother and friends vouch for her but because she has very little motive, as Dan says, apart from the normal jealousies of young women in competition for either men or career. No one's reported her as likely to hurt others, let alone kill someone. No history of tempers or personality disorders. Besides, she had a very small window of opportunity to kill

Alex and if, by a long shot, Ed Collins was also deliberately killed, although we have no idea how, she was nowhere near his farm at the time.'

He looked around. The other three were nodding, so he went on, 'We need to know more about Alex's personality. Her life. What did she do, for example, when she wasn't at the stables or on a racecourse?'

Dan said, 'What do you suggest?'

'I thought I'd visit this Tim Booth, the lad who knew both Belinda and Alex. He should be able to fill in some details.'

'Good idea,' Dan agreed. 'Any other ideas?'

Adam nodded. 'There's plenty more to do. Steph, maybe you could keep looking out articles John Harris has written in the past, and talk to him again while Dan focuses on yard gossip. I'll track down any medical details on the deaths of Alex and Mr Collins, looking for links. It's time we began to strike a few suspects off our rather long list soon.'

As the meeting broke up, Adam walked through the reception area with Steph. She was looking even more attractive than usual. Her eyes gleamed with the thrill of the investigation.

'Do you need any help with that John Harris?' he asked. 'He's a slippery customer.'

She chuckled. 'I was a journalist for years. I learned how to handle the John Harrises of this world. I know how to flirt. But, I'd like to have you with me. Shall I entice him back to The Plough?'

'Good idea.'

She continued, 'But before I meet with him, I'd love some research help. He's written such a lot. I thought I'd spend a morning checking it out online before I meet him again, but it would be quicker if there were two of us on separate machines. Do you want to come over to my place and help?'

Adam shot her a sideways glance. He certainly wasn't about to turn down the chance for a few hours alone with her.

'I'll bring my laptop. I'm supposing you have a good internet connection?' he said.

'That was the first thing I wanted to know when I was buying the house. See you tomorrow.'

Adam grinned. 'I'll bring pastries.'

24

HARRIS

On Friday morning, Adam and Steph sat comfortably in her cosy sitting room. The furnishings were as cheerful as her clothes, the cushions, rugs and curtains collected with a love of colour and light that lifted Adam's spirits.

This morning he'd revisited his resolution to get fit, and run around the village, the kind female voice of the Couch to 5K coach murmuring encouragement in his ear. Just as well she couldn't see his red-faced, puffing attempts at jogging for a full minute. Who would have thought a single minute could last so long?

By ten thirty, showered and dressed, Adam sat at Steph's circular dining table with his laptop open, salivating like Harley as she produced coffee and plates for their Danish pastries. 'My favourites,' she said, 'How did you know? Although I try very hard not to eat too many. It's difficult not to bloat like a balloon when you're small and you live alone, like I do. I try to make myself walk straight past the baker's down the road, but I fail more often than not.'

Adam, remembering his morning's exercise, decided not to

spoil its effect and cut his apple Danish in half. That would save a few calories, wouldn't it?

Munching happily, they searched for articles and blogs carrying John Harris's byline. They had quite a task in front of them. Harris had been a journalist for more than thirty years and during much of that time he'd specialised in horse racing. He'd worked for many, many newspapers and magazines and he blogged regularly on his own site.

Steph said, 'You take his blog, and I'll sift through back articles to check if there's anything in his past we need to know. Imogen and I went through most of his recent stuff before we met him.'

'Good idea. Anything that mentions racing stables, or the names of the grooms and jockeys at Leo's yard, or the other one – Ann Clarkson's.'

He stopped talking as he noticed Steph's wry smile. 'I'm mansplaining, aren't I?' he sighed.

'Well, just a little. It's endearing, though, in you.'

They worked in perfect harmony, accompanied only by clicking keys and the occasional curse.

Adam concentrated on past articles from Harris's blog. He ploughed through acres of horse-related material until he found a section featuring rider profiles. They zinged with malicious humour.

'This ageing trier,' Harris wrote under the photo of an older jockey, 'near the end of his undistinguished career, notched up an undeserved win today. His opponents, writing him off as a loser, wasted energy outmanoeuvring each other while the also-ran slunk past and snatched an unmerited win.'

In the comments an argument between supporters and detractors rapidly descended into trolling.

Adam assumed Harris had a friendly lawyer on retainer to keep him just this side of a libel suit.

Tiring of the man's sneery style, Adam replenished the coffee cups and, after a short battle with his better self, swallowed the remaining half of the Danish pastry in one gulp.

Steph kept her head down, scrolling doggedly through one article after another, often chuckling to herself. Adam turned back to his laptop, oddly irritated. Steph seemed to be enjoying Harris's work.

She looked up. 'I might have something, here.'

Adam moved to a chair next to her and together they scanned one of Harris's pieces.

She said, 'It's another of his puff pieces about his niece, Alex, but there are some interesting points.' She pointed to a paragraph halfway down the screen.

Newcomer Alex Deacon scores an early win on Morning Soul, a likely star of the future from Leo Murphy's stable. Winning the ride over the head of other upcoming jockeys, notably Belinda Sandford from Murphy's own yard, she proved her mettle by leading the field from the start and maintaining a cracking pace through the final furlong.

Murphy's praise for her was unstinting. 'There's no denying Alex's quality as a jockey.' He'll no doubt be offering her more rides in future.

Asked about the quality of his own conditional jockeys Murphy claimed he'd be grateful for one with half Alex's ability.

The article continued,

It's unusual for a trainer to prefer another stable's up-and-coming jockey to his own. Is there some kind of merger in the wind between two of the most successful racing yards in Somerset? Leo Murphy's long been friendly with Ann Clarkson. Does their friendship go beyond business, and are we looking at a private and professional merger?

'That's a pretty incendiary piece of writing,' Steph said. 'I wonder how he persuaded Leo to make remarks like that about his own protégée.' She sounded impressed. Adam shot a glance at her. Was she interested in Harris for more than information?

'If he really did,' Adam said. 'Most aren't quotes, just Harris's opinion. When did he write this?'

Steph scrolled to the top of the post. 'The end of January. I wonder what Leo Murphy made of it.'

Adam mused aloud, 'A merger between Ann Clarkson and Leo Murphy. Does John Harris know something, or is this all speculation?'

They found no further references to a possible yard merger.

'In fact,' Steph remarked, 'it looks to me as if Harris made the whole thing up. I wonder why. Well, there is one way to find out. It's time for that chat with John Harris, I think.'

* * *

Harris showed no objection to returning to The Plough. 'So long as the drinks are on you,' he told Adam.

'The first round anyhow,' Adam smiled, keeping his temper. 'Red wine or white?'

Harris glanced at the bar. Looking for something stronger, maybe. Whisky? Adam waited, his hand halfway between a bottle of red and one of white. 'I can recommend the white,' he said.

Harris shrugged. 'I prefer red, if it's all the same.'

Steph swirled her drink around her glass. She'd agreed to

take the lead in the conversation. Adam had said, 'If he wants to muscle in on this book you claim to be writing, he'll be willing to dish the dirt to you.'

She dropped any pretence at small talk. 'We know you're busy, John,' she said, 'so I'll get to the point. I've been reading your work. Is there something going on between Leo Murphy and Ann Clarkson?'

Harris blinked at the direct question and gave a slow nod. 'There's been gossip around Somerset's racing circles for a while. Ms Clarkson is an attractive woman, you know. She's a widow, with a successful yard, so she's very eligible.' Adam sighed. Of course, Harris judged a woman on looks and money.

'I thought there might be something brewing, although Murphy's been married to his wife for over thirty years, and she's a feisty lady. I wouldn't want to rub her up the wrong way. But a few weeks ago, I started to wonder. I saw Ann Clarkson with that older groom from Leo's yard.'

'Callum?' Steph suggested.

'That's the one. Likes the ladies, does Callum. Ann and he were all over each other, like a pair of schoolkids behind the bike sheds.'

'Except,' Steph suggested with a twinkle, 'they substituted horseboxes for bike sheds.'

'Exactly. And he's half her age. A toy boy.'

They laughed together. Adam looked from one to the other. What did Steph see in this man? 'So, there's a link between the two yards, but it's not the trainers,' he said, 'or at least, not both of them. So no merger on the cards.'

Harris sniggered, 'Not a business merger, anyway. I made that bit up in the piece – it got me a few more commissions from the editor. They like a rumour, do editors. You just have to phrase it right.'

He'd drained his glass, and looked hopefully at the bottle. Adam picked it up, holding it, tantalisingly, over Harris's glass. The man's eyes never left it. Some kind of problem there, Adam thought. No wonder Harris's eyes were bloodshot.

'Look,' Harris said, 'there's all sorts of goings-on between those yards. Well, it's what you'd expect, isn't it? They're only a few miles from each other, and they are heaving with athletic men and women? No wonder they get together, have relationships, break up and start again.'

Adam said, 'Kind of like a chessboard,' He tilted the bottle above Harris's glass. 'And with your niece working for Ann, I bet she kept you in touch with all the gossip.'

Harris nodded absently, his attention on the wine as Adam half-filled his glass and replaced the bottle on the table, close to his elbow. 'Help yourself,' he smiled. 'And there's something you can do for us.'

Harris stiffened. 'What would that be?'

Adam said, 'We'd like details of all – all – liaisons and friendships between the staff at the two stable yards.'

Steph joined in. 'We want every bit of scandal, John. I know you're good at it. Your blog's gripping.'

Harris stroked a stubbly chin. 'Romantic relationships or business?'

Steph waved a hand in the air. 'Everything you know. Ring me, would you? Here's my number.'

Harris turned her business card over in his hand.

'And I'll run you home,' Adam added. He didn't want Steph alone with this man. 'You're welcome to take the bottle.'

'Good man.' Harris looked less than impressed at the prospect of a ride with Adam.

'I'll bring your car over, if you like,' Steph added.

'Quite the five-star treatment.' Harris attempted a sneer, but his eyes darted from left to right. 'I'll get back to you if I hear anything.'

What, Adam wondered, was bothering the man?

* * *

'Adam.' A call from his old friend, James, usually brought a smile to Adam's face. Permanently rushed off his feet, the father of a busy household, James lived the fullest life of anyone Adam knew, and still had time to feed titbits to his old friend.

Since Oswald's revelations, though, Adam hadn't spoken to him. For a moment, he was lost for words.

He gathered his wits and said, 'What have you got for me today?'

James's rich chuckle echoed through the ether. 'Well, I'll tell you, but it will cost you another meal. I liked that last one in the posh Streamside Hotel. How is the lovely Imogen? Still seeing her most days, are you?'

'We meet up often and she's as nice as ever,' Adam said, 'but if you're hinting that there's anything between us apart from friendship, you're mistaken.'

'I believe you, mate. I know your heart belongs to Maria Rostropova, more's the pity.'

The back of Adam's neck burned. 'Actually...' He stopped. Maybe he'd let James imagine he still pined for Maria. It would protect his feelings for Steph. He wasn't ready to share them, not even with his old friend.

James said, 'Actually, what?'

'Actually, I'm hoping you've got a bit more information to share.'

'Nothing exciting, I'm afraid. There's no chance of an autopsy for Ed Collins. The doctor's convinced it was a heart attack. The man had been to a heart specialist only two weeks before he died and the surgeon was planning a bypass. So, if you've got any evidence suggesting someone engineered his death in some way, you'd better hurry because the body's been released and the family are planning the funeral. It's at the end of next week.'

Adam heaved a sigh. 'This is all very frustrating.'

'You're not the only one hitting your head against a brick wall. I hear DCI Andrews is pinning his hopes on the public giving him a few leads into Alex Deacon's death. The coroner returned an open verdict, so they can't shut the case. There's going to be a ceremony at the next Wincanton race day, and the police will be there in force, hoping to jog some memories.'

'That's good news.'

'Sorry, I have to go. Ring me with details of the next over-priced, ten-course meal you're treating me to. Cheers.'

As Adam put down the phone, it rang again. DCI Andrews sounded perkier than Adam had ever known him as he detailed the arrangements for Alex's memorial event.

Adam did his best to sound surprised. There was no need for the DCI to know that James had already passed on the news.

25

HAIR

It was all very well, Imogen thought, saying she would look into the details of Alex's life, but it wasn't easy. Unlike Dan, who had free entry to Murphy's yard, Imogen had no reason to talk to anyone at the rival racing stables and she wouldn't intrude on Alex's family.

She'd need to approach Alex's circle in a less direct way.

She could use some thinking time to puzzle this out. Donning her gardening clothes, she went outside. She did her best thinking while she dug, or pruned rosebushes, or spread fertiliser on flowerbeds.

Harley by her side, she opened the door to the potting shed.

Oswald was there in his rickety old chair, drinking tea from a cracked mug.

He beamed at her through two perfect rows of false teeth. 'Looks like we'll be busy, now the weather's so mild.'

'I love this time of year,' said Imogen. 'Everything is so hopeful. Buds bursting all over the place.'

'You're right there, and no mistake. My eldest's wife is expecting another baby in six months. Life just keeps on coming, don't it, Mrs Bishop? Like I said to that Edwina at the shop, there's never a dull moment.'

Imogen opened up the lid of a propagator to admire a row of small plants in a peat-free compost and sand mix. 'I'll pot these foxgloves, shall I?'

'They're overdue,' Oswald said. 'I planted them seeds too late last autumn, so they never got into their pots. They're about ready to grow on now, though, so I thought we'd move them up to the cold frames and plant them out in a couple of weeks.'

Imogen loved the feel of compost in her fingers. Delicately, she held each tiny plant by a leaf, eased it out of the seed tray with the end of a pencil, and dropped it in a hole in the compost, one seedling to each pot.

As she worked, she chatted. 'Edwina knows a thing or two about the area, doesn't she?'

Oswald laughed, with a croak that turned into a cough. Covertly, Imogen watched him. He was getting very old. One of these days she'd have to persuade him to retire. But not yet. Self-ishly, she'd miss his company too much.

He recovered from the cough. 'That woman knows it all, and no mistake. If you're looking for a chinwag, that's the place to go. If Edwina Topsham doesn't know something, she'll know someone who does.'

Imogen's hands stopped working. 'Oswald, you deserve a medal. You've given me an idea.'

Pausing only to transport the tiny plants to the cold frames, she hurried up to her private rooms to scrub her hands and change into more respectable clothes.

Harley was asleep in reception, on his back, all four legs in the air. 'Come on, Harley, wake up. We're off to the shop.'

They found Edwina alone. Imogen collected a couple of

random items from the shelves. She could easily find a use for Belgian chocolate biscuits and a tin of salmon.

'Mrs Topsham,' she began politely. 'When I was in here the other day—'

The shopkeeper interrupted. 'Now, then, Mrs Bishop, I promised that old gardener of yours some of this Yorkshire Tea when it came in.'

Absentmindedly, Imogen took the packet. 'I'll give it to him, but I wanted to ask you something—'

'His wife likes it, you see. Good, strong, English tea.'

Resisting the temptation to quibble that English tea was grown in Asia, Imogen ploughed on, 'I wanted to ask you about one of Jenny Trevillian's daughters. She was in the pony club, I believe.'

'That's right, along with all the horsey girls in the area. Young Sarah, it was. She hung around with Belinda Sandford and Alex Deacon, the poor girl who died at Wincanton. Sarah had a nice little chestnut pony, if I remember rightly. She would have liked to be a jockey but she didn't have what it takes. You have to be tough to work in a stable yard. Long hours, heavy lifting, and all for a pittance.'

'What does Sarah do now?'

'She works over in Camilton at the hairdressers. You know, that posh place in the arcade next to the teashop.'

Imogen had been there. The place was expensive and full of young professionals having something called balayage, which, to her mind, made their hair look like an unfortunate hair dye error.

'Thanks, Mrs Topsham.'

The shopkeeper scratched behind Harley's ears. 'Call me Edwina, my dear,' she said.

'Th— thank you.' Imogen stammered as she left. The use of Edwina Topsham's first name was granted to very few. 'Harley,'

Imogen said, 'it seems I'm in her good books. Who would have thought it?'

* * *

Back at the hotel, she made a quick phone call to Crimpers, to check that Sarah Trevillian was working that day. As cover, she begged for an emergency appointment, explaining her hair was entirely out of control and she'd been invited to dinner with an oil executive and his wife.

After a great deal of huffing and tongue clicking at the other end of the phone, the receptionist, in a muffled voice that suggested her hand was over the phone, hissed to an unseen colleague, 'Can you fit in this Mrs Bishop today? She's got her knickers in a twist.'

After a few moments of muttering, she unmuffled her voice and announced graciously that Sarah would see her if she could get into town within the hour.

Wishing she'd eaten lunch, Imogen turned Harley over to the care of the receptionist at the hotel, who, judging from the bored expression on her face, had little else to do. She looked at Harley as though he were an annoying toddler pulling at her skirt. 'Cheer up. Our guests want to see a friendly face,' Imogen said. The girl flushed and sat up straight. Imogen would have a word with Emily later. Young Kelly wasn't going to be a receptionist for much longer if she didn't up her game.

The journey to Camilton took only twenty minutes and Imogen had time to park the car in the multistorey car park, pop into the cafe next to the hairdresser and eat an egg mayonnaise roll. She washed it down with a bottle of something that seemed unsure whether it was water or fruit juice, and tasted of neither, before entering the hairdressers.

The place was intimidating. A girl half her age looked her up and down, offered a professional smile and asked if she were Mrs Bishop.

Admitting she was, Imogen said, 'And you're Sarah?'

'Oh no,' said the girl. 'Sarah's with a client. Please take a seat. She'll be with you as soon as she's finished.'

Imogen sank onto a fashion-forward but uncomfortable chair, picked up a glossy magazine from the coffee table and pretended to read. After two or three minutes, Sarah emerged through the swing door. Imogen was sure she'd been waiting, out of sight, for just long enough to impress on this new client how busy she was.

Soon, Imogen found herself wearing a nylon smock, flicking through photos of expensive-looking haircuts and choosing between several almost identical shades of brown. 'You see,' Sarah explained, holding a strand of Imogen's hair between finger and thumb, a sad expression on her face. 'You need something to bring out your highlights.'

Imogen looked at the strand, dark brown fading gently to grey.

'I think I'll leave it up to you, 'she said, fingers crossed inside the smock. Praying she wouldn't find herself looking like mutton dressed as lamb, she added, hopefully, 'Nothing too young.'

'I know exactly what you mean,' Sarah said. 'My mother lets me do her hair. She says, if I didn't, she'd probably let it grow until it reached right down her back, like her grandmother's, and she'd have to wear it tucked around one of those rolls women used in the forties. Actually, my great granny looked rather sweet and lovely.'

Imogen began to like Sarah. For one thing, her fingernails were short, scrupulously clean, and painted a pleasing shade of an in-between colour Imogen believed to be taupe or, possibly, beige.

'Now,' said Sarah, pointing at two of the little swatches of hair on the colour chart, 'I suggest we go for a mix of this one here and this other one. We'll cover your hair all over, and you will see where your hair's lighter—'

'You mean grey?'

'Well,' Sarah waggled her head, preferring not to call a spade a spade, 'those paler bits will look as if you've had expensive highlights.'

Imogen remembered she hadn't come for the sake of vanity, and submitted with a good grace.

A trainee scurried off to mix up the potion, and within minutes Sarah was smearing it all over Imogen's scalp, lifting strands of hair to make sure she covered every single centimetre.

Imogen said, 'Your name came up when I was talking to Mrs Topsham at our local shop.'

'Oh yes, I know who you are,' Sarah sounded thrilled. 'You live in that gorgeous hotel in Lower Hembrow, don't you? I'm planning to come and visit your gardens when they open to the public.'

'Well, make sure you let me know when you come and I'll show you around. We've done a lot of work out there. But, I was saying, Mrs Topsham said you were keen on horses.' The girl's hands stopped moving for a moment.

'That's true.' The warmth had left Sarah's voice.

Imogen ploughed on. 'She said you were friends with Belinda Sandford and Alex Deacon. You know, the girl who died at the races.'

Sarah gave no reply and Imogen cursed her own tactlessness. Sarah must have been horrified by her friend's death. 'I'm very sorry for your loss,' Imogen said.

'Thank you.' There was a long silence, while Sarah combed colour carefully through Imogen's hair and pulled a wheeled electric heater closer. 'I'm just going to put a little heat on your hair.' Her voice was distant, professional.

She adjusted the heating elements so they pointed at Imogen's hair, and seemed to give in to the urge to talk. 'I did know Alex,' she said. 'We grew up together. I mean, we weren't at school, but I knew her in the pony club. Everyone around here knew her and Belinda. There were loads of us in the club, but Alex and Belinda were the best.'

Now, she was a chatty teenager again. 'Actually, Alex struggled, because she was a bit too tall. Even for a jump jockey. She was always on one diet or another, trying to lose weight. My mum used to say she looked anorexic.'

She stood back. 'There, I'll leave you for twenty minutes. Would you like a coffee?'

* * *

Imogen was left to herself, enjoying the warmth of the heater on her head, sipping excellent coffee and reading last month's edition of *Somerset Life*.

By the time Sarah returned, she'd admired houses she couldn't afford, read about a local woman who made wedding cakes, and skimmed a brief report of a concert at a local school.

Sarah lifted a strand of Imogen's hair and wiped it down, staring for a long moment.

'Not quite ready. I'll give you seven more minutes.'

Imogen was keen to keep Sarah with her for a moment. 'I don't know if you heard, but Belinda Sandford's mother asked me and my friends to help her. She's very worried that Belinda will be blamed for Alex's death.'

'Belinda?' Sarah gave a little snort. 'Belinda couldn't kill anyone, even if she wanted to. She'd be too scared. We used to laugh at her in pony club. She's very – sensitive – I suppose is the right word. Like her mum. You know the sort, if you come up behind them, they jump in the air. Belinda's better now, of course, she's toughened up since starting work in the racing yard. We're all amazed, really, but, although she likes to win, she's much too gentle to try to hurt a fly.

'Now, if Belinda was killed, everyone would suspect Alex. She was much more likely to be violent.' Sarah stopped with a gasp. 'I'm so sorry, I shouldn't have said such a thing. What with Alex being – you know...'

'Dead?' Imogen was deliberately blunt. She wanted the placid Sarah to be shaken up enough to tell her everything she could about Belinda, Alex and their relationship.

She said, choosing her words carefully, 'I've heard that Alex could be a little – difficult?'

Sarah shifted from one foot to the other. Imogen felt sorry for her. It was obvious she hated speaking ill of anyone, but Imogen was sure she knew secrets that could be useful.

'Come on, Sarah,' Imogen said. 'Belinda's mother's worried to death that her daughter will end up in prison.'

The stark words did the trick. Sarah gave another little gasp. 'If there's anything I can do...'

'Tell me about Alex. Any detail might be helpful. She wasn't perfect, no one is, but that doesn't give anyone the right to kill her. We have to bring them to justice.'

Sarah said, 'Look, let's go over to the basins. It's quieter there. I'll wash the colour off your hair myself – and we can talk.'

Imogen followed her across the room and leaned back in a chair, her head in a basin. It felt odd holding such a serious conversation with a hairdresser, when you couldn't see her face.

Sarah sprayed water onto Imogen's hair. 'When Alex was feeling good about things, she was great company; laughing, telling jokes, she was always the centre of attention. All the lads liked her, not just our crowd. I mean the lads in the stable yards.'

'Ann Clarkson's stables?'

'Not just them. Is the water too hot?'

'What?' Imogen said, startled. 'Oh, no, thanks, it's great.'

'Well, not just the Clarkson yard. Some of the lads at Leo Murphy's had been in the pony club with us. They used to hang around Alex as well.'

Imogen heard the hesitation in Sarah's voice, and waited, holding her breath, sure she was on the verge of hearing something important.

Sarah let out a sigh. 'My boyfriend works there. His mate, Tim, went out with Alex for a bit, but then she dropped him when that Callum came along.'

Imogen stiffened. 'Callum from Leo Murphy's yard, you mean?'

Sarah started to talk fast. 'That's right. Callum was one of the reasons Alex and Belinda fell out. He'd been going round with Belinda – well, he goes through all the girls in Leo's yard. He's older, you see, and good-looking, too. All that blond hair. Not my type, though,' she added.

'Let me get this right, 'Imogen said, wishing these young jockeys didn't lead such complicated social lives. 'Belinda had been friends with Tim, but he started to go around with Alex. Belinda and Callum were together for a while, and then Callum also moved on to Alex?'

'That's right, but, but—'

Sarah's overdeveloped conscience was at work again, Imogen took a shot in the dark.

'But Alex and Callum had a row? Did you see it?'

She felt rather than saw Sarah's nod. By now she'd washed

Imogen's hair, combed through conditioner, and rinsed it off. 'Sit up and I'll put this towel round your head.'

Imogen obeyed. Sarah said, 'It was at a race in Exeter. Me and my boyfriend were there, and Tim Booth as well, come to think of it. We placed a few bets, not that we usually win. But this time, one of our horses won at 4-1, so after the race we went into the bar for a drink. Callum and Alex were there, having quite the barney.'

'And you heard it all?'

'Couldn't help it,' Sarah said, sounding a little self-righteous. Imogen imagined her growing into the kind of middle-aged mother who'd disapprove of bad table manners, or rolling down hills, or jumping in puddles.

Sarah went on, 'Callum told Alex she was a tart and she'd better watch out because some men were after young girls like her and it was disgusting, and if that was the kind of guy Alex liked, he – Callum – wanted nothing more to do with her.'

She took a breath. 'I don't know who he was talking about. Alex said she didn't care, Callum wouldn't be getting any more out of her and she'd see whoever she liked. Then she jumped up and left, and Callum looked up and saw me and Colin. He came over and talked to us, and he called Alex all sorts of names,'

'Did he say any more about the man she'd been with?'

'Sorry,' said Sarah, 'that's all I know. Now, let's decide how we're going to cut your hair today. The colours look amazing.'

That was all the information Imogen was going to get out of Sarah.

26

HOTEL

'Well, look at you,' Emily gasped, as Imogen popped her head around the door of the office to announce her return. 'You look amazing – there's no other word for it. Just wait until your Dan sees you.'

Imogen, who'd spent much of the journey back from town stealing glimpses of her hair in the rear-view mirror, gave an awkward laugh. She'd entered the hotel by the front door, secretly pleased to show off her new 'do'. She tucked a strand behind her ear. 'You don't think the colour's too bright?'

'Absolutely not,' said Emily. 'There's just a tiny gleam of copper and it suits you.'

'Well,' said Imogen. 'At the price I've just paid, it jolly well should.'

* * *

Dan planned to visit that evening and Imogen's heart was fluttering. I wish, she thought, I could behave like a proper grown-up. Her head was a mess. She couldn't decide what she really wanted. Neither, she supposed, could Dan. He certainly hadn't made any advances on her. It was as though they were keeping each other at arms' length, trying to make up their minds.

Nevertheless, this evening she'd found one excuse after another to hover between the dining room, the main lounge, and the reception area, knowing that from any of these vantage points, she'd catch sight of him as soon as he entered.

She soon had to leave the dining room. Her presence made the staff uncomfortable. They tiptoed round the room, adjusting knives and glasses, polishing the silver and removing invisible specks of dust from tablecloths, constantly glancing Imogen's way, looking for approval.

It was exhausting for all parties, so she found a window seat in the lounge, facing towards the front. The French doors at the other end of the room were firmly closed. The afternoon was turning to evening and it would be dark, soon.

It was close to seven o'clock when he arrived. Imogen had drunk three mugs of coffee in addition to the one at the hairdressers'. Her hands were beginning to tremble slightly. It was definitely time for a glass of white wine.

'Imogen?' Dan looked at her for a long moment, finally announcing. 'You look fabulous. Great hair.'

'You like it?'

'It's wonderful. I didn't know you were planning a transformation.'

'Come and have a drink,' Imogen said, wondering how bad she'd looked before. 'I've got so much to tell you.'

'And I had an interesting time today. Not so much with the horses as the lads. Those beautiful, and very expensive, racehorses intimidate me a bit. All teeth and hooves. I keep well away from both ends, I can tell you.'

He made himself comfortable by her side.

'How's Mrs Hammond?' Imogen asked.

'She's back home with her brother, now. The hospital let her out. I looked in at her bungalow and she says she's fine, though she looks pretty shaken up, to me.'

Imogen said, 'Flowers, I think, and chocolates.'

Dan gave a lopsided grin. 'Already sorted, days ago.' He sat opposite Imogen at the table they'd last occupied a few days ago. 'By the way,' he said, 'I'll be buying you dinner tonight. I sold a painting this week so we can drink champagne and choose the most expensive dishes on the menu, if you like.'

'That sounds wonderful,' Imogen agreed, feeling suddenly shy.

'Who's going to go first? Dan asked.

'I will. I've had a busy day,' Imogen said. She explained her progress, from the chat with Oswald, that led her to seek inspiration from Edwina Topsham's local knowledge, and from there to her conversation with Sarah, the hairdresser, and the news that Alex had gone through boyfriends, from Tim to Callum and on to some unknown older man.

As she talked, Dan watched her face, intently. She felt a little thrill of excitement. It was many years since anyone had looked at her with half that degree of interest.

Her insides tied themselves in a little knot and she took two or three gulps of champagne, feeling it go straight to her head. She'd eaten little today apart from the sandwich in town, and her head was beginning to swim.

She liked the fuzzy feeling, but replaced her glass on the table. There was no hurry; no need to rush. She had the whole evening alone with Dan. She watched him talking, liking the way he ran his hand through his hair.

'So, Alex went through boyfriends like a knife through butter?' Dan commented.

'So it seems. And, by all accounts, Callum does the same with women.'

'The stable yards seem to be hotbeds of sex. I can tell you, most of the lads at Leo's had their eye on Alex. She was pretty well flavour of the month there, even though she worked in the other yard.' He grinned and his eyes glinted with sudden excitement.

Imogen said, 'You look like the cat that's stolen the cream. Have you made some kind of breakthrough?'

'I didn't find much in the way of secrets. In fact, I think my career as a sleuth is probably over before it began.'

He shrugged, but he wasn't fooling Imogen. He was bursting to tell her something. 'Get on with it before I throw wine over your head,' she said.

'I overheard one thing that made me think. It's probably nothing but—'

'Yes,' Imogen encouraged.

He narrowed his eyes. 'I heard one of the lads having words with Callum. He said, "You don't seem too upset about Alex Deacon. I thought you and she were having a thing." And Callum said, "Didn't mean anything. Course, it's a shame she died, but Leo didn't like me hanging around her. I'd decided to move on, anyway. She was just a kid." And he went on, "Now you get on with your job".'

Imogen, disappointed, said, 'I'm not sure that takes us much further...'

Dan leaned across the table. 'It's not so much what he said, as the way he looked. He walked away, out of the box, and I caught sight of his face. He looked like he was about to take a swing at someone. All bright red face and screwed-up eyes. He's not the friendly, happy-go-lucky guy he seems. One of the other lads, the chap who shares a flat with Belinda, he was standing near me and he gave a funny little whistle and said, "You don't want to get on the wrong side of our Callum, and that's a fact".'

Imogen thought about that. 'So, he has a temper. I heard he was angry about this older man? Could he have killed Alex?' She puffed out her cheeks. It was hard to keep track of these people and their love affairs.

Dan refilled Imogen's glass, and his own. 'I don't know any more. That's all I have to tell. Your friend, Adam, won't be impressed by my lack of detective skills.'

Imogen glanced at his face. 'Nonsense. It was your photo that alerted us to Callum, you know. Maybe it will turn out he's the villain, and you spotted him first.'

27

TIM

Tim Booth, Alex's ex-boyfriend, lived with his parents in a small semi-detached house not far from the hairdressers'. Rex had provided Tim's address and phone number, but despite ringing two or three times, all Adam ever got was a recorded message from Tim asking for his number.

Adam couldn't bring himself to leave condolences on an answer machine, so he continued to call from time to time and Tim continued to ignore the messages. Adam wasn't surprised. The boy's ex-girlfriend had just died, he wouldn't want to chat, and he'd probably been plagued by a local journalist or two who'd tracked him down as one of Alex's friends.

Adam preferred not to descend, uninvited, on Tim's doorstep. The poor family had enough to cope with.

On the fifth try, Adam's call to Tim's mobile was answered, although not by Tim. A female voice said, 'This is Gina Booth. Tim can't come to the phone just now, I'm afraid.' Tim's mother, Adam guessed.

He said, 'Mrs Booth, my name is Adam Hennessy. I'm a friend

of Belinda Sandford's mother and she asked me to help clear Belinda's name. I'm hoping Tim might talk to me.'

'Oh, I know who you are. I saw your name in the papers over that business of Greg Bishop. But Tim had nothing to do with Alex's death. He wasn't even at the races that day. He's dreadfully upset. That's why he won't answer his phone, not even to his friends.' She sounded exhausted.

Adam said, gently, 'I'm not accusing him of anything. I just need to know more about Alex, so I can help Belinda. I'm sure Tim will want to lend a hand with that. They're friends, aren't they?'

'I don't really know...'

In the background, Adam heard a male voice, muttering something Adam couldn't catch.

'Yes, dear,' said Mrs Booth.

'Look,' she talked fast. 'I have to go. My husband isn't well and he needs me. Tim will be here, at home, this evening. He's hardly been outside the door, except for work, since Alex – you know.' She cleared her throat. 'If you come around about seven – we'll have eaten by then – he might talk to you, but—'

'Yes?'

'Please don't upset him.'

She sounded near the end of her tether.

When Adam arrived, she welcomed him politely. She was small and frail and her face bore the pallor of long-term ill health. Her smile was tremulous.

'I'm so sorry this has happened,' Adam said. 'It must be hard for Tim. Sudden death like this upsets so many people.'

'Come inside,' she said. 'Tim's waiting for you.'

Tim Booth was a fresh-faced youth, shorter than average, and slightly built, but Adam noticed a pair of bulging biceps on the verge of bursting from a short-sleeved T-shirt.

He half rose as Adam entered the room, sank back into his chair and slumped, gazing at his fingers, his right thumb picking at a nail on his left hand.

'I'm sorry for your loss,' Adam said, formally.' Tim jerked his head, but said nothing.

Mrs Booth said, 'Tim, mind your manners.'

She was hovering in the doorway. Adam said, 'It's fine.'

Mrs Booth dithered. 'I'll leave you alone together, shall I?'

Adam gave her a warm smile. 'That would be best, thank you.'

He sat on a chintz-covered chair. Tim kept his face turned away and Adam decided not to beat about the bush. 'I expect you know you're one of the suspects, if Alex Deacon's death was murder.'

'Course,' Tim mumbled, his voice a monotone. 'Me and Belinda, too. People seem to think it's one of us. I expect you do, too.'

'Not at all. In fact, as Alex's friend, I would have thought you'd be one of the last people to want to hurt her.'

The boy crossed and uncrossed his legs once, and then crossed them again. One ankle rested on the other knee. He moved his attention from his fingernails to the knee of his jeans, which was fashionably ripped, and pulled at a loose thread in silence.

Adam said, 'I heard you and Belinda used to be a couple.'

Tim grunted. He flashed a look at Adam's face, and dropped his eyes again.

Adam waited. This boy would make a terrible witness in court. He was likely to incriminate himself and end up in prison, innocent or not. Neither police nor juries liked sullen teenagers.

Adam took off his glasses, pulled a large white handkerchief from his pocket, breathed on the glass and rubbed it vigorously.

He'd give Tim a chance to think, hoping he'd decide to tell him everything he knew.

Finally, Adam looked up. He said, 'Belinda told me Alex stole you from her, deliberately. Is that true?'

Tim bit his lip.

Adam held onto his patience. 'You can tell me the truth, you know. I'm not a copper. I used to be, but these days I'm just a pub owner, trying to save Belinda from an unfair and very serious accusation. If you won't cooperate, you'll be letting her down. You may no longer go around with her, but I bet you won't want to see her in prison for thirty years. Unless she did kill Alex, of course.'

That got Tim's attention. He heaved a sigh. ''Course she didn't. Those two, Alex and Belinda, they were always at each other's throats, ever since they were kids. They both had to be best, all the time. The best rider, groom to the best horses, who got offered the best ride – you know what I mean? My mum used to say it would end in tears.'

Tim's voice squeaked at the end of the sentence. 'Belinda wouldn't kill anyone, though. And nor would I.'

* * *

Tim seemed to make his mind up. He pushed back his shoulders, took a deep breath, blew it out and began to talk.

'The three of us go way back – to when we were about twelve. None of our families have money to throw around, but we're from farms and like everyone in this part of the world we lived around horses.'

'I thought Belinda's father was a lawyer?'

'He was, but her mum, Diane, grew up on a farm. Alex's dad used to work for the Collinses on their farm, and Alex kept her pony in one of Mr Collinses fields.'

He gave a watery grin. 'You don't have to be rich to keep a horse in Somerset and the pony club's not just for stuck-up kids. None of us had expensive riding clothes, like you see on those kids at the Horse of the Year Show – just a hard hat and a pair of jodhpurs. The pony club makes you wear hats or helmets.' He chuckled. Adam guessed he'd had some arguments with Pony Club officials in the past.

'We were all horse mad. There were about eight of us in our crew, but Alex and Belinda were the best riders. I knew I'd never be too great as a jockey but I like working with horses. Being part of a racing yard is about all I ever dreamed about, but the girls set their hearts on becoming champion jump jockeys.'

Adam said, 'And I suppose, as you all grew older, you paired off.'

'We did, but for most of us, it didn't mean much. By the time we had full-time jobs at the stables, Belinda and I were a sort-of couple, but I don't think either of us was really serious. More like friends, really. Useful to go around with, to parties and things. Good for a chat.'

Adam nodded. Tim was looking at him at last, frowning earnestly, and Adam felt inclined to believe he was telling the truth.

Tim continued, 'I was always a bit in awe of Alex, to be honest. For one thing, by the time we were sixteen, she was an inch or two taller than me. I used to be a bit sensitive about my height.'

Adam nodded. 'I know the feeling.'

The boy gave a short bark of laughter. 'Maybe you should have thought about riding.'

Adam patted his stomach. 'Not with the weight I carry. I don't know how you riders keep so thin.'

Tim was nodding. 'It can be a problem. My mum says we're like ballerinas.' He laughed again. An old family joke, Adam guessed. 'We have to keep our weight down. I don't have any trouble, but I've known people make themselves ill. Sometimes, jockeys don't even take a drink of water on a race day in case they don't make the weight.'

Adam raised his eyebrows, genuinely shocked. 'That's not healthy, surely.'

The boy shrugged. 'Like I said, ballerinas. Jockeys suffer for their art. Even if you're a groom, you have to watch your weight if you want to ride the horses out.'

'So, it's not all rosettes and prize money in your world?'

'I wish.' Tim rolled his eyes.

Now that the lad had relaxed and was talking freely, Adam brought the conversation back on track. 'So, you were with Belinda then, as a sort-of couple. Did something happen to break you up?'

'We rubbed along okay, but I think we were both looking around. I don't know if you've seen Callum, at her yard?'

'The tall, good-looking, older guy?'

'Exactly that. Why would Belinda care about someone like me, someone she'd watched fall off a horse a million times, never going to make a name for himself? She had her eye on Callum. In any case, Pat isn't keen on relationships between the two yards, although he doesn't seem to mind what Callum does.'

'Why's that?' Adam was pretty sure he knew the answer to that one.

'The yards are in competition with each other. Oh, they get along fine, but no trainer wants his lads telling the other yard how training's going.' He chuckled. 'We can watch each other riding out, of course. There's no way to stop that, and every trainer worth his salt has someone with a pair of binoculars keeping an eye on the other yards.'

Adam thought about that. 'Would Callum be part of that?' he suggested. He'd wondered why an older stable hand like Callum, with no real future prospects, seemed to be so highly regarded at the yard.

'Everyone knows he goes in for a bit of spying.'

Adam tucked that piece of information away in his brain and returned to Tim's relationship with Belinda. 'You and Belinda were tired of each other, then. No shame in that. It's perfectly normal, happens all the time. Maybe, one day, you got talking to Alex.'

Tim hesitated, as though reluctant to admit what had happened. 'We got together one day at the races and went out a few times,' he said, at last.

He fidgeted, crossing his legs and uncrossing them. He clearly felt bad about dumping Belinda. 'Alex was fun. There was never a dull moment when she was around. You can't blame a man for having fun, can you? It's not as though Belinda and I were really serious.'

'Was that relationship with Alex likely to last, do you think?'

Tim rose to his feet, wandered across to the window, and looked out, his back to Adam. 'I thought it might but after a week or two she seemed to cool off a bit. You know, she couldn't come out when I asked her. She needed to wash her hair, or she'd agreed to watch a film with her flatmates – that kind of thing.'

Typical signs of a relationship going sour.

Tim turned around. 'Then, she started seeing someone else. She went around with Callum for a bit, but one day I saw her leave the yard and get in a car. A flash affair, it was. Everyone around here drives four-by-fours, nothing unusual in that, but this one was brand-new. Top of the range, I'd say. And it was quiet. You couldn't hear the engine. Like one of those new electric cars.'

Adam asked, trying not to look excited. 'Who was she with? Do you know?'

Tim opened his hands in a gesture of ignorance. 'I couldn't see.'

Adam's spark of excitement died away. 'So you wouldn't recognise the driver again?'

Tim sat down, crossed his arms and puffed out his cheeks. 'No chance,' he said, shaking his head. 'The car flashed past, heading towards Camilton. I noticed Alex more than the driver. She looked at me, and I know she saw me, but she didn't even wave.'

He swallowed. 'That was the last time I saw her. It was a week before the Wincanton races and I had the week off. I went to Cornwall with Mum and Dad.' He swallowed hard. His eyes were suspiciously bright and Adam guessed his mother could be sicker than she'd seemed. The family might not be going on too many more holidays.

'So, you were in Cornwall on that Saturday?'

'We drove home in the afternoon. I was with Mum and Dad all day and I didn't even check my phone. Mum doesn't like it if I do that when we're all together. She says it upsets Dad.' He managed a smile. 'I think it annoys her, really. She phones her friends on our landline, would you believe? I gave her my old phone but she won't use it. Anyway, I didn't find out about Alex until after we got home.'

Tim gave Adam the address of the Airbnb cottage they'd rented for the week. As Adam left, Mrs Booth hovering politely, he remarked. 'Cornwall's a lovely place for a break.'

'We think so,' she said. 'My husband loves it there, even in February. The sea's so wild and invigorating.'

Adam could check Tim's alibi with DCI Andrews but he

believed the story. The lad wasn't at the races on the day Alex died. Adam liked Tim. He bore the weight of looking after his vulnerable parents with grace beyond his years. Perhaps Alex should have stayed with him, instead of dropping him in favour of either Callum or her other unknown suitor.

28

FUNERAL

The morning of Ed Collins' funeral dawned bright, the sunshine warm, and the crocuses in The Streamside's garden in full bloom. Mrs Collins had phoned Imogen and begged her to attend. 'After all, you were there when it happened, and you were so helpful.'

'It was nothing, but I'd be honoured to come.' In fact, she wished she had an excuse to avoid another funeral. The last church funeral she'd attended had been her father's. Her husband, Greg, had been cremated in a bright but impersonal crematorium and his ashes left under a stone that stated only his name and the dates of his birth and death.

Mrs Collins said, 'I've booked The Plough for his – well, we call it a wake, these days, don't we? I hope you're not offended, but he wasn't the kind of chap to want anything grand, like your hotel. He drank in The Plough many times over the years, and he liked the new landlord, that Adam Hennessy. Oh, and do bring that lovely man we met. Dan, I think? If he wants to come...'

Now that the day had arrived, Imogen hesitated over what to wear. It used to be easier when she was a child and people wore black to funerals. Nowadays it was harder to judge. Finally, she opted for charcoal as Emily suggested. 'It's near enough to black but less draining on the face.'

Dan and Imogen took their seats in church, a few rows back from Laura, her husband and family in the front pews. Imogen shot a look at Dan by her side and caught her breath. Black suited him perfectly.

Laura's eldest sister gave a short eulogy, describing her father's love of nature and the countryside. Helen Pickles, the vicar, managed the event with thoughtful competence and the packed congregation sang 'All Things Bright and Beautiful' with gusto.

* * *

Afterwards, The Plough was packed. Ed Collins had been a popular member of the Somerset community. Imogen found herself surrounded by all the Collins family, who wanted to thank her for her kindness. Dan, who'd only arrived at the end of the drama of Ed's heart attack, tactfully moved away and chatted to Helen Pickles about the upcoming Spring Fair, their heads close together.

Embarrassed, for she felt she'd done no more than any reasonable human being would do, Imogen drank coffee and listened as the family swapped old stories about Ed.

'At least,' Mrs Collins said, 'he died happy and that was thanks to you, Laura.' She gave Laura a hug. 'He was so pleased you'd come to help with the lambing. He said it was like the old times when you girls were at home, running around with your friends and quarrelling over whose turn it was to ride the pony.'

Laura rolled her eyes. 'So many of us,' she laughed, 'in our hand-me-down jodhpurs. We shared everything – clothes, friends, ponies – you name it.'

'And look at you now,' one of her sisters said, 'with your

gorgeous husband, living the life of Riley in that mansion of yours. And now you even own race horses.'

Laura laughed, 'Or, at least, part of one.'

Magnus arrived with a tray of drinks. 'Is there room for me here with you ladies?'

Mrs Collins pulled up an empty chair for him and he sat between her and Laura. 'We were talking about Laura as a child. She was easily the naughtiest of the girls.'

'I can well believe it.' Magnus slipped an arm around his wife and gave her a squeeze.

'Let's change the subject,' Laura said. 'Look, they're bringing out the food. Let's go and grab some. The lads from the Young Farmers are here in force. Most of them have helped Dad out on the farm at some point, and they'll scoff the lot if we're not quick.'

Mrs Collins watched her daughters pounce on the food, leaving Magnus and Imogen as her only company.

'I don't think I can eat anything,' she said. 'I've lost my appetite and I'm not a great one for food, anyway. Ed used to say I was small enough to be a jockey, unlike our Laura. She wanted to be a ballet dancer, you know, but by the time she was five we could all see she was going to be too tall.'

Imogen nodded politely. She was glad Magnus had joined them. He was the syndicate member she knew least well. He wore all the hallmarks of a successful man, his suit immaculately cut and his fingernails short and neat.

Magnus looked like a man who appreciated neatness and order.

Mrs Collins was revisiting her husband's death. 'Of course, Magnus, you weren't there that day. I keep forgetting, but Laura was such a help. I didn't want to say this in front of all the girls, but Ed had a real soft spot for her – and he was so pleased she married you. "A doctor", he said. "A nice, steady job, not like farming. She'll be set up for life."' She sighed. 'Laura's missing her dad and she's also missing Alex. They were friends in the pony club days, although Laura was quite a bit older. I think some of the locals – Alex, Laura and Belinda – formed a kind of united front against some of the other girls in the club. One or two were richer than the others, and a bit snobby. It hit Laura really hard when Alex died. And then the shock of Ed's...' She snatched a handkerchief from her bag and pressed it to her lips. Her voice shook. 'I'm glad Laura has you to look after her, Magnus.'

Imogen, awkward to be part of what was fast becoming a very private conversation, half rose, planning to cross the bar and chat to Helen and Dan. They were surrounded by a small group of laughing parishioners, and Imogen heard Helen twisting arms to gather support for the Spring Fair. 'If we all chip in and help, we'll raise enough to fix the roof of the village hall and have enough left over to buy more toys for the playgroup.'

Mrs Collins' next words stopped Imogen in her tracks. She'd moved on to her husband's last day. 'Yes,' she was saying, 'my Ed was laughing and joking that day he died. We'd just taken over from Laura in the lambing shed. She was looking after one of the new lambs that had been rejected. It was one of triplets, with a new mother, and the poor ewe couldn't manage all three. Laura took the weakest one that looked as though he wouldn't make it, but she did such a good job. The lamb's still with us, growing fast.'

She frowned. 'Ed was worried about Laura because she was so upset about Alex. She'd been inconsolable the day after the death. That's why Ed persuaded her to stay with us for a few days and help out. Such a pity you couldn't stay, Magnus.'

'Hospital business, you know. It never stops. I'd like to have been there—'

Mrs Collins laughed. 'Now then, Magnus, we know you're not

really a country boy. I was surprised when I heard you owned horses. Was it Laura who persuaded you?'

She went on without waiting for an answer. 'Ed said he'd talked to Laura in the shed about that day at the races and Alex's death and what a terrible thing it was. And then, while he was talking he stopped. He gave a big gasp and a sort of shudder. He said, "Magnus. I need to talk to Magnus about her", and his face went red, and he was grabbing at his chest.'

She mopped her face and took a deep breath. 'Now then, I'm not going to cry. Ed wouldn't like it. I was just so pleased he died happy, doing what he liked best. Lambing time was always his favourite. And he was proud of you, Magnus. Such a wonderful husband for our Laura. Imagine, you were the very last person he mentioned, just before his heart attack.'

* * *

Later, when the funeral mourners had left – or at least, those that hadn't settled in for an evening with their mates – Imogen perched on a stool next to Dan.

Rex was busy at the other end of the bar, so Adam had a few moments to chat. Imogen said, 'There's something I wanted to run past you.' She told them about the conversation with Mrs Collins and Magnus. 'Magnus said a funny thing. Mrs Collins asked him if he went into horse ownership because of Laura, and he sort of hesitated, as though he'd joined the syndicate because of someone else.'

'But he didn't say who?'

'No, Mrs Collins went on talking and I didn't get a chance to ask. Maybe Henry persuaded him, or Rupert, Belinda's father. It probably doesn't mean anything.'

She shrugged. Dan said. 'But it might be important.'

Adam's elbows were on the bar and his eyes, behind his glasses, gleamed. 'Did they say anything else?

Imogen nodded. 'Mrs Collins told us about Ed's last moments. He'd said how much he loved his daughter and how pleased he was with Magnus as a son in law. Mrs Collins said he died happy, but—'

Imogen picked up her glass, circling it in her hand until the liquid swirled like a whirlpool.

Adam was silent for a moment or two, thinking. 'What car does Magnus drive?'

She swallowed a mouthful of wine, not really tasting it.

'I think he has several. Today, he came in a brand spanking new hybrid Range Rover with not a speck of mud on it. Nothing like the old wrecks the farmers drive around here, covered in mud and muck.'

Adam said, 'Do you remember when I went to the yard? I met the other members of the syndicate there, but Magnus had left. He had a meeting to go to, Laura said, but I saw a Range Rover travelling away from Leo's yard...'

Imogen said, 'You're wondering if Magnus could be Alex Deacon's secret lover?'

'It could lead to a motive. Did Magnus say anything else?'

She shook her head. 'But there was one more thing. Ed Collins' last words were, "Magnus. I need to talk to Magnus about her—" and then he had the heart attack.'

Dan was frowning into his empty glass. 'So, who did Ed want to talk to Magnus about?'

She shrugged. 'I don't know. Mrs Collins assumed that 'her' meant Laura, but it could have been someone else.'

Dan and Adam spoke together. 'Alex.'

Imogen's eyes opened wide. 'He might have wanted to talk to Magnus about Alex's death, you mean?'

'Because,' Dan said, excitement ringing in his voice, 'while he was talking about Laura and Magnus, Ed put two and two together about Magnus and Alex. Maybe he'd heard something about Alex's older man, and suddenly it all clicked in his head.'

'In fact,' Adam said, 'Ed might have come to the same conclusion that we have. He thought Magnus was cheating on his daughter with Alex, and the thought upset him so much he had a heart attack. He had a history of heart failure and he'd been up all night, lambing, so that thought could have raised his blood pressure so high, it killed him.'

The three looked at each other. 'It makes sense,' Imogen said, 'but it's all conjecture and guessing. There's no evidence and we'll never know what Ed was thinking, but if we're right, Magnus is a slimebag and maybe even Alex's killer.'

29

MEMORIAL

The day before Alex's memorial, as The Plough filled with regular drinkers, Adam and Imogen retreated to the peace of Adam's private rooms in one wing of the old building.

'It's looking neater since Harley came to live with me,' Imogen said, 'But where's your easel? You haven't started on that still life?'

'Not while Dan's around the place. I don't want him to see my amateur daubs.'

Imogen stiffened. 'Why not?'

Adam grinned. 'Too embarrassing.'

'Well, that's just silly.'

'He has a painter's eyes. He never misses anything. He'd fall over laughing if he saw my work.'

'Painter's eyes? He's the most absent-minded person I've ever met. If he's thinking about his work, he never notices anything else. You could let off a firework behind him and he wouldn't flinch, if he was in the middle of painting a blade of grass. He even managed to lose that photo of Belinda and Callum.'

Adam sighed. 'He did a good job of picking out Callum and he caught Harris in one shot. It's a pity he wasn't at the races when Alex died. He might have taken a few of those snaps of his, shown someone following Alex Deacon into the stabling area.'

Imogen peered at Adam. 'Is everything all right? You haven't been your usual cheery self.'

'I'm fine.'

'Come on. We're friends, aren't we? And friends tell the truth.'

'You wouldn't say that if you were in the police.'

'Stop it. You know what I mean. It's time for you to come clean about Steph. Everyone can see you're crazy about her. She must know it. Why do you think she invited you over to her house and ate your Danish pastries? She hasn't exactly pushed you away, has she? But you need to talk to her. Have you said anything at all?'

He frowned, blinked, snatched off his glasses and polished them furiously.

She put her hand on his wrist. 'You'll break your specs if you go on like that. Now, answer my question.'

'Look here,' he said. There was a long pause. Imogen waited. He sighed. 'Steph would never look at someone like me. You saw the way that Harris creature behaves – all over her like paint. And she likes him. I can't think why – he's a toad. But, they understand each other. They're in the same business. She laughs at his jokes.'

'She laughs at yours.'

'Mine are funny.'

Imogen leaned over and kissed him on the cheek. 'Of course they are. I won't bug you any more, but if you want Steph, I suggest you do something about it – and soon. Don't let a sleaze like John Harris get in your way. If you want my advice, you should seize your chance at the racecourse on Saturday. Steph's going.'

* * *

That Saturday, Wincanton Racecourse opened the day's racing with a short tribute to Alex Deacon. Standing by a large montage of photographs showing Alex from childhood, already clutching rosettes, through to her recent triumphant appearance in the winners' enclosure with Season's Greetings, Ann Clarkson described Alex's popularity with colleagues in the yard and her growing brilliance as an outstanding young jockey. 'Her potential, already realised so tragically by a win on the very day of her death, would, I am certain, have astounded us all over the coming years.'

Alex's parents listened, heads high, fighting back tears with dignity, and a lump rose in Adam's throat. DCI Andrews spoke briefly, solemnly, encouraging anyone who'd attended the races that day in February and had seen Alex, or had anything to add to their investigations, to talk to one of his officers. Adam heard the familiar phrases, glad his own retirement meant he'd never have to deliver such a speech again.

As the short ceremony ended, the throng of racegoers dispersed and the buzz of a racing day returned. In need of a stiff drink, Adam made his way towards the grandstand and caught sight of Steph. She was striding purposefully into the bar, scarf flying, as though on a mission.

Adam hesitated.

Was this his chance? Imogen had practically accused him of cowardice. Maybe he should ask Steph out? He gulped. Was he ready? What if she said yes?

Come on, he muttered. Be a man.

He followed Steph into the bar. Just the sight of her made his heart race, from her curly hair, carelessly tied up in some kind of headscarf arrangement – Adam never understood what women did with their hair – to her boots, polished until they shone like a pair of conkers newly fallen from the tree.

Before he could reach her, Steph took a step sideways. Small and slight, she almost disappeared from view in the crowd of enthusiastic punters. Was she hiding from someone? Adam moved until he could just see her profile.

She stood, unmoving, focused. He followed the direction of her gaze. In a corner, their heads together, were John Harris and Callum. Adam wished he could hear what they were saying, but the noise level in the bar rose as the first race was announced.

Adam shouldered through the crowd, to Steph's side. 'What's going on?'

She turned to him, her soft brown eyes bright with excitement. 'Adam? I didn't see you. Look at those two. What are they up to, do you think?'

'Probably nothing.' Adam said. 'They're old friends chatting about the races.'

Steph scoffed. 'Nonsense. My journalist antennae tell me they're up to no good. And Harris never came back to me, although he said he'd let me have any gossip he picked up. Oh, look—'

Callum shot a quick glance round the room, snatched something from his pocket and thrust it into Harris's hand. Harris barely glanced at it, but dropped it into his own jacket pocket.

'Got him,' Steph said. Quick as a flash, she ran across the ten metres separating her from Harris, Adam in close pursuit. 'Hello John. Fancy meeting you here.' Her tone was friendly, bland, but Harris jumped, his face as pink as a baby's, guilt written all over it.

Callum slipped away, quickly losing himself in the crowd. Adam hesitated, ready to give chase, but on second thoughts, let him go. He could find him later. Just now, he wanted to hear what Harris had to say.

Harris had recovered quickly, and was smiling at Steph. Leering, Adam would call it.

Steph took Harris's arm. 'I hoped you'd be here,' she said, her smile bright, 'but I thought I might not see you in such a crowd. The place is heaving.' Harris grinned complacently. 'Steph. What a surprise. Doing more research? Can I buy you a drink?' Adam imagined punching him. Just there, on the point of that weak jaw.

'No thanks,' Steph said. 'Oh, look. Isn't that Leo Murphy over there?' She pointed. Harris's head jerked to the right, suddenly wary. Steph, with one smooth movement, slipped her hand into his jacket pocket and pulled out a folded scrap of paper.

'Hey,' Harris made a grab for it, but Steph was too quick.

'Let's have a look at this.' She backed away.

Harris took a step forward, menacing. 'Give me that—'

Adam blocked his path. For a second, he thought Harris was going to hit him. He rather hoped he would. Harris might be tall but Adam was stocky.

Steph unfolded the paper. 'I don't understand this,' she said. 'It's just a list of horses?'

She waved it at Adam.

Harris shrugged. 'It's nothing to do with me. I picked it up from the floor – someone must have dropped it...'

Adam said, 'Don't bother. We both saw Callum give it to you. Witnesses, you see.'

He moved closer, keeping Harris from moving past him. 'It seems our Callum's passing on information – a few facts and figures about today's horses. If you'll pardon the expression, we have you bang to rights.'

'I think,' Steph said, grinning broadly, 'you should go now, John. We'll pass this on to the police. I'm sure they'll be in touch with you about it, soon.'

Adam put out a hand to keep Harris close. 'There's one more

thing. What did you have to do with Alex's death? You were one of the last people to talk to her and you know your way around the racecourse. Everyone recognises you. It would be the easiest thing in the world for you to creep up behind her and push her head under water.'

'Oh no.' Harris's face blanched white. 'You can't pin that on me. Why would I? You used to be a cop. You know you need a motive.' He was gabbling. 'I don't gain anything by her death – in fact, quite the opposite. I made plenty of money writing about her.'

'And using her as another source of insider information?'

Harris bit his lip. 'Look, I'm no saint, and if I can make a few bob from under-the-radar information from my contacts, I will. There's nothing illegal in that.'

'Unethical, though,' Steph pointed out. Harris glared at her, his lip curling. He seemed to have lost interest in her charms. She went on, 'You can forget any collaboration with me.'

Harris muttered something Adam couldn't catch. It didn't sound complimentary.

Adam said, 'Did you pay Alex for tips on Ann Clarkson's yard, and Callum for info on Leo's horses? Playing both against the middle, I think that's called. Had Ann found out Alex was selling info?'

'I don't know about that.' He was blustering now, ready to admit everything and throw the blame on his niece if he could. 'Alex made a nice income on the side, selling information. She wasn't earning much yet from riding.'

Adam nodded. Buying information wasn't a crime unless the courts decided Harris knew the information had been come by illegally.

Harris saw Adam's hesitation. Encouraged, he said, 'Besides, I never saw Alex again after taking that photograph of her and

Belinda. I went home to write my piece and she went off with that bloke; her new boyfriend. Not that he's exactly a boy,' he sniggered, relaxing.

Steph said, 'You know who the boyfriend is?'

'Don't know the name, but he's one of that bunch of owners. You know, Belinda Sandford's crew. Always hanging around the young girl jockeys, that one. Smooth old goat.'

Adam pulled out his phone, scrolling until he found photos of Henry Oxon and Magnus Wilson. 'One of these two?' he asked, showing them to Harris.

Harris didn't hesitate. 'That one,' he pointed.

Adam looked at Steph. 'Magnus Wilson,' he said. 'The doctor.'

'Now, if that's all, I need to be somewhere else,' and Harris was gone.

They watched him disappear. 'Do you think Magnus Wilson's the killer?' Steph breathed.

Adam shook his head. 'Not necessarily, but he's moved a space or two up the list of suspects.'

'Above Harris, or even Callum?'

'I think Harris told us the truth. Paying for information's not against the law. Alex and Callum were breaking the terms of their employment, I'm quite sure, and I'll be talking to Leo about it. Callum will be out of a job, you mark my words. But Harris is just a small-time chancer with the morals of an alley cat. He's right – his niece was valuable to him while she was alive. We'd better decide what we do with this bit of paper.'

Steph held it so he could see it. 'Roving Dawn,' he read. 'Underweight, losing power on the uphill gallops.' She looked up. 'Is that the best Callum could do? Not worth much, that. I don't think the police will care, but I'm glad we gave Harris a shock.'

She broke into a laugh. 'He didn't look too pleased, did he? I don't think we'll be seeing much of him around Somerset for a while.'

Adam met her eyes and she fell silent. Their gaze held.

'Well,' she said at last.

Adam cleared his throat. 'Maybe we'd better – um...' He was lost for words. Then, in a rush, afraid that if he didn't say it now he never would, he said, 'You're not interested in John Harris, then?'

She wrinkled her nose. 'You're joking. He's a creep. Oh—'

She stood a little closer. 'Is that why you've been funny lately?'

'Have I?' His heart lurched.

'Distant. Remote.'

His head swam, as though he were perched on a high diving board, screwing up his courage to jump. 'I didn't want to get in the way. You know, if you liked him.'

'Like him? Do me a favour. He's the slimiest toad I've met for a long time. I was after information, that's why I've been hanging around with him. I knew he was up to no good.'

'In that case—'

'Yes?'

Adam hesitated for a split second, then swallowed hard and dived. 'In that case, I'll buy you that drink he offered you. And then, let's go out and eat somewhere.'

Steph's eyes twinkled. 'Adam Hennessy, I do believe you're asking me out on a date at last. I thought you never would.'

30

SPRING FAIR

The sky was grey, and a light drizzle dampened the bunting-decorated stalls. Imogen peered into the hotel gardens. 'Is it going to rain all day? It's been like this since I woke.'

Emily pointed to the wall clock. 'It's not ten o'clock, yet. My granny used to say, 'Rain before seven, fine by eleven.'

'I hope she's right. I love these country forecasts – did you know Oswald hangs a piece of string on the potting shed wall? He says if the string's dry it's about to rain, and if the string's wet it's already raining.'

Emily frowned. 'But that's nonsense. It means – oh, that was a joke, wasn't it?'

Poor girl, Imogen thought, she's losing her sense of humour.

Already, the stallholders from the village were arriving. Helen, juggling bags of jumble for the Church bring-and-buy table, grinned through the window.

'I'll go out and help,' Imogen said. 'You relax – have a cup of coffee. You've been running yourself ragged these past few days, organising everything. Today's going to be fabulous and I'm sure the weather will improve. Michael's dying to show us how efficient he is. He's hoping to be acting manager, when you go on your summer holidays.'

As though he'd heard, Michael's voice exploded from the sound system. 'One, two, three, testing,' he announced, tapping the microphone. It screeched. A nearby gang of schoolboys shrieked and covered their ears.

Emily said, 'I'll just show him how to work the thing.' A determined look on her face, she strode through the lounge, and out of the French doors. Imogen sighed. Emily was a control freak. There was no doubt about it.

She followed, joining Helen. 'Well, I'm liking the look of Edwina Topsham's cake stall,' Helen said. 'I think your chef may have contributed a few items – French patisserie, no less. Just look at those strawberry tarts.'

'Early strawberries from the fruit tunnels in the walled garden. The tunnels are a bit of an eyesore, to be honest, but we hide them right at the back, surrounded by bushes. We're hoping to grow most of the fruit and veg for the hotel from now on,' Imogen held up crossed fingers. 'Oswald's taken charge of the flower stall today. He won't let anyone else touch his precious tulips. They're the last of the season, and his pride and joy. He may refuse to sell them. He's a bit stressed anyway, with all these people tramping on his cherished lawns.'

'It's amazing, what you've done with this garden,' Helen said. 'I'm afraid your father let it go in recent years, but you've got it back to its best – maybe even better than in the old days. Are you getting many visitors, since it opened to the public last month?'

'Quite a few. I'm pleased so far, although I have to stop Oswald following them around, checking they're not stealing cuttings.'

A burst of music echoed through the garden as Emily helped Michael, who fancied himself as a DJ, gain control of the sound system. Edwina Topsham danced a jig, wobbling cheerfully, an enormous raincoat knotted tightly around her waist and a bright red headscarf protecting her hair from the drizzle.

Adam and Steph arrived together. Adam looked ready to burst with happiness. Imogen grinned. His contentment was infectious, now that he and Steph had finally got together.

Steph said, 'Is Dan on his way?'

Imogen groaned. 'He's coming. He promised me – promised faithfully – he'd be here for the Grand Opening, but you know how he is when he's painting...'

Adam grunted. 'Have you seen the prison young Alfie Croft and his mates have set up? They're planning to lock the head-master inside.'

'Last year, they chained him in a pillory and threw wet sponges at his head,' Helen said. 'Luckily, he's a good sport.'

Adam looked around. 'Things are going well here, apart from the drizzle.'

Imogen put in, 'Emily says it will stop soon.'

'Does she? I'll take her word for it.' He turned. 'I'd better go. Here are the members of the Butterfly Charm syndicate. Hooray Henry and his friends have taken quite a fancy to Lower Hembrow.'

Sure enough, Ling Oxon waved madly at Adam, and Henry ushered Diane Sandford across the grass to shake his hand. 'Magnus and Laura will be here in a few minutes.'

'Good of you to come,' Adam said.

'Wouldn't miss it for the world,' Ling smiled. 'And the weather's clearing nicely, isn't it?' She twinkled at Imogen. 'I've learned how to talk about the weather since coming to England. We don't bother in Thailand. It's always either hot and dry or hot and wet.'

Helen, as ever the perfect vicar, engaged the newcomers in conversation, and Imogen drew Adam to one side. 'I didn't know you'd invited the syndicate,' she hissed.

He smiled, blandly, but his eyes glittered behind his spectacles.

She said, 'I hope nothing's going to ruin the Spring Fair.'

'Everything will be fine,' he said. 'There's nothing to worry about.'

* * *

By half past eleven, Dan had still not arrived. Imogen sent a text message. He replied,

Sorry, got stuck into something. On my way...

So, he was letting her down. Today of all days, when the hotel was hosting Lower Hembrow's biggest annual event, he couldn't put her first.

Well, at least she knew where she stood in Dan's priorities – always some distance behind his work.

But she wasn't going to let Dan ruin the day. Her head high, she dropped the phone in her pocket and accosted Michael. 'Are you ready for the ribbon cutting?'

'You bet. I've got my autograph book handy.'

Imogen rolled her eyes. 'Leo Murphy is an honoured guest – one of the top trainers in Somerset. We're lucky he's agreed to come, so please, don't annoy him or his wife.'

'As if I would, Mrs Bishop.' Michael opened his eyes innocently wide, unsettling Imogen. He was good at his job, but he could do with a spot more training in tactfulness if he wanted promotion.

Just then, a horsebox drew into the hotel car park. 'Has Leo brought Butterfly Charm?' Michael gasped.

'Not likely. That horse is far too grand for our Spring Fair. I don't know what—' Imogen stopped talking, suddenly lost for words. 'Well, I never,' she managed as Dan jumped down from the driver's seat, let down the ramp at the back of the box and led one of the donkeys through the gate. 'I thought some of the kids might like a donkey ride.' He thrust the reins at a speechless Imogen. 'Here, you hold Smash while I fetch Grab.'

Harley bounded across the field. Imogen slipped her spare hand into his collar but Smash nosed at him, snuffling happily, Harley's tail thrashed from side to side and Imogen let him go.

Dan returned with Grab. 'There, I knew they'd be friends.'

Imogen, bewildered, shook her head. 'Why didn't you say you'd be bringing the donkeys? Where are we going to put them?'

'No problem.' Steph was at her shoulder. 'It's all arranged. It's a surprise. Dan's idea.'

Imogen fanned herself with her free hand. Just when she'd made up her mind she couldn't trust Dan to keep his promises, he'd arranged this. The donkeys were going to be the biggest attraction of the day. Already, a babble of excited children surrounded them. One of the Trevillian children clapped his hands, shrieking, 'This is the best fete, ever.'

Imogen murmured, faintly, 'I think I've had enough surprises for one day.'

'Let's hope so,' Dan said. 'Oswald's cleared out the potting shed, and there's water and hay there, so they have somewhere to go when they need a rest. He said as the whole of Somerset would be ruining his lawn, he might as well let the donkeys finish the job, and I've promised to keep them down near the stream, where the grass is tougher.'

Leaving Steph and Dan to set up the donkey rides, Imogen walked back to the gate, where Adam was waiting to greet Leo Murphy.

'Are you okay?' he asked. 'You look as though you've had a shock.'

'I have – but a nice one.'

'The donkeys?' Adam's eyes twinkled. 'Steph was in on the plan. She told me yesterday, but swore me to secrecy.' In companionable silence they watched Dan and Steph patiently sort the rabble of squabbling children into a tidy queue. Imogen felt an unfamiliar, warm feeling steal through her. Happiness? Contentment?

Before she could put a name to it, Adam exclaimed, 'James? What are you doing here?'

'How could I resist a day in Lower Hembrow, with the promise of a large beer tent serving, I hope, plenty of best Butcombe.'

But Adam was greeting the woman at James' side. 'Elinor?' he said. 'So nice to see you.'

As his wife pecked Adam's cheek, James grinned. 'We're thinking of making a move to this part of the world. Elinor's had enough of Birmingham, and of me working all hours.'

Imogen shared a glance with Adam. Since Oswald told her he'd seen Elinor at the hotel, they'd wondered who she'd been with.

A move to Somerset suggested some kind of heart-to-heart between the pair. With a wide smile, Imogen showed them to the beer tent, leaving Adam to greet the guest of honour.

Leo arrived accompanied by his wife, a doughty woman with a kind face and hair like a grey haystack. 'Good to see you, Adam. Let's get this Spring Fair open before the sun goes in again. Then we can enjoy ourselves.'

They walked across to the tent Michael called the Sound Studio, situated alongside a blue ribbon that stretched between two beflagged tables.

Michael called for attention over the tannoy. 'I'm sure everyone knows Leo Murphy, our foremost National Hunt trainer, fresh from another tremendous season. He's kindly agreed to open our Spring Fair. So, with no more ado, Mr Murphy, I'll ask you to say a few words and then cut the ribbon.'

Leo said, 'Well the weather's looking fine, the going's fair, and it's a good crowd, today, so I'll declare the Lower Hembrow Spring Fair well and truly open.' With a flourish, he cut the ribbon. 'Welcome everyone. Have a wonderful afternoon and raise plenty of money for your village hall.'

* * *

Imogen heaved a sigh of relief. All was going well, so far. Leo happily signed posters for a queue of star-struck village boys, while Dan and Steph led the donkeys up and down the field.

Tim Booth and his friends leaned against the back of a garden seat, watching Smash and Grab plodding steadily backwards and forwards as though they would never tire of carrying bouncing, excited children.

Imogen found Adam. 'I take it we've got certificates and insurance and everything, in case one of those children fall off?'

'Emily helped to sort it all out,' Adam said. 'We kept it secret because Dan wanted to surprise you. He said something about proving he wasn't a selfish oaf.'

She raised her eyebrows. 'Are you two getting along, then?'

He shrugged. 'We're fine. I have a suspicion he was jealous of me and you,' he chuckled. 'Imagine. Ever since Steph and I got together, he's been more friendly. And I've forgiven him for his talent with a brush. He's offered to give me a few lessons.' He wrinkled his brow. 'I'm not sure I'm quite ready for that. Anyway, perhaps you'll make a human being of him yet.'

He looked at his watch. 'I need to start the auction for his painting—' he broke off, his gaze slid past Imogen.

'What is it?' Alarmed, she spun round. What had Adam seen? Nearby, all the syndicate members stood laughing with a group of girls from Leo's yard, clutching plastic mugs full of beer. 'I can't see anything wrong.'

Adam growled, 'Look at Magnus.'

She looked. He stood with his back to Imogen and Adam, relaxed, laughing, with his wife, Laura, on one side and one of the stable girls on the other.

Imogen gasped. Magnus Wilson's free arm circled the stable girl's waist, casually, like an old friend, but his hand had slipped inside her jacket. 'What's he up to?' Imogen exclaimed.

The girl leaned in a little closer to Magnus.

Imogen said, 'That's a bit – you know…'

'Unsettling,' Adam suggested. 'I agree. She's half his age.'

'Our public-spirited anaesthetist seems keen on young women. His own wife is twenty years younger than he is.' But it was the disloyalty that upset her. The man was fondling a girl while his own wife stood barely two metres away. Did Laura know? Did the whole group? Imogen wasn't close enough to see their faces.

She turned to Adam. 'So, we thought he might be the man having an affair with Alex, and we could be right. He seems to prefer younger women. Could that affair with Alex mean he's our killer? If they had a row, perhaps?'

Frown lines showed on Adam's usually cheerful face. 'I don't know…'

Imogen wasn't listening. She shivered. 'I don't like to see him fawning over a young girl like that, let alone while his wife's there. I'm going to do something. Follow me.'

She marched across to Laura, Adam a short pace behind. 'So

glad you could come,' she said to Laura. 'Hello, Magnus.' Briefly, their eyes met. Imogen let her gaze drop to his arm. With a lift of one eyebrow, Magnus moved away from the girl. Imogen turned away and chatted to Laura.

* * *

Soon, the group broke up into ones and twos, wandering from one stall to another, laughing, as the Spring Fair gathered momentum and the sun shone.

Adam auctioned Dan's painting, raising several hundred pounds, the final bid coming from the owner of Haselbury House, the local stately home.

Imogen visited every stall, squirting water at balloons balanced on bottles, buying jars of jam she didn't need and watching Jenny Trevillian's four-year-old trying to pin the tail on a paper donkey at Joe's stall. 'He's going to have a ride on one of the real donkeys in a moment,' Jenny said. 'He hasn't sat on a horse yet, but our eldest rode her first pony at his age, so it's time he started. Just so long as that artist fellow brought a riding hat that fits a little one.'

Fancy Dan being so thoughtful. Imogen wished she could relax. Her nerves felt raw, and there was a twinge in the pit of her stomach that she couldn't shake off, even though the sun had come out.

Across the garden, people removed their coats, moved into the lunch tent and tucked into sausage rolls, bacon sandwiches and hot dogs. Adam's chef, Wyatt, and Imogen's own Gerald had made peace and were frying onions, flipping burgers and cracking jokes at the barbecue.

She joined Dan, forgetting about Magnus and the stable girl. 'Shall we take Smash and Grab for some refreshment?' she suggested, stroking Grab's nose and feeding him an apple. 'A good drink of water and a rest?' She looked at the sweat on Dan's brow and added, 'You should treat yourself to a beer, first. You look exhausted. I'll take Grab, and you bring Smash along in a moment.'

Such kind creatures, donkeys, Imogen thought, taking Grab's reins. Still, 'I've got a funny feeling,' she confessed.

'Fancy that.' Dan grinned. 'Care to be more specific?'

She leaned against the donkey. 'I can't. It's that feeling you have when you're about to go into an exam and you haven't done the work.'

'Ouch.' Dan winced. 'I still have a dream like that.'

'You do? Me too. Fancy that.'

'We should have told each other when we were at school. A problem shared, you know.' He disappeared towards the beer tent, leading Smash.

Imogen hardly noticed. Something was horribly wrong. Was it just the sickening sight of Magnus Wilson with that girl, or was something else going on?

She surveyed the garden. What could it be? Steph was deep in conversation with Ling Oxon, probably talking about pad thai and tom yum goong, Imogen thought. Steph adored food.

Imogen scanned the stalls. There was Henry, or 'Hooray', as Adam called him. He'd buttonholed Leo Murphy and their heads were close together. Was that sinister in some way? Adam had told her Callum sold information to John Harris. Was Leo doing something similar? The two men suddenly roared with laughter and Henry took Leo's arm to lead him towards the beer tent. Imogen relaxed. There was nothing shifty there, after all.

Laura Wilson appeared by her side, stroking Grab's neck. 'It's going well.'

'I think it is.'

'Look, can I have a word with you?' Laura seemed to have aged several years. That might be due to her father's sudden death, but more likely, Imogen thought, she was waking up to reality. She must have seen Magnus and that girl.

Imogen groaned, silently. This was a tête-à-tête she could do without. Where was Michael with one of his silly questions, just when she needed him?

Instead, she smiled. 'Of course. I'll just take Grab over to the potting shed for a rest. Dan's going to follow with Smash.'

31

POTTING SHED

Adam caught up with Leo in the beer tent, where he'd retreated for a few moments respite from the never-ending stream of horse-mad teenagers wanting selfies and middle-aged punters begging for tips on upcoming races.

Rex, behind the bar, broke off from flirting with Belinda, filled a foam cup and thrust it in Adam's hand. 'There you are, Boss. Enjoy.'

Leo's wife had drifted away to huddle with Helen, chat about their husbands and eat cake. Adam walked Leo to a quieter corner. 'You're a big hit, here,' he said.

Leo laughed. 'Somerset folk love their racing. And that's where it all starts—' He pointed through the tent entrance to Smash, waiting patiently while Dan downed a plastic mug of cider. 'That chap's painting a couple of my horses. Seems to like being around the yard.'

Adam nodded. 'I wanted to talk to you about your set-up.'

'Still up for horse ownership?'

'Oh. Yes, definitely. Well, probably. But, I was wondering about your grooms. Do you have any trouble with them?'

Leo put his glass down. He peered, shrewdly, at Adam. 'Sure we do. You saw that fight in the yard, back in the day. They don't normally come to blows, mind. Tempers are a bit high at the moment, so they are. Everyone's wondering how Alex Deacon really died and no one seems any nearer to solving the mystery. While there's a suspicion she was killed, the grooms are nervous. They watch each other like hawks.'

Adam nodded. 'Of course, that's understandable. But there's something you need to know.' He told Leo about Harris's confession.

Leo's lip curled. 'So, Callum's been spying on my yard. I've suspected someone was selling information but I couldn't work out who it was. Luckily for Callum, he's not here today.' His enormous fists were clenched in fury and his voice, loud with anger, rose above the babble of voices in the tent. His wife looked round and glared. He unclenched his fists. 'He'll be out of my yard first thing tomorrow,' he said, more quietly, 'and Harris won't set foot there ever again.'

He took a breath. 'I won't be sorry to lose Callum. He's a bad influence. Good-looking – too much so, I reckon, and with the morals of an alley cat. I've had to warn him off the girl grooms more than once and I told him if I saw him pawing at them once more in my yard, he'd be finished.'

Adam nodded, barely listening, remembering something Dan and Imogen had said about their visit to the yard. What was it?

'The trouble is,' Leo went on, 'he's popular with the owners, especially the ones that like to think they're one of the lads. I should have got rid of him, long ago.'

'Any owners he was especially friendly with?' Adam asked.

'Well, there's Magnus Wilson. He's another one for the ladies.' Adam hid a sigh. He'd been right. 'I've seen the two of them gossiping together in corners, like best mates in the pub. Mind you, he was good to Diane Sandford when her husband was ill. She was in a state, poor woman. All the owners rallied round her.'

Adam told Leo he'd seen Magnus with his arm around one of the stable girls. 'And it was more than a comforting squeeze.'

Leo's lip curled. 'That makes me sick to the stomach.'

'I suspect Magnus was Alex Deacon's "mystery man",' Adam said.

'You do? Could be right. I hear she liked men almost as much as Callum likes women.'

Adam nodded. 'All the boys seem to have been partial to Alex. She went through them like a dose of salts. First there was Belinda's old friend, Tim, and then your Callum, and finally, Magnus.'

Leo drank the last of his beer. 'Do you think one of them killed Alex? After a quarrel or something?'

Adam was silent. Parts of the jigsaw were finally clicking into place. He ran through them in his head; Alex and men, Alex and Belinda in competition, Magnus and Callum moving from one woman to another. He thought about Ed Collins' heart attack, the theft of Dan's laptop, Magnus cheating on his wife, Alex beating Belinda in the race...

He stood up, his mind clear. At last he knew what had happened.

While Adam and Leo talked, Imogen and Laura set off towards the potting shed. 'Let me lead Grab?' Laura begged, and Imogen handed over the rein. Laura brushed a hand across her eyes, as though dashing away tears.

Imogen sighed. This was going to be a difficult chat. She waited, patiently. Laura would talk when she was ready.

Above the hubbub of the fair rose a different noise.

A shout. Sudden. Sharp.

It came from the shed. Some of the boys must have broken in.

Imogen burst into a run. 'I don't want the village kids hurting themselves.'

The shed door hung on its hinges, swinging half open. She pushed inside and stopped in the doorway.

Diane Sandford's back was turned to Imogen, but sunlight from the windows on the sides of the shed glinted on the garden shears in her hand.

Slumped against the far wall, gripping his chest, gasping for air, lay Magnus Wilson.

Imogen stopped and with a cry, Laura pushed past. Diane swung round to face her, the shears raised. 'Stay there,' she shrieked. 'Don't come any closer.'

Her face was ugly, her features twisted with fury.

Imogen grabbed Laura's arm. 'Keep still.'

Laura pulled her arm away. 'Diane? What have you done?' she gasped. 'Magnus – Magnus—' She took a step towards her husband, but Diane barred the way. 'Don't come any closer.'

Magnus groaned.

He was alive, his body crumpled against the old weathered brick of the potting shed wall, dark blood seeping through his green jacket. Laura's eyes were dark pools of horror, her hand outstretched.

Somewhere, miles away it seemed to Imogen, a child laughed. Another screeched with excitement. In a parallel reality, the Spring Fair continued.

In the potting shed, the only world that mattered at that moment, no one spoke.

Imogen licked dry lips. She must stay calm, talk to Diane, try to take the shears. She held out a hand that trembled. She drew a shaky breath and spoke quietly, trying to sound calm, soothing. 'Give the shears to me, Diane. There's no need to make things worse. We can sort this all out. Just pass them to me.'

'Sort it out?' Diane cried. 'You can't sort it out. He's a monster – a beast – and he deserves to die.' She shuddered. 'I saw him, touching that girl.'

Magnus roused a little. 'It wasn't anything.' His voice was faint, hard to hear.

If only there were another entrance to the building – but this was a potting shed, almost emptied for the day, still smelling of compost, just a couple of spades on the wall next to a space where the shears had hung.

Imogen said, still calm, 'There's time to put this right. Magnus needs a doctor. Give me the shears and this will all be over.'

The shears wavered. Diane bit her lip. 'It won't,' she gasped. 'Never. It will never be over.'

Imogen's heart thudded. Diane seemed almost ready to let go of the weapon.

As she stretched out a hand to take the shears, Magnus grunted.

The sound broke the spell. Diane sidestepped, her eyes on Imogen and Laura, the shears at chest height. Now she was leaning against the side wall, and Magnus, Imogen and Laura were all in her sights.

Through clenched teeth, she snarled at Magnus. 'You lied to me. You told me you loved me and you were lying. You said I was the one you wanted, and you lied again. Lies after lies after lies.'

Her voice rose to a shriek. 'I cheated on my dying husband for you, but you betrayed me – and,' the shriek turned to laughter, 'you cheated on your own wife – your very own pretty little wife, with her blonde hair and her perfect teeth.'

As her laughter faded to a whine, she jerked the shears at Laura. 'Didn't do you much good, did they, those glamour-girl looks? You didn't know, did you? You thought you had it all, but for years, your precious husband loved me. Not you. Me.'

She gasped. 'Didn't you wonder why the hospital called him in so often? Didn't you ask why he spent so much time away from home – from you? Didn't you see you could never be enough for a man like him?'

Imogen stole a glance at Laura. She looked green and sick. She muttered, 'But, I—'

'Shut your stupid face,' Diane snapped. She waved the shears and Laura fell silent.

Diane grinned, in control, enjoying the moment. She leaned back against the wall, as relaxed as though they were chatting outside at the fair. 'You're just a fool. A pretty, stupid fool, but he's a monster.'

She pointed the shears towards Magnus. 'And then he took up with that little slut, Alex Deacon.' She almost spat the name. 'A spoilt, selfish little twister.'

Imogen's breath caught in her throat. Adam had been right. Magnus was Alex's mystery man. Had he killed her?

Diane made a noise in her throat, like an animal. She was sick, crazy – hovering on the brink of madness, and Imogen knew the truth.

She gulped. 'You killed Alex Deacon. Not Magnus – you?'

Laura whimpered. Magnus groaned.

Diane pushed herself away from the wall. 'Alex Deacon stole my man. And she cheated my daughter out of that race. She deserved what she got.'

She took a step forward. The points of the shears hovered inches from Imogen's face. Diane and Imogen faced each other, their eyes locked. Silence fell.

* * *

Meanwhile, in the beer tent on the other side of the garden, unaware of events in the potting shed, Adam bought Leo another pint. He left him venting his fury at Callum's betrayal to his wife and Helen as Adam made his way through the throng towards Henry and Ling. They were arguing amicably over the rival merits of the few remaining baskets at Maria's stall.

Harley appeared, fresh from an exhibition of his jumping skills over a set of jumps Michael had constructed near the stream. He leaped at Adam, still full of energy.

Gently, Adam pushed him away. 'Not just now, Harley.'

'Have you seen Magnus?' he asked.

'Not for ages,' Henry boomed. 'Probably been called away again. Happens all the time. I reckon he has a secret lover—' He chortled.

'But where is he?' Adam insisted. 'And Laura? And Diane?'

Ling said, 'Laura's with Imogen. I think they were taking one of the donkeys for a rest in the potting shed. I don't know where Diane went. Why?' With mounting tension. 'Is something wrong?'

Adam didn't wait to answer. Magnus and Diane, both missing at the same time. If his theory was right, he had no time to lose.

'Come on, Harley.' He set off at a run towards the potting shed, Harley galloping at his heels, with Henry, Ling and Belinda close behind.

Grab was quietly grazing outside as Adam reached the shed. He looked from the donkey, unaccountably deserted, to the shed and stopped dead. The door hung awkwardly on its hinges.

Adam raised his hands, warning the others to be quiet, tiptoed forward, and looked inside.

Diane's shears hovered close to Imogen's face. Diane, focused on Imogen, hadn't seen Adam. He stepped back, out of sight, thinking fast. There was no other entrance to the shed. No handy door at the back.

But there was another way.

He turned to Harley. 'Come on,' he whispered, and for once Harley obeyed him as he led the way to the side of the shed.

* * *

The shears were almost within Imogen's reach. Could she seize them in time?

She took a deep breath. It was now or never.

But before her brain could make her muscles obey, the window in the wall behind Diane crashed open.

Diane spun round, distracted by the noise, and froze as Harley, teeth bared, scrambled through the window.

She raised the shears, but Harley was already on top of her and she fell back. Imogen lunged forward, trying to catch hold of the arm that held the shears, but she was too late. Diane stabbed wildly and Harley fell to the floor, still growling.

Then Adam was at Imogen's side, twisting Diane's arm behind her back.

The shears clanged on the stone floor.

Within seconds, the shed was full of people.

Dan, his donkeys left to fend for themselves in the lush grass outside, grabbed Diane's other arm. She sagged, sobbing, between the two men.

Laura ran to Magnus. Steph followed, stripping off her jacket and held it, bunched tight, against Magnus's chest.

Imogen knelt beside Harley, sick at heart, as he lay on his side, blood staining his coat. He was no longer growling, but whimpering. 'Oh, Harley,' Imogen whispered. 'What have you done?'

32

AFTERMATH

For the villagers, Lower Hembrow's Spring Fair had never been so exciting. One moment the garden was filled with children stuffed with burgers and high on sweets, badgering their cider-drinking parents for more money to spend, and the next, the bucolic calm was shattered by the arrival of an ambulance, sirens blaring, closely followed by a pair of police cars.

Local people gathered to watch as Diane Sandford was led away weeping and loaded into one of the cars, while the ambulance crew took a stretcher into the potting shed and returned carrying a still figure.

'Is he dead?' A child cried, quickly shushed. Two police constables ushered the crowds away. 'Nothing else to see here, ladies and gentlemen.'

The vet left his children with his wife and examined Harley in a hastily-vacated lunch tent. 'Nothing serious,' he said. 'Just a scratch.' He stroked Harley's nose. 'You'll never be short of a treat, after this, old fellow. You're the hero of the hour.'

Joe Trevillian, hands on hips, watched from the entrance.

'Never a dull moment at this hotel,' he told his children, grinning with ghoulish glee. 'And that there dog deserves a medal.'

'Now, come away, Joe,' Jenny said. 'You should be ashamed.' Joe followed, meekly.

Steph, watching with Dan, said. 'I think we can see who wears the trousers in that house.'

Oswald, nearby, complained loudly. 'I said they could feed the donkeys in my potting shed. I never said nothing about a fight. I'll have a few words to say to Mrs Bishop about that later. I hope there's not too much damage, that's all I can say.'

Emily and Michael ushered everyone involved away from the potting shed and into the hotel, providing endless comforting cups of tea.

Imogen, Dan, Adam and Steph compared notes.

'How did you know it was Diane?' Imogen demanded of Adam. 'By the way, thank you for rescuing me.'

'Not me – that was all Harley,' Adam said. 'And I didn't suspect, not for a long time. After all, she'd asked me to investigate. But something didn't seem right. She was too hysterical, too anxious that Belinda would be blamed for Alex's death, too tearful. It wasn't as though she even liked Alex Deacon.'

'But she'd lost her husband recently, and she's a nervous kind of person,' Steph said.

Adam smiled. 'Yes, that's what everyone said about her. She was recently widowed, upset when Belinda lost the race, protective of her daughter, scared of horses, twitchy, frightened of her own shadow.' Everyone in the group nodded.

Adam went on, 'There's another way of seeing her personality. She wasn't just a widow trying to cope with her husband's death. She was a neurotic woman, having an affair while her husband was dying, eaten up with guilt, unbalanced and desperately jealous of the younger woman – Alex – who stole her lover. She became fixated on her daughter's success, clinging on to that while her own life fell into pieces around her.'

'So,' Steph said, 'Alex winning that race pushed her over the edge to murder?'

Henry and Ling were sitting nearby. Henry had lost his usual bluster. 'I told Diane that Alex pulled her horse up to steal the race. I don't even know if that was true – I said it to cheer her up. If only I'd kept my big mouth shut. She might not have attacked Alex—'

Adam interrupted. 'You're not to blame. Diane was already hovering on the brink. There's a thin dividing line between normal levels of anxiety and psychotic thoughts. I'm no psychologist, but I wouldn't be surprised if she gets a short sentence.'

Henry grasped at the idea, visibly relieved. 'You're right,' he said. 'The defence shrink will try to pin it all on a psychotic condition. I've heard forensic psychiatrists describe similar things in court. There's a build-up of jealous rage over a long time, until finally, a single event tips the balance and the killer explodes. Diane had no idea, when she went to Wincanton, that she'd finish the day by committing murder. She hadn't planned it – I bet she hardly even knew what she'd done afterwards.'

'So, there was no premeditation,' Steph mused. 'No planning, and she had no weapon. She must have followed Alex into the stables at the racetrack – there was plenty of time. The others were having a last drink and Belinda was taking a shower and changing, ready to go to the hotel.

Dan, sitting beside Imogen, said, 'But, why did Diane turn on Magnus today, if she blamed Alex for all her woes? Did something happen at the fair?'

Imogen said, 'You were busy with the donkey rides, but Adam and I saw Magnus with his hands all over a stable girl. We interrupted him and he stepped away as though nothing had happened, but Diane was there at the time. She must have seen it, too, and realised she wasn't going to get him back. He'd betrayed her again, and that was simply too much to bear.'

Imogen shivered. 'It pushed her over the edge again, then?'

Adam shrugged. 'Who can say? I imagine a psychiatrist will get involved, but ultimately, the jury will decide.'

* * *

Steph said, 'There are a couple of things I don't understand. Why would Diane kill Ed Collins? Surely she didn't blame him because his daughter was married to her lover? That's too twisted, even for Diane's mixed-up logic.'

'No,' Imogen agreed. 'She had nothing to do with his death. We can let her off that hook. At Ed's funeral, his wife described what happened in the lambing pens. Ed's last words were 'Magnus.' Ed had been talking about Laura, his daughter, and how proud he was of her. Then he mentioned Alex's death, and suddenly said, "Magnus. I need to talk to Magnus".'

She swallowed. 'What if Ed had seen Magnus once or twice, at the races, standing a bit too close to Alex? Talking about Alex's death must have reminded him. He suddenly suspected his son-in-law had been unfaithful to Laura. He didn't know for sure – he wanted to ask Magnus about it. We'll never know exactly what he meant, or whether that was why he had the heart attack, but it makes perfect sense.'

Imogen went on, 'There's something else I remember from Ed's funeral tea. Magnus was asked who persuaded him to join the syndicate. He didn't answer, which seemed odd at the time, as it seemed obvious he joined for Laura's sake. In fact, I suspect he joined to be with Diane.'

'And, possibly, to be around all the young women at the yard.'

Adam described his conversation with Leo. 'Magnus and Callum were like an infection; a pair of older men leering over the young female jockeys. Leo will be glad to see the back of them.'

'It's Laura I feel most sorry for,' Imogen said. 'She had no idea her husband was straying. He had a perfect alibi for all his absences. I bet, when the police talk to the hospital, they'll find no record he was there, all those times he claimed to be called in for emergencies.'

'That's right,' Adam said. 'The day I had lunch at Leo's yard, neither Magnus nor Diane were there. Diane had sent her apologies, saying she couldn't face it, and Magnus pleaded a call-out from the hospital. I saw him drive past me.'

Ling said, 'On his way to see Diane. So, Magnus and Diane were carrying on their affair almost in front of our eyes, even after Alex died, and we never noticed a thing. Magnus had no idea he was playing with fire.'

'One last question,' Steph said, 'before we all glaze over with exhaustion. Who hit Mrs Hammond over the head and stole Dan's laptop? Was it Diane?'

'Now, that's interesting,' said Dan, 'and I think I know. Do you remember, Imogen, you and I were at Leo's yard talking to Pat and we showed him the photograph – the one with Belinda. Callum told us that tale about Belinda hurting herself, but he knew his job would be on the line if Leo saw it.'

'That's right,' Adam said. 'Leo told me he'd given Callum a final warning about his behaviour.'

So,' Imogen put in, 'Callum must have pocketed the photo. No wonder we couldn't find it later, Dan. Then, he left the yard, jumped in his car and drove to your studio. He thought the place would be empty, as we were still at the yard, and he could have a good look around for any more incriminating photos. Unfortunately, Mrs Hammond was there. Callum heard her, panicked, followed her outside and attacked her. Then, on the way out, he grabbed the laptop, in case Dan had more pictures of him there.'

Henry stood up and paced around the room. 'Not the brightest knife in the drawer, Callum. Hitting an elderly lady over the head won't endear him to a jury.'

He took a few more steps. 'What about these racing yards? Leo's going to have his hands full, getting his place back on track.'

'That reminds me,' Steph said. 'John Harris dropped a few hints about Leo's yard merging with Ann Clarkson's. Is there any truth in that?'

Adam chuckled. 'I don't know, but having met Leo's wife, I'm sure any merger would be strictly business. She's a feisty-looking woman. In any case, I suspect Harris was letting his imagination run away with him.

'And with any luck,' he went on, enjoying the thought, 'the police investigation into Harris buying stolen information will go some way to spoiling his career, even if there's not enough proof to get a conviction.'

Steph gave a wicked grin. 'My publishing friend will be giving him a wide berth in future, and she definitely won't be looking at any trashy book he writes.'

33

AFTERNOON TEA

'Do you think, once the dust has settled, Laura will stay with the syndicate?'

Imogen and Adam sat around a table in Adam's garden, enjoying a private tea party with Steph and Dan.

Steph looked at Imogen. 'You've seen her a few times since the Fair. What do you think?'

'It's going to take her a long while to adjust. She's staying with her mother on the farm, and she says she won't be seeing Magnus until they meet in court for the divorce. She mostly worried about her boys – they're devastated. She told them the whole story.'

Adam poured tea from a huge pot and helped himself to one of Wyatt's doughnuts. 'At least their father's not a murderer. Just an adulterer. But that may not be much better, from their point of view, and with Magnus in prison I suspect Laura will have to take them away from their boarding school.'

Steph put in, 'Once Magnus is out of hospital, he'll be pulled up in front of the General Medical Council, pleading not to be struck off. He was one of the team involved in Rupert's care during his final illness. Adultery with a patient's wife could see

Magnus lose his licence, so life will never be the same for that family.'

'Or,' Dan spread cream and jam on a scone, 'for Belinda. Imagine, losing your father and then discovering your mother's a killer.'

Harley interrupted, begging for scraps. Imogen said, 'I suppose we should indulge you, since you're the hero of the Fair. But no cake. Dog biscuits only.'

Disappointed, Harley turned his attention to Adam. 'He knows who's the weakest link,' Steph sighed, as Adam slipped half a sausage roll under the table.

'The thing is,' Imogen admitted, 'that despite our best efforts, we didn't suspect Diane.'

'Not the best investigators in the world, were we?' Steph agreed. 'She took us all in with that innocent, fragile widow act – except for you, Adam. You worked it out.'

'Only just in time!'

Imogen said, 'Well, I was running out of options in the potting shed until you came along with Harley. I believe Diane was genuinely willing to stab me with those shears. She'd lost all sense of reality by then. What could have pushed her so far away from any sort of normal behaviour?'

Adam chewed, thoughtfully. 'Possessiveness and jealousy. She had a long-standing affair with Magnus, cheating on her husband, even while he was sick and dying. Then, when she discovered he'd been with Alex Deacon, she was eaten up with jealousy. The last straw was Alex beating Belinda, Diane's own daughter, in the race. To everyone else, it was just a race. I spoke to Belinda a few days later, and she was managing to put it behind her, but on the day, it was too much for Diane.'

Steph objected. 'But, when she thought Belinda was about to be blamed, why didn't she confess?'

Adam shrugged. 'You would think she would have, but that would suppose she was thinking clearly. In her muddled, over-wrought brain, Diane wanted Belinda's name cleared and that's why she came to me. She never asked me to solve the murder, remember. She didn't want that. No wonder she sobbed with relief when I told her the police were leaning towards accidental death. She thought she was off the hook.'

The others digested these thoughts, along with their tea. 'Well,' Dan said at last. 'I can't say I'm sorry for Magnus Wilson. In my opinion, he deserved what happened.'

Imogen said, 'The goings-on in Leo's yard muddied the picture, didn't they?'

Adam agreed. 'Most of that was down to Callum. He was the bad apple in the yard, selling information and spreading rumours about Ann and Leo and their yards, aided and abetted by his crony, John Harris. But Callum wasn't as clever as he thought. DCI Andrews tells me he's admitted to the assault on Mrs Hammond and to stealing your laptop, Dan, all because he panicked at the thought of losing his job at the yard and wanted to get rid of the photographic evidence of his canoodling with the young jockeys.'

'With any luck he'll get a custodial sentence and be out of circulation for a long while,' Dan said. 'Just don't let me near him.' His eyes were angry slits. 'Mrs Hammond's bounced back, and she's been cleaning for me again, but I make sure I'm around while she's there. I won't leave her alone. Callum deserves a good, long sentence for what he did to her.'

Adam nodded. 'I agree with you, and so does Leo. He's delighted to be rid of him.' He paused, before saying in a more cheerful voice, 'He's been trying to persuade me to invest in Butterfly Charm, now Magnus and Diane are both out of the syndicate.'

Steph chuckled. 'What did you tell him?'

'Nothing definite, but I've been thinking, why not? I'd no idea racing could be so exciting. My old mate, James, is interested too.' He grinned at Imogen. 'We were worried about his marriage, but we were barking up the wrong tree.' Steph and Dan exchanged a puzzled look.

Imogen explained, 'Oswald saw James' wife having dinner with another man.'

Adam laughed. 'Turned out, he was Elinor's brother and he's an architect. They were looking around the area for a place to renovate. Elinor was on a mission to get James out of Birmingham, and she's finally succeeded. He's going for early retirement and moving nearby.'

He turned to Dan. 'How's that painting of Leo's yard coming along?'

'Well, since you ask, I've brought it along to show you, before it goes to Leo. Hang on a moment.'

He left the garden, jingling his car keys, and returned moments later clutching a heavy canvas. He set it gently on a garden chair, suddenly sheepish. 'What do you think?'

Steph whistled. 'It's gorgeous, Dan.'

Pink Gin, Leo's champion steeplechaser, stood in the yard with one hoof raised, nostrils flared, eyes bright, as though he couldn't wait for his next race. But the friends were far more interested in the other horse, half-hidden in the background.

'It's a terrific painting,' Imogen smiled. 'Pink Gin's a handsome beast, but for my money, it's Butterfly Charm that looks like a winner.'

Steph agreed, 'Especially with Belinda in the saddle. Does Leo know she's in the picture?'

'It was his idea. There's a soft old heart beating behind that tough-guy trainer exterior.'

'Well,' Steph looked from Adam to Dan. 'We might have taken a while to solve the mystery of Alex Deacon's death, but one or two good things have happened, at least.' She grinned at Adam. 'Imogen and I are so relieved you boys have learned to play nicely. It will make a good ending to my book.'

She beamed and reached for the last doughnut. 'If I ever find time to write it.'

ACKNOWLEDGMENTS

To be a writer during the Coronavirus pandemic has been (almost) a blessing, because I can work quietly at home, happily lost in my imaginary world of Lower Hembrow.

However, restricted movement across the UK meant I needed even more expert help than usual with fact checking, and for that I'd like to thank Carol Ridding and Don Stickland along with Caroline Ridding herself, my trusty editor, for the encyclopaedic knowledge of racing they've so kindly shared with me.

This story is entirely fictional, which means I can make things up and move dates, times and locations at will to fit with the plot, but I'm pleased to say that no horses, dogs or people were harmed in the writing of this book.

As ever, I've been helped immeasurably by the team at Boldwood Books, by Cari Rosen and Rose Fox, and buoyed up by the constant support of my family and my loyal and helpful readers.

Thank you everyone.

MORE FROM FRANCES EVESHAM

We hope you enjoyed reading *A Racing Murder*. If you did, please leave a review.

If you'd like to gift a copy, this book is also available as an ebook, digital audio download and audiobook CD.

Sign up to become a Frances Evesham VIP and receive a free copy of the Lazy Gardener's Cheat Sheet. You will also receive news, competitions and updates on future books:

https://bit.ly/FrancesEveshamSignUp

Discover more about the world of Frances Evesham by visiting boldwoodbooks.com/worldoffrancesevesham

ALSO BY FRANCES EVESHAM

ABOUT THE AUTHOR

Frances Evesham is the author of the hugely successful Exham-on-Sea Murder Mysteries set in her home county of Somerset. In her spare time, she collects poison recipes and other ways of dispatching her unfortunate victims. She likes to cook with a glass of wine in one hand and a bunch of chillies in the other, her head full of murder—fictional only.

Visit Frances's website: www.francesevesham.com

Follow Frances on social media:

- facebook.com/frances.evesham.writer
- twitter.com/FrancesEvesham
- instagram.com/francesevesham
- bookbub.com/authors/frances-evesham

ABOUT BOLDWOOD BOOKS

Boldwood Books is a fiction publishing company seeking out the best stories from around the world.

Find out more at www.boldwoodbooks.com

Sign up to the Book and Tonic newsletter for news, offers and competitions from Boldwood Books!

http://www.bit.ly/bookandtonic

We'd love to hear from you, follow us on social media:

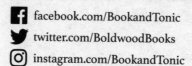

facebook.com/BookandTonic

twitter.com/BoldwoodBooks

instagram.com/BookandTonic